SATAN'S DOORSTEP

A bald eagle floated effortlessly down out of the clouds to tear a crimson-bellied fish from the sky-blue water. Riding beside the immense lake made Juanita aware that the heart of Yellowstone was cradled in a vast basin surrounded by range after range of towering mountains. No wonder so few whites had entered this hidden paradise!

"There she is!" Hawk cried. "The biggest geyser basin in Yellowstone. A great big smoking hell-hole!"

Juanita stared at the unworldly scene—dozens of spouting geysers and countless pools of blue-green boiling water. The earth seemed angry in this place. She could hear it growl, hiss, spit, and belch, and she tasted something foul on the wind.

"It's as if we are looking at Satan's doorstep," she said.

"Yep," Hawk agreed. "The water is hot enough to boil a human in seconds. When we ride down there, I'll let you take a close look. Some of those pools, the water is so clear you think you can see down more than a hundred feet."

"What if one of the geysers erupts while we're down there?" Quinn asked. "Seems to me we'd be running a big risk of getting scalded."

"That's right, Pilgrim," Hawk said. "But wasn't you the one that told me life was just one big gamble?"

<u>BOOK YOUR PLACE ON OUR WEBSITE</u>
<u>AND MAKE THE</u>
<u>READING CONNECTION!</u>

We've created a customized website just for our very special readers, where you can get the inside scoop on everything that's going on with Zebra, Pinnacle and Kensington books.

When you come online, you'll have the exciting opportunity to:

- View covers of upcoming books
- Read sample chapters
- Learn about our future publishing schedule (listed by publication month *and author*)
- Find out when your favorite authors will be visiting a city near you
- Search for and order backlist books from our online catalog
- Check out author bios and background information
- Send e-mail to your favorite authors
- Meet the Kensington staff online
- Join us in weekly chats with authors, readers and other guests
- Get writing guidelines
- AND MUCH MORE!

Visit our website at
http://www.pinnaclebooks.com

YELLOWSTONE

Gary McCarthy

Pinnacle Books
Kensington Publishing Corp.

http://www.pinnaclebooks.com

ORCHARD PARK

PINNACLE BOOKS are published by

Kensington Publishing Corp.
850 Third Avenue
New York, NY 10022

Pinnacle and the P logo Reg. U.S. Pat. & TM Off.

First Printing: June, 1998
10 9 8 7 6 5 4 3 2 1

Printed in the United States of America

*"Climb the mountains and get their good tidings
Nature's peace will flow into you as
sunshine flows into trees.
The winds will blow their own freshness into you
and the storms their energy, while cares will
drop off like autumn leaves."*

John Muir, after
visiting Yellowstone
in 1885.

Prologue

My name is Juanita Henry King and I should have begun this diary many years ago because my seventeen years have already been filled with great happiness . . . but also great sorrow. My existence has now become unbearable and I would lack the strength for life were it not for my devoted servant girl, Inez. She is five years younger than myself, a California Indian whose parents died of the pox which has killed so many of her native people.

I have only recently become the unwilling wife of Mr. Lucius King. In fairness, had it not been for his generosity, my father would have died many years ago. In return for this, I had no choice but to agree to this marriage. I consented in my fourteenth year. At the time, it did not seem a sacrifice. I could think of nothing but the welfare of my father, who was too ill to work. The agreement between my father and Mr. King—money for marriage—once seemed heavensent. Now, I believe it conceived by Satan in hell.

I never knew my mother because she died while giving me birth. Being Catholic and Mexican, she was allowed to rest peacefully in the holy mission cemetery. I know very little of her because my father could not even speak her name without tears and too much drink. But he never blamed me for her death and I have—until now—always been treated with love and respect.

As the wife of the wealthy Mr. Lucius King, I am expected to learn the management of his large casa. My husband is often away on cattle business for which I am grateful. He returned only yesterday and, once again last night, I was used for his pleasure like an animal. Inez trembles at the sight of Mr. King and carries the terrible scars of his cattle whip on her thin body. I cannot bear to think what other injuries or outrages Inez has suffered at his cruel hand.

Were it not for Inez, I might kill myself. I know this is a great sin in the eyes of the Church, but I have no fear of eternal damnation. For reasons that even I do not understand, I am sure that this is not my first life. I believe that this present earthly existence is our most difficult test and, after death, we become pure light and happiness. This is why I do not fear death and am willing to risk everything in order to escape into the wilderness with Inez.

No good can come from remaining in this evil house. I can neither abide the touch of my husband nor stand to hear the screams of the servants under his whip. If I remain much longer, I believe that those screams will become my own and I will certainly go mad. Better, much better, to die with my face to the sky and my spirit again free.

Chapter One

When Lady Luck smiled, Quinn Wallace always rode her hard. Never mind that his brain felt fried from drinking too much bad tequila or that his mouth tasted like old sawdust. So far, he'd won more than three hundred dollars at this poker table and, if his luck held, he was about to win a shot glass brimming with gold nuggets.

"Hawk, it's your bet," Quinn said to the haggard old giant slouched in his worn, stinking buckskins.

"Don't rush me."

"I'm not. Take your time."

Hawk glared across the table, his sunken eyes leaden slugs resting on pillows of wasted flesh.

"You have no idea what it cost me to get this gold."

Quinn was tired. Ten straight hours of poker had left him feeling rotten. Far too rotten to start that boat-building job he had promised Don Miguel Hernandez. The coastal hide trade was in full season and the rich

Mexican ranchers couldn't deliver them out to the schooners fast enough to satisfy the growing appetite for bartered American goods.

"Hawk," he said, trying to remain civil because the old man was becoming desperate, "I don't know or care where you got those gold nuggets. Now, are you going to fold, or raise the ante so we can call it a night?"

"No man's luck can last this long. Damn Blackfeet nearly scalped me gettin' this gold," Hawk muttered, caressing the gold-filled shot glass.

"How about another tequila?" Quinn offered, hoping the small gesture might avert bloodshed.

"If you're buyin'."

"I'm buying." Quinn motioned toward Arturo, their bartender and his friend. "A bottle, *por favor.*"

Arturo returned with the tequila and placed it before Hawk, who grunted with approval. Quinn paid for the bottle, remembering how his father had taught him always to leave a loser something. And besides, Hawk was a genuine frontiersman. He was among the last of those wild mountain men who had opened up the western frontier, fighting grizzly bears and Indians while trapping icy mountain rivers for beaver. Once proud lords of the American wilderness, the remnants of this dying breed were not pathetic relics.

Hawk was not the first of this breed that Quinn had skinned at cards, but he was the most desperate and, therefore, explosive. Desperate because he was way too damned old and battered by the years to enjoy California's warm climate and far warmer señoritas.

Hawk drank deeply and sighed. Impatient to end this game, Quinn asked, "What's your play?"

Hawk wouldn't be prodded. "Have you ever lived in far country where the grizzly rule?"

"I like Santa Barbara."

"You don't know what you're missin'."

"I can live with that."

"I don't expect you've lived much yet at all," Hawk said.

He shook his head and his voice lost its edge. "But I have. I trapped the Rockies for nigh on twenty years, then moved into the Tetons and then Yellowstone country."

"Then you should leave California and go back to Yellowstone. But, right now, please either fold or up the ante."

"I been uppin' the ante all my life," Hawk said to himself as he drummed his fingers on the table. "I was always searchin' for the wildest and tallest mountains where the rivers run sweet and full of virgin beaver. I even knew John Colter. Now *he* was a man and the first to see that Yellowstone country. He died in bed, though. Died of the fever in St. Louis some years back. Say, do you want to see where an Indian put an arrow in my hide?"

"I want you to bet . . . or fold."

"Shortly, I will."

Hawk laid his cards facedown and petted them with his big, liver-blotched hands as if they were each a haunting memory needing to be stilled. "I was at the first rendezvous in 1825 at Henry's Fork on the Green River. I was at the last one, too. Back then, I was considered somethin' special, even by the likes of Joe Meek, old Tom Fitzpatrick, and Jim Bridger. Sometimes we worked for the American Fur Company but mostly we worked for our own damned selves. The finest men ever to climb the mountains respected my words about

Indians, trappin', and the changes of weather. And I was considered handsome."

He grinned a little sheepishly and added, "Pilgrim, believe it or not, Indian women favored me above all other whites. But everythin' passed way too fast—it was all over in just fifteen years."

Quinn yawned. "Hawk, I'm *real* tired. So would you . . ."

Hawk lovingly poured the shot glass full of gold nuggets into the palm of his left hand, then stroked them with his right index finger. "This is the last of my smaller ones," he said. "I won't give up the others."

"What does that mean?" Quinn asked with sudden interest because Hawk's "smaller one" was very large indeed. "Do you have any big nuggets?"

His eyelids drooped low. "Yep."

"Maybe they're worth enough to finally change your luck tonight."

"I can't take that chance," Hawk replied, picking up the pea-sized nuggets one by one and dropping them back into his shot glass, while gently nudging it toward the pot of already-wagered money. "Not with the last three, I can't. They're my 'get-back-to-Yellowstone' stake. Son, I raise you this gold nugget. Ought to be worth a hundred dollars."

Quinn pushed a stack of chips forward, wondering if he had misjudged the old man and actually could lose this hand. The thought of it caused his gut to twist. He heard a chair scrape close by and someone coughed. Other than that, he couldn't hear anything except a brassy buzzing in his ears and the throb of his headache.

"Call."

Hawk grinned broadly and turned his cards faceup.

"Three kings. Just like in the Bible story of the three wise men."

"Sorry," Quinn said, turning up his own cards. "I've got another full house. You lose."

Hawk paled. "Pilgrim, I guess I shoulda quit a long time ago."

"Take the bottle and don't gamble anymore," Quinn told the man in his gentlest voice, "because you're not very good at it."

"And you are?"

"I'm good," Quinn admitted. "I win more often then I lose."

"You're a gambler."

"We're *all* gamblers. Life is nothing but a gamble. Hawk, you've lived plenty long enough to know that."

Hawk inhaled deeply and squared his still-impressively-wide shoulders. "Yeah, you're right. I got things yet to do. Someone that I got to see in Yellowstone."

"Go back, old timer."

"First, I want to show you somethin'." Hawk reached into his coat pocket and shouted, "Gather 'round, boys! I want to show you what old Hawk is *really* worth!"

He opened the pouch and spilled three gold nuggets so massive that any one of them could have bought the Rana Verde Cantina—lock, stock, and barrel.

"You're rich!" Quinn whispered in astonishment.

Hawk cackled and rested big hands on his narrow hips. "Yep, and there's a whole lot more where these came from."

"Where?"

"In Yellowstone."

Quinn hadn't realized he'd jumped to his feet when the nuggets tumbled across the table. Now, he sagged back in his chair. "Then why didn't you get them *all*?"

"Pilgrim, can you ride a horse and shoot a muzzle loader? Can you winter in freezin' weather and kill an Indian set on takin' your scalp?"

"I can ride and shoot. I've never wintered in hard weather and, in California, the Indians are all friendly."

"The Blackfeet ain't."

"I'm going to fill my hat with the pot and then I'm leaving," Quinn said. "But, if it means anything, I'm glad you didn't gamble with those last three nuggets. I'd have won them just like I won the small ones."

"You're cocky and you're quick with that gun. Have you killed men before?"

"I have."

"More'n one?"

"Yes, but I'm not boasting. I'm no fool, either."

"That's why I got somethin' to talk to you about."

"No," Quinn said, pulling his eyes away from the biggest gold nuggets he'd ever seen. "I'm going to bed."

"Son, I believe that when a young man is offered the biggest opportunity of his lifetime, he ought to grab it by the neck."

"I'm doing fine here. Quit gambling."

Hawk snickered. "I've just offered you the chance to get rich and you're givin' *me* advice?"

"Good night."

Quinn gathered his winnings and dumped them into his hat, feeling Hawk's hot eyes. Never mind. He was a boat-builder by day and a gambler by night, when it suited him. And he was doing very, very well in this Santa Barbara paradise.

Outside the cantina, a pretty Mexican girl was waiting at the door and tried to take his arm but Quinn shook his head. "Not tonight."

Her lips formed a provocative smile and her dark eyes

grew wider at the sight of all the money filling the hat Quinn cradled against his chest. "You win very big! You need someone good to take care of you, Señor."

"I can take care of myself," he answered, knowing that if he took this girl to bed, he might never wake up again.

She followed him out into the street, talking, touching, but Quinn wasn't interested. "Leave me alone, Señorita."

She spat, and yelled into the darkness. Quinn hurried on. An owl hooted from the canopy of a cottonwood tree and then silently launched itself across the rutted street toward the crumbling and abandoned mission fields overrun with weeds and rodents.

The hour was very late. He heard a woman's shrill laughter float down an alley. Quinn breathed deeply and the ocean air was a tonic.

"Mister, your winnings or your life!"

Three armed thieves, all wearing bandannas drawn across their lower faces, emerged as silent as ghosts. Quinn scooped up his hat. If he could retreat around the corner and onto the main street, perhaps someone would notice his plight and raise a call for help. But then, he heard the ominous clicking of a pistol's hammer and his hand slid toward his derringer. If he could get a little nearer to Rana Verde Cantina, then . . .

Quinn tripped just as he saw two muzzle blasts of fire split the darkness. A slug burned his cheek and another struck him in the foot. He collapsed, spilling his winnings to grab the toe of his boot. A third shot caused dirt to sting his eyes and he blindly rolled over and over, certain that he was about to be slaughtered like a helpless lamb.

"Ahhhhh-yeeeiii!"

It was the scream of a panther. No, it was Hawk. One moment Quinn was almost a dead man, the next he was listening to hideous howls, more gunshots, and the pounding of boots fading into the night.

"Pilgrim, you dyin'?"

"I need a doctor," Quinn gritted. "How bad is my face?

"Can't see well enough to tell. Maybe you ain't gonna be so handsome and cocky as before."

"Go to hell!"

"Some people call Yellowstone 'Colter's Hell' 'cause of all them geysers and boilin' mud pots."

"What are you talking about?"

"Colter's Hell! Why, that Yellowstone country is plumb full of boilin' water spouts that shoot . . . maybe a half mile straight up into the sky. That water is boilin' and smokin' and it stinks somethin' terrible. And the earth belches and booms—oh, it's the Devil fartin', all right! Them mud pots are his poisonous stew. I seen an elk fall through what looked like solid ground. He was boiled alive and, if I'd had a rope, I'd have lassoed and ate him."

"I'm shot!"

"You'll live," Hawk said. "I'll show you Yellowstone where it can be blowin' a blizzard but, if you're camped close to them geysers and mud pots, you'll be as hot as Mexican chilies!"

"Dammit, I'm not leaving California!"

"You gotta."

"Why?"

"Because you owe me your life."

Quinn knew he should argue, but pain and too much bad whisky sent him tumbling into darkness.

* * *

Morning brought sunlight and excruciating pain. Quinn gazed around, realizing they were in Pablo Escobar's stable and Hawk was snoring hard enough to wave spider webs back and forth in the rafters.

Quinn saw that the toe of his left boot had been cut entirely away. He was relieved to see that only the very tip of his middle toe was missing. But it was ugly. He steeled himself for the worst and fingered his cheek. The cheek was grooved and crusted with blood, but the wound was only superficial.

"It's a miracle," he said, eyes coming to rest on his hat filled with last night's poker winnings. Quinn scooted over to a post and levered himself erect, causing a pair of chickens to scatter, cackling with outrage. A horse whinnied and shafts of dusty light lanced through gaping roof holes. Quinn hobbled over to a barrel and immersed his head in cool water. He held his head under for a full minute, then straightened, shaking himself like a wet dog.

I'm alive. By jingo, I'm alive and I'm going to be all right!

Quinn doused himself in a water barrel, deciding to leave Hawk fifty dollars and all of his Yellowstone nuggets. That was generous, very generous. It was more than fair. He managed to hop back to his hat, empty it of Hawk's share, then turn to leave.

"Hold up, Pilgrim!"

Quinn swayed around, his toe throbbing like crazy. "I *am* leaving! I've paid you well for saving my life. Just look and you'll see your nuggets."

"I want more."

Quinn blinked. He hugged a post and swayed, trying

to understand. His hand automatically reached for his derringer.

"Your hide-out pistol is gone. I saved your life and I want more."

"Too bad."

"You owe me everythin'," Hawk said, slowly coming to his feet before raising his buckskin tunic to reveal a terrible knife wound. "The first thief cut me good before I broke his back. I shot another. The last one escaped. I reckon we can track him down and kill him."

Quinn stared at the knife wound. "What do you *really* want from me?"

"I need a partner for the Yellowstone country. All my old trappin' friends have died so now I need a young man with guts. You still got yours . . . thanks to me."

Quinn slid down the post and leaned his head back against it, closing his eyes and breathing deeply. This conversation seemed unreal. But there was his bloodied middle toe and horrible old Hawk was telling him there were two dead banditos lying out in the street. Suddenly, a woman outside screamed.

"She musta found their thievin' bodies," Hawk said matter-of-factly. "I doubt they're a pretty sight."

"I'll pay you extra money," Quinn said. "But I'm not going to Yellowstone."

"If you don't go, I'll damn you with a Shoshone curse. That, and you won't get rich."

Quinn cared nothing about the Indian curse, but the word "rich" sounded good. Still, he had no intention of going far away with this crazy old coot.

"Hawk, let's go to my room. We can send for a woman to feed us."

"Okay, but I won't trifle with a woman." Hawk shook his head. "Can't trifle at all."

"Then don't," Quinn replied, remembering that old men often had difficulty doing what young men most desired to do. "But let's get out of this barn."

Quinn slung an arm across Hawk's shoulders and reminded himself again that he owed the mountain man his life.

Chapter Two

"Señor King is leaving for Monterey!" Inez whispered late one dark and overcast April morning.

Juanita had been brushing her black hair, burnished with the reddish highlights of an Irish heritage. She placed her comb on her vanity and turned to look at her only true friend and confidante. "Are you certain? Mr. King said nothing to me about leaving last night."

"I just overheard," the Indian girl replied. "Señora, are you sure that we should run away and hide in the hills?"

Small wonder that poor Inez looked so frightened whenever they spoke of fleeing. After the death of her parents, the orphaned Inez had been raised by a succession of poor Chumash Indian families, passing from one to another like an unwelcome hand-me-down. And while she was terrified because of the abuse she had received from Mr. King, she trusted and adored Juanita. Sometimes they played and laughed like sisters but most of the time Juanita was like her mother and her protector.

"Inez, listen to me," Juanita said, reaching out her arms and hugging the girl tight. "We have talked much and nothing has changed. I must be free. You must be free."

"But where can we go that his men will not find us?" Inez asked, chin trembling. "If we run, Señor King will send men after us. They would kill me and *hurt* you!"

"I am already being hurt," Juanita said, feeling a sickness in her belly where Lucius had just planted his evil seed. "And besides, I would not let them kill you. I would never allow that to happen. I swear it."

"But where . . ."

"You have Indian people who left the abandoned missions and went back to live into the wild country."

"They say my gone-away-people are all dead!"

Juanita had heard the same grim speculations. The California Indians who had lived almost four decades under Spanish bondage not only had suddenly been relieved of their mission responsibilities but also of their food and shelter. They had lost their ability to hunt and survive in the wilderness. The more fortunate ones had gone to work for the new Mexican rulers of Alta California but many others had no choice but to become beggars and thieves. Yet perhaps, Juanita prayed, a few had survived and readapted to freedom. Surely there were at least a couple of small bands of Indians surviving in the nearby coastal mountains where game remained plentiful.

"I believe some of your people yet live free," Juanita again reminded the worried girl. "We can hide among them until we decide what is best. This is our only hope."

"Yes," Inez said, trying to act brave but sounding doubtful. "We just have to find them."

"That is why we have packed our clothes and some jerky. We have chosen good horses and . . ."

"But I still cannot ride!" Inez exclaimed. "I have only *touched* a horse."

Juanita had promised weeks earlier to find a way to get Inez on the back of a horse. But, since this would have been extremely unusual and attract great attention, it had never been possible.

"I know, but you will learn quickly," Juanita promised. "It is not hard and the horse we have chosen for you is gentle."

"But Señora, the vaqueros can race their horses very fast! How can we escape them?"

"Maybe they will not come after us if Mr. King is gone and cannot give the order. Besides, Chaco Diaz will accompany him to Monterey. The others only act upon the orders of my husband and Chaco. With any luck at all, both will be gone for at least two weeks."

Inez nodded so vigorously it seemed as if she were struggling to convince herself that all would turn out well. "Yes, Señora, two weeks."

"Today, we need to sell more household silver for money," Juanita said. "Inez, this is very important. Without money, we cannot get help."

"But, if my people still live free, they would not use money."

"*Everyone* needs money. As much money as they can get. Always remember that."

"I will never have money."

Juanita understood the Indian girl. In Alta California, there were many wealthy Spaniards and Mexicans. People so rich that they did nothing except enjoy life and indulge in lavish entertainments, each attempting to be grander and more colorful than their equally rich neighbors.

There also were a few very successful Anglos—men like her husband, who had made a great deal of money raising cattle on leased land and brokering shipments between the Californios and the American ship captains. Sometimes, her husband also imported shoddy factory goods from New England that he resold at large profits in the ports of San Francisco, San Diego, and Monterey. Another remarkable American success story was that of the already legendary John Augustus Sutter, a penniless Swiss who had landed in California and charmed the Mexican officials into giving him an inland empire up on the American River.

There were *no* rich California Indians. Indians were just as much of a subclass now as they had always been under the strict parochial rule of the Spaniards. And, if the Americans ever seized control of California, as many predicted they soon would, the native Indians would still be considered vastly inferior beings. Always poor, always little more than slaves to a tenuous survival. Even now, they were still the first to die from every new epidemic and usually buried without benefit of clergy or blessing—as her father had been in his pauper's grave.

"Señora, it is all right," Inez was saying. "I do not need money. Only food."

"You will have much more than food. I will take care of you," Juanita vowed. "As long as I have life and breath you shall never go hungry or cold or taste the bite of a whip again."

Inez's eyes filled with grateful tears. "I believe you

but I am still afraid. I pray, just as you have told me, but God does not comfort.''

"He will protect us, and so will I. Now go outside again and listen to the vaqueros and my husband. Listen well, for we cannot afford to make a mistake when we leave this night.''

The Indian girl paled. "Tonight?''

"It is perfect. If the rain begins, it will wash away the tracks of our horses so that not even Chaco and his vaqueros will be able to find them.''

They held hands for a moment, each praying for rain and their freedom. Then, they parted to make their preparations.

The storm held off all morning but the air tasted of rain. In their courtyard, the flowers swayed in a rising wind that whistled over the courtyard wall. Juanita heard the distant rumble of thunder and prayed that it would not cause Lucius to postpone his trip to Los Angeles. That was most unlikely for he always traveled in an enclosed carriage but if El Camino Real, known by the early Spanish as The King's Highway, became too slick with mud, it would make travel impossible.

"I want rain,'' she whispered to Inez that afternoon as they prepared to cut some roses for the house, "but not if it makes him decide to stay here tonight.''

"Will it, Señora?''

"I don't know. He's been packing and going over figures all morning in preparation for what must be a very important business meeting. I'm hoping that he will have no choice but to leave as soon as possible.''

"Inez!'' Lucius shouted, suddenly emerging from the

house. "My boots weren't polished this morning and damned if I can find clean underwear!"

Juanita dropped her fresh-cut roses and stepped in front of Inez. "That's my fault. I had her working on my mending. And besides, I thought Inez was *my* helper."

"Don't question my authority!"

Juanita stood her ground, well aware that she was Inez's only strength and protection. "I am questioning nothing," she told her husband, "but Inez is my personal servant. Please ask someone else to polish your shoes and wash your clothes."

"Sonofabitch!" he shouted, papers scattering from his hand. "We're going to get a few things straight right here and now. *I* am the master of this house. *You* are nothing! You came from nothing and by gawd, if I decide to throw you out of my house, you will become nothing except the used daughter of a pathetic drunk!"

Something snapped inside Juanita. One moment she was protecting little Inez, the next throwing herself at this animal who had robbed her of her innocence and precious childhood dreams. Lucius had taken everything except her spirit and that spirit now inflamed her mind. Juanita wanted to beat his ugly, brutish face and curse his name.

Chaco started to jump between them but stopped when Lucius took three long strides and punched Juanita in the chest. Her rage was instantly replaced with agony and she crumpled to her knees, hearing Inez call her name. She turned her head to see Inez snatch up their rose-pruning knife. Juanita had no doubt that the Indian girl would have buried the knife in Lucius except that Chaco drew his pistol and fired but missed. Dropping his weapon, he reached for his wicked fighting knife.

"No!" Juanita yelled, sprinting to shield the terrified girl.

Lucius was right behind her. "Chaco, this savage bitch was going to knife me! She *would* have put a knife in me if you hadn't fired at her!"

Chaco calmly began to reload his weapon. "That Indian girl is not to be trusted, Señor King. She has a devil's spirit."

"By gawd, you got that right! Hurry and get my whip."

"Please!" Juanita cried. "Inez was just trying to protect me. She forgot herself."

"Hurry up in there!" Lucius bellowed, then turned back to Juanita. "I'm gonna peel away that girl's hide and sell her cheap as a dirty Indian whore!"

"I *swear* that she did not mean to kill you!"

"What else was she planning to do with that knife? Now crawl away from her!"

When Chaco appeared moments later with his master's rawhide whip, Juanita dragged the cringing girl to her feet, shouting, "Run for it!"

Inez was so paralyzed by fear that Juanita had to practically shove her toward the courtyard gate. She fumbled with the latch as Lucius's whip bit through her cheap cotton dress and into the flesh between her shoulder blades. Juanita heard the girl's hysterical shriek.

"Inez, run!"

But the Indian girl seemed frozen with one hand on the gate latch, the other raised as if giving a benediction to the busy street beyond. Juanita grabbed the fallen knife and lunged after her husband, who was following Inez, whipping and cutting her back to shreds as she staggered out into the street. Juanita knew that his rage and savagery would not allow him to stop until the girl was dead.

"Damn you!" Juanita cried, grabbing up the pruning shears and attacking Lucius from behind. She drove the knife into his shoulder and felt its tip glance off bone. She heard his cry and it sounded like music.

Lucius spun around and knocked her into the street. "Chaco!" he howled. "Kill them! Kill them *both!*"

Chaco drew his knife again. It was said that he was the best knife fighter in Santa Barbara and he carried the scars of his bloody victories like badges of courage. Juanita struggled up and faced the Mexican with her little knife clenched in her fist.

"This will be my pleasure," Chaco told his boss, advancing toward Juanita with a wicked smile on his scarred face.

"Inez, run!" Juanita cried, choking down rising terror. "Run and don't ever stop!"

Quinn and Hawk's wounds had almost mended that gray and overcast afternoon when they rounded a corner and saw a bloody-faced woman and a small Indian girl being attacked, one with a cattle whip, the other with a knife.

"Gawdamn!" Hawk swore, clawing for his old flint-lock pistol and bellowing, "Get away from that poor little girl, you ornery sonofabitch!"

Quinn began to hobble as fast as he could toward the knife-wielding Mexican, scooping up a rock since he was unarmed. "Stop!"

Lucius King was so enraged he did not hear Hawk's terse order. He was still mindlessly lashing the squirming, shrieking Indian girl when Hawk's lead ball struck him in the right knee. His mouth opened wide and he collapsed, twitching.

When Chaco Diaz turned, Quinn planted his feet and hurled the rock with all his might, striking him in the face. Chaco staggered and tried to recover but it was too late. Quinn landed a thundering haymaker against the side of his face. The knife spilled from Chaco's fist and he bent over, allowing Quinn to drive an uppercut into his exposed ribs, spilling him to the ground, gasping for air.

Quinn spun around to confront the woman. "What the hell is going on here?"

Juanita was dazed but the pruning knife was still clenched in her fist. When she saw Lucius, she might have killed him if Quinn hadn't pinned her to his chest, kicking and screaming.

"Easy!" he shouted, his eyes jumping to hawk, who was kneeling beside the Indian girl and covering her mutilated back with his dirty buckskin jacket. "Who are . . ."

"We've *got* to get away before the vaqueros come!" Juanita cried, her words sounding thick because of her mashed lips. "When my husband's vaqueros hear of this, they'll kill us all!"

"The hell they will!" Hawk snorted. "Who is this little Indian girl?"

"Her name is Inez. She works in my husband's household."

"Bastard deserves to die," Hawk hissed, glancing over at the writhing American. "I never seen no animal whipped like he was doin' to this girl."

Juanita knew that there was no time for even the briefest of explanations. The gunshots would bring people in a hurry and some of them might be her husband's vaqueros, coming to his aid. Certainly it would not be long before Chaco's equally dangerous and despicable brother Xavier and the other vaqueros discovered him beaten almost beyond recognition. They would be duty bound to seek revenge.

Escaping Quinn's grasp, Juanita ran into the house to grab the things she had packed for their escape. She found Lucius's wallet, knowing it would be filled with money, then ran down the hallway and out the back door. When she reached the stables, two Indians were standing with round, fearful eyes beside her husband's waiting carriage. When she started to speak, the pair turned and fled. Juanita hauled saddles and bridles from the tack room and loaded them into the carriage.

Satisfied that she had accomplished everything that time permitted, Juanita clambered into the driver's seat. As a girl, she had driven a team of horses for several months after her father had become too drunk to handle a brief freighting job. It had been easy and pleasant. Gathering the lines, Juanita figured that she could escape with Inez and drive this coach out of Santa Barbara following El Camino Real north. When the four horses grew tired of their hard laboring, she would cut them free of their harness, saddle two and ride them as far and as fast as possible, allowing for Inez's awful condition.

Wiping blood from her lips, Juanita threw her head back and gazed up at the dark and troubled sky. "Rain! Please rain!"

She drove the carriage around to the street and saw Inez weeping, out of her mind with pain and confusion. Juanita hauled the sorrels up and shouted, "Put her inside! Hurry, please!"

"Where the hell are you goin'?" Hawk shouted, arms still wrapped protectively around Inez. "This girl needs a doctor!"

The sorrels were fractious and almost impossible to handle. They probably smelled blood and wanted to run. "Please, listen! My husband and that Mexican you hurt will have you both drawn and quartered!"

"Your husband is shot," Quinn said.

"My knee!" Lucius cried. "I'm bleeding to death. Help me!"

"Help you?" Hawk roared. "After what you done to that poor Indian girl, you deserve to be castrated!"

Juanita had seen farm animals castrated and it would have given her immense pleasure to watch her husband suffer the same fate. When Hawk marched over to Lucius, Juanita dragged Inez into the carriage. A piercing scream spun her around and she saw Hawk standing over her husband.

My God, he actually did it! Juanita thought, hearing the young man beside her draw a deep breath. She turned to him and said, "Mister, get out of Santa Barbara just as fast as you can! If my husband doesn't bleed to death, he'll see you *both* dead."

Quinn had heard all about Lucius King and knew she was right. "Thanks for the warning. I promise we won't be far behind." Juanita gave the team free rein and let them run. The carriage whipped back and forth, almost overturning as it barreled through the poor Indian district of Santa Barbara.

Dear God, help us and help those two Americans, she thought as the carriage swerved up El Camino Real and into a storm.

Quinn ran to grab Hawk and yelled over the rumble of approaching thunder, "Hawk, we've got to run!"

"Pilgrim, if we run, we run to Yellowstone! Is that clear?"

"Yes!"

"Okay, then," Hawk snorted, sheathing his bowie and clapping Quinn on the back.

It took them less than thirty minutes to gather their belongings and buy two fast horses.

"Which way?" Quinn shouted.

"North up the coast, then we cut east and cross over the coastal mountains."

Quinn felt cold raindrops begin to pelt his face as they galloped out of Santa Barbara, following the same road that the woman had taken with the half-dead Indian girl. Maybe they would overtake the carriage, but maybe not. As far as Quinn was concerned, perhaps it was best if they didn't.

That pair had already brought them the very worst kind of bad luck.

Chapter Three

As she drove the carriage deeper into the onrushing storm, Juanita tried not to imagine the chaos taking place back in Santa Barbara. When the image of Lucius clasping his wounded knee and then his groin appeared, Juanita remembered how her husband had been shot and . . . She shuddered at the thought. *Castrated.* What kind of a man could maim and degrade another so horribly?

The answer was clear—only someone wild·and completely uncivilized. A throwback to a barbarian, a pirate, or a savage. And what about Chaco? Proud, cruel Chaco, who had been defeated by a handsome young man who hobbled on a bad foot and, at first glance, appeared harmless.

My God, Chaco and his family will be honor-bound to seek revenge.

The storm was intensifying, the rain coming down in icy, wind-driven sheets. *Good! This will wash out our tracks.*

Just ahead, a bolt of lightning lanced out of the sky and a tree exploded in flames. Thunder cracked like cannon and the terrified horses swerved, sending the carriage into a shuddering slide on the muddy road. Juanita fought the team but it was too late as the carriage yawed badly, teetering on two wheels before slamming over onto its side. Juanita struck the ground, rolling over and over until she came to rest against a large rock. Dazed, she managed to stand. The sounds of the thrashing and screaming horses competed with the thunder. Jumping to her feet, Juanita ran to the carriage and had to jump up on its side to reach the door handle.

"Inez!"

The Indian girl looked like a broken rag doll covered with saddles and loose tack. Tearing the door open, Juanita had to move the heavy Mexican saddles before she could reach her. "Inez, please don't die!"

The girl's eyes fluttered. "Where are we? What . . ."

"It's all right," Juanita whispered with relief. "We've . . . we've escaped."

Inez tried to move, but Juanita held her still. "I've made an awful mistake," she confessed. "I was driving the team much too fast. I lost control and we over-turned."

Inez gazed around, then said, "I'm all right. But I can hear the horses struggling."

"They're going to be fine," Juanita said, making a poor job of hiding her doubts. "I just have to get them saddled so we can ride away and never be found."

"Yes, we must go far away." Inez blinked rapidly against the rain. "But Señora, I don't think we're ever going to . . ."

"Don't you worry. I'll be right back." Juanita covered

the girl with the horsehair saddle blankets, knowing they would offer some protection from the storm.

"Promise me you won't move." She could feel the horses thrashing violently. She was glad she still had the sharp pruning knife to cut them free.

"Inez, you must gather strength for what is yet to be faced. I'll be back soon."

Juanita crawled outside and studied the destruction. The carriage was destroyed. One of the sorrels was standing, but the other three were hopelessly entangled, kicking and slamming their heads up and down in the mud.

Juanita drew the pruning knife out from her coat. "Easy," she crooned to the struggling animals as she slowly began to cut them free of their tangled harness.

"Easy," she repeated again and again. The moment the first horse was free, it bolted forward, bucking like the devil up the soggy highway.

I can't afford to let that happen again, Juanita thought as the animal disappeared into the storm.

Her mind clearer, she began to use pieces of harness to hobble each horse before it was free to escape. It was easy, for she had often seen her husband's vaqueros hobble horses with loops of stiff rawhide.

"Inez?" she asked, returning to the carriage. "Can you climb out?"

"I think so."

Inez pushed to her feet and, somehow, she got outside. Juanita retrieved the saddles and readied two of the horses. "Maybe I can lift you into the saddle," she said.

Inez nodded and Juanita could tell that her friend was very near the breaking point. It seemed unfair to expect her to climb onto a horse for the first time in her life and ride to God-only-knows-where in the hope of finding sanctuary.

"God will help us, won't He?" Inez asked weakly.

"Of course," Juanita replied, leading the child over to what seemed the more calm and sensible of the two animals. "Speak softly to this mare and tell her that you expect her to be good."

"I expect you to behave and not hurt me," Inez told the nervous sorrel mare. "In return, you will never feel the whip from my hand as I have felt it today from your master."

"All right," Juanita said, aware of each precious passing moment. "I will lift you into the saddle but I am afraid that I cannot shorten the stirrups."

Inez grasped the saddlehorn as if it were her salvation and sat upright, eyes staring straight ahead.

"Try to relax," Juanita urged.

Inez struggled to relax and Juanita felt that perhaps they could really elude their pursuers. They were now in possession of three very fast horses. Inez was managing, and Juanita quickly made sure that her money and precious food was still packed into the saddlebags.

"I'll lead off slowly at first," Juanita said. "As soon as I'm sure our horses will behave, I'll remove their hobbles."

Juanita mounted her own horse, keeping a tight rein so the animal could not bolt. She was quite tall for a woman, as tall as most of the vaqueros, so her stirrups were the correct length. "Inez, even though these hobbles are loose, they will force our horses to hop. Do not be afraid. Just hang on tight!"

"I will."

"Someone is coming!" Inez cried, looking back down the road.

Juanita's first impulse was to jump down, cut the hobbles, and try to outrun the vaqueros. But that was ridiculous. Inez would fall off and they would both be returned to Santa Barbara as prisoners. Certain that they were about to be captured, she even considered killing herself rather than endure the humiliation and degradation of facing her vengeful husband.

"It is the Americanos!" Inez cried.

Juanita almost sobbed with relief as they waited until the two men galloped up.

"Can you help us?" she cried.

"Damn right," Hawk bellowed, jumping from his horse and using his awful knife to cut the hobbles free. "Where are we goin'?"

"We don't know," Juanita admitted, realizing how foolish that must sound. "We are running for our lives. Where can we go that is safe?"

"Yellowstone!"

"Hawk," the younger man protested, "this woman don't even know . . ."

"Never mind!" the mountain man thundered. "Let's ride for the high mountains."

Juanita let the mountain man untie the reata from her saddlehorn and lead Inez. She followed close behind and the young American brought up the rear, leading their extra horse. The rain intensified and they turned east, climbing steadily into the coastal range. Long, miserable hours passed until Inez rolled sideways off her horse.

"Tarnation!" Hawk shouted, jumping off his horse. "We've got to make a shelter and get this girl warm!"

"I can do that," Quinn said. "I brought some tools."

"Well, then do it!" Hawk yelled over the storm.

Quinn felled several trees. With a saw and hammer,

he quietly fashioned them a shelter. It was crude but effective, and the mountain man had no difficulty starting a fire.

"Señorita," Hawk said, "in case you're wonderin' about your husband, he's goin' to live."

"Did you . . ." Juanita was too embarrassed to complete the question.

"Naw! He ain't gelded. But I sure put the fear of God in him, didn't I?" The old man cackled with mirth but, Juanita was filled with dread. Lucius was not a man to forgive or forget. Yellowstone might be far, far away, but—for the sake of revenge—Lucius would send men with orders to track them to the end of the earth.

Two days later, they had crossed the coastal range and dropped into the great Central Valley of Alta California where bands of wild horses grazed on the rich native grasses. The sun gleamed like burnished copper and huge clouds sailed on warm westerly winds. Inez was handling her pain and her fear. Best of all, she had fallen in love not only with her sorrel mare, but also with the old mountain man who doted on her as if she were his own flesh and blood.

And so, riding free with Inez across this virgin wilderness, Juanita thought that life could not have been finer were it not for the realization that they were being hunted.

That evening, Juanita said to Quinn, "Your friend talked in his sleep last night."

"He did?"

"Yes. He kept calling out for Hocina."

"He's never mentioned anyone with that name."

"I think she is Indian."

Quinn threw a couple of twigs on their struggling campfire. The night was cool and they were camped in an arroyo, sheltered from a persistent southerly wind. "I've heard that the mountain men often married Indian women and fathered children."

"Has he ever spoken of such a woman?"

"No. Hawk talks constantly about Yellowstone and the Shoshone Indians along with their friends, the Bannock, Nez Perce, and Flathead. I gather the Shoshone are his favorites and have a number of scattered bands, each named after their principal livelihood."

"What does that mean?"

"Well," Quinn explained, "some of them are called Sheepeaters because they live in the higher mountains and their main source of meat is wild sheep. Others are Fisheaters, and so forth."

"The merino sheep being raised on the California ranchos could not survive in mountains," Juanita told him. "What kind of sheep are raised in Yellowstone?"

"I don't know but they must be very different from the California flocks." Quinn smiled. "All I care about now is outrunning your husband's men and finding a glory hole filled with Yellowstone gold. That's part of our deal."

"What if he has no gold?"

"Well, he does!" Quinn exclaimed. "He's shown me some nuggets already, And he carries a map drawn by no less a famous man than that John Colter. It shows a dead tree lying in the Yellowstone River and . . ."

"A dead tree?" Juanita couldn't help but stare because Quinn seemed so naive. "There are probably *hundreds* of dead trees resting in Yellowstone rivers."

"Yeah, but we'll find the right one with Colter's map."

Quinn was about to say more but their conversation

was interrupted by the sound of racing hoofbeats. He and Juanita kicked dirt over the fire, then grabbed their rifles and scrambled up to the rim of the arroyo. The hoofbeats grew louder and Quinn wondered if the smoke from their pitiful campfire had been enough to betray their presence.

"Don't shoot unless I do," he ordered as his heartbeat matched the drum of the flying hooves.

A band of mustangs burst out of the darkness and seemed to leap over the moon, then landed on the far side of the arroyo before thundering away like ghostly apparitions.

"Nothing to worry about," Juanita said, breathing a sigh of relief.

Hawk had awakened and thought otherwise. "Somethin' must have spooked 'em. Let's give it time."

A quarter of an hour passed before they heard the squeaking of saddle leather and saw the glitter of silver conchos. Quinn felt a chill down his spine as their pursuers, holding at a steady trot and moving along in single file, entered and exited the arroyo as they trailed the wild horses.

"They're far enough away now," Juanita said after a long, anxious while. "The dust of those wild horses must have blotted out our campfire smoke."

Quinn realized how lucky they'd been. "I think we should ride to the base of the Sierras rather than stay in this open valley," he said.

"If that's what you think, we can do it," Hawk agreed, "but I'd as soon shoot 'em as not."

"There were too many," Juanita said, feeling very tired. Tired, and anxious about what would befall them in the days, weeks, and even years that lay ahead.

* * *

The Sierras were big-shouldered and mantled with snow. Juanita wondered how they would ever cross them, but Hawk told her he knew a good pass.

"What kind of birds are those?" Inez asked, pointing up at a pair with immense wingspans.

"They're vultures," Hawk answered.

"Condors," Quinn corrected.

"Same thing," Hawk grumped as the great birds soared effortlessly on the updrafts, necks craning as they searched for carrion. Once, Juanita saw an eagle plunge thousands of feet into the forest, then emerge with a struggling creature whose dying shrieks echoed across the mountain canyons.

Their plan was to ride to Sutter's Fort and buy whatever provisions they would need for a Yellowstone expedition. But that all changed one afternoon. "Hawk, wouldn't Sutter's Fort be the most logical place for anyone from Santa Barbara to intercept us?" Quinn asked.

"Yeah," Hawk agreed. "Everyone who comes or goes over these mountains must pass through Sutter's Fort."

"Then perhaps we should outfit somewhere else," Juanita suggested. "There must be other posts."

"There's a fair-sized tradin' post on the far side of these mountains," Hawk replied. "But it's owned by a low-down, double-dealin' scalawag named Custis Crowder who profits off immigrants who have just crossed the Nevada desert. By the time they make that last waterless fifty miles to the Truckee River, their livestock are in no shape to pull wagons over the Sierras. Crowder buys them used-up animals cheap and resells 'em later after they're fat and rested. Nothin' wrong with makin' a profit, but Crowder is gettin' rich off folks' misery."

"Well," Quinn said, "Crowder won't make much of a living off of us. We have good horses and they'll still be in fine shape after we cross the Sierras. All we need is a couple of pack animals and a few extra supplies."

"Pilgrim, you seem to know a lot for a man that has never been more'n a hundred miles from any damned ocean. You came around Cape Horn on a sailin' ship, right?"

"Yes, but . . ."

"Well then, you got *no* idea what we'll need to reach Yellowstone."

"Maybe not," Quinn said, stung by the old man's bluntness, "but one thing I do know is that what funds I have left I mean to save for emergencies."

"In Yellowstone, emergencies happen every day. And ladies, you might as well understand we'll live in a wickiup like the Shoshone. Ain't nothin' better."

"I don't want to live in a wickiup," Juanita said.

"It won't be so bad," Quinn assured her. "We'll only stay in Yellowstone long enough to find the gold and then leave before the Blackfeet catch us."

"Glad you told her about them murderin' Injuns we might have to fight," Hawk said. "I'm not tryin' to scare any of you, but just want to make sure you all understand Yellowstone ain't like Santa Barbara."

Juanita put her hands on her hips. "We know that."

"Glad you do. Can you shoot?"

In reply, Juanita went over to her bedroll and retrieved her pistol.

"Try and hit the tree yonder," Hawk suggested, pointing to one about fifty yards away.

"All right. Do you see that little pine cone?"

"I see a lot of pine cones."

"Watch the one hanging lowest on the tree."

Before Hawk could reply, Juanita took aim and fired, all in one smooth, unhurried motion. Hawk's eyes bugged when the pine cone shattered.

"Sonofa . . . gun!" Hawk choked, catching himself before he cussed. "That's fine shootin'! But what about a rifle?"

"I'm even better with a rifle," Juanita told him. "My father did teach me a few valuable lessons. But now we need to break camp."

"Yes, ma'am!," Hawk said with sudden respect. "Anythin' else?"

"Yes, as soon as you're feeling better, take a bath. And when you pass wind, do it away from our camp."

"Why, sure!" Hawk winked at Quinn. "Maybe it's that blood-suckin', card cheatin' Crowder and the Blackfeet that ought to start worryin'!"

Chapter Four

They spent the following days skirting the Sierras and fording the many powerful rivers that flowed off the western slopes until they reached the American River, about seventy miles northeast of Sutter's Fort where pines had replaced oak and sycamore.

"Pilgrims, it's time to put ourselves to the test," Hawk grandly announced one morning. He pointed up toward the soaring, snow-capped peaks. "We're strikin' for the summit pass. There'll be snow up to our bellies in another couple thousand feet. It'll be cold and tough goin'."

"More snow than usual?" Quinn asked.

"A hell of a lot more snow," Hawk replied. "Double or triple normal, I'd guess. We got to watch out for avalanches. They happen when the snow is meltin' and starts to break loose underneath."

Hawk checked Inez's cinch, then his own, making it clear that Quinn and Juanita would be wise to do the same. "Child, you hang on tight and stay in the midst of us. Don't let this mare turn and head back down."

"I won't," Inez promised.

"I know that. You and this horse are friends, right?"

Inez grinned. "I love her."

"And she loves you."

Juanita couldn't help but notice how Hawk's eyes went soft and his voice gentled whenever he spoke to Inez. It convinced her that the old man had a girl of his own somewhere. There was a softness, but also a sadness in Hawk when he talked to Inez. If Juanita had to guess, she was afraid that Hawk had lost his own daughter and that Inez had already taken her place.

Hawk's prediction about deep snow in the higher elevation proved all too true. A few miles farther and they could see the peaks where only the tops of the tallest trees were visible.

Juanita fretted because their horses soon had to buck the snow. "Hawk, what will it be like on the other side of these mountains?"

"Won't be as much snow on the eastern slopes," he promised. "Never is. But I reckon it'll be June before anyone can drive a wagon through this pass. Gonna be mud-sloppy for weeks after the snow is gone and these rivers are runnin' high."

"It sounds like you've been over this pass more than a time or two," Quinn remarked.

"That I have!"

Hawk kept a sharp vigil for dangerous footing as he forced his mount through the melting snow. "This wagon road is gonna be washed out and need a lot of work when the first immigrant trains attempt a crossin' later this spring."

"Bet it doesn't stop them, though," Quinn called as

they rode in single file, winding their way higher and higher through a stand of majestic Ponderosa pines whose boughs were still drooping with melting snow.

"Naw, it won't stop 'em," Hawk agreed. "Put yourself in their shoes. If you'd already come a thousand miles across every kind of bad country, would you quit a hundred miles short of California?"

"Never."

"And neither will they," Hawk declared, letting his wary horse pick its own sound footing.

It took them four hours to climb five miles that afternoon and threatening weather turned nasty at the summit. Shivering, exhausted, and with a rising wind blowing snow into their half-frozen faces, they made an early camp and even Hawk was put to the test starting a fire while Quinn constructed a hurried shelter. It grew bitterly cold as darkness fell. The wind strengthened, hurling icy crystals while they huddled together for warmth, feeding their struggling campfire.

"You warm enough, girl?" Hawk asked worriedly.

"I am now," Inez said as he dragged her between himself and their campfire.

"How is your foot?" Juanita asked, noting the way Quinn still limped.

"It's healing."

"Maybe I should look at it."

"Naw. It's just the toe but it's taking longer than I expected."

Such a wound should have almost healed by now, Juanita thought. "Take off your boot and let me see."

"No, thanks," he snapped.

"Do what she says, Pilgrim. Go lame and you won't be any use to me in Yellowstone."

Quinn knew that the toe was festering but he'd

checked it every morning and there was no evidence of gangrene. Still, it was swelled up and he wished it would quit throbbing.

"All right, dammit." He removed his boot and let Juanita peel off his dirty stocking.

Juanita drew in a sharp breath. "We must boil some water and then I will use a knife to open this wound so it can drain."

"Not a chance." Quinn pulled the foot back under him. "It's going to be fine. Besides, you're no doctor."

"It doesn't take a doctor to see that the toe is infected," Juanita said. "And that the infection will soon spread into your foot. Do you want to *lose* that foot?"

All three of them were staring at Quinn. The idea of losing his foot chilled him right to the bone.

"Okay," he said, "but go easy. It hurts enough already."

"You'll live," Juanita said.

It took some time to boil water—then Juanita used a hairpin to lance Quinn's shattered toe. He managed not to howl and, when she was finished applying steaming compresses to the toe, she let him stick a snowball around it. Quinn sighed with relief. "You are very stubborn, Señor," she told him.

"And you aren't?"

Juanita smiled at that; they were all stubborn and strong-willed. Inez was no exception, although she still hadn't completely recovered from her beating despite the healing salve Juanita had applied to her back. Juanita knew the Chumash Indian girl had a lot of grit and spunk. Hadn't she attacked Lucius and stabbed him with that pruning knife? That took great courage.

No one said much of anything the next morning as they saddled the horses, though Quinn thanked her for doctoring his foot and mumbled, "Feels a whole lot better than yesterday."

"We'll need to do that every night until the healing is finished and all the redness is gone."

"Okay," he said, throwing the heavy Mexican saddle on her horse in what Juanita supposed was repayment.

After a quick breakfast, they attacked the summit with every intention of getting through the pass and well down the eastern slope before sundown. But they were surprised to come upon the tracks of many horses. Juanita took a deep breath. *So, my husband's vaqueros are waiting for us up ahead,* she thought.

"Hawk, what do you think?" Quinn asked. "Is it our friends from Santa Barbara here to settle the score?"

The mountain man didn't bother to dismount or even lean down for a closer look. "Not likely. They'd be warmin' their toes down beside the American and probably have paid a couple of Sutter's men to be their spies. These tracks are only two or three hours old. We'll catch 'em beyond the pass headin' for Nevada."

"That'd be fine," Quinn said. "Just as long as they aren't King's henchmen."

"Señora," Hawk said, pointing back to the tracks. "Some of these people are afoot. Vaqueros wouldn't walk, would they?"

"Not unless they had to," Juanita answered. She couldn't see any boot tracks, but that didn't mean they weren't there. Hawk was a tracker and she knew better than to argue. "Any idea how many?"

"I'd guess a dozen. Could be more, though."

"Maybe there are some children." Inez smiled. "Like me."

"Maybe," Hawk said, favoring her with a smile. "We'll find out soon enough."

The air was thin, the going hard, and no one said anything until they finally crested an icy, windswept ridge where Hawk dismounted and stood behind his horse. The harsh, buffeting wind cut like a blade and whistled through the bent and beaten pines. "There it is!" Hawk shouted, resting an arm across his saddle to point eastward. "That's Nevada desert and it stretches all the way to the great Rocky Mountains."

They dismounted, loosened their cinches, and stood behind their horses using the steaming, panting animals as a windbreak while they gazed down at the hazy brown panorama that marked the beginning of the infamous Humboldt desert lands.

"There's a pretty lake," Juanita said, pointing to a place just a few miles off to the north. "It's below the snow line. Perhaps we could camp there tonight and . . . look, people!"

"About time one of you saw 'em," Hawk remarked.

It took Quinn a few seconds to see what they were talking about. "That must be the party whose tracks we found," he said. "But why would they veer away from the most obvious trail down to the Washoe Crossing?"

"They ain't movin', are they?" Hawk asked with a frown.

"No," Juanita answered, "they've stopped in a clearing. What I really don't understand is why the treetops around those people are all chopped off high above the ground."

"Maybe they are in trouble and need our help," Inez offered.

"Maybe," Hawk replied. "I can't figure why they'd gather on this mountainside with snow up to their eyeballs. Another hour, they could be on the dry. Makes no sense a'tall to me. Might be we oughta check 'em out."

Juanita nodded in agreement. "I think there are women among them—but no children."

"Then maybe we should detour around 'em," Hawk suggested. "I haven't much use for women."

"I know that," Juanita replied, "but what about your Indian wife, Hocina? Or is she your daughter?"

Hawk's cheeks corded with ropy muscle. "Humph!" he snorted, checking his cinch.

"Hocina must be *very* important," Juanita continued, determined to press him for the truth, "because you kept repeating her name in your sleep."

"Mind your own business!" He jammed a foot into his stirrup, hauled himself up into his saddle, and booted his horse forward, leaving them behind.

"You really angered him," Quinn said.

"I don't care. We had better understand this man well before he leads us into that desert."

"Do you think he's tricked me and all the Yellowstone gold is gone?"

"I don't know what to think, but I don't want to find out after it's too late," Juanita answered.

"Hawk is good and honest," Inez told them.

"I'm sure you're right," Juanita said, hoping her little friend was not becoming too attached to the old man.

Nothing more was said until they overtook Hawk. He had reined in his horse about a hundred yards above the group. Juanita saw that there were more than a dozen men and women arranged in a loose semicircle, hands clasped and heads bowed.

She could feel their sorrow. "Maybe we should just ride away."

"Now you're talkin'!" Hawk agreed, lifting his reins.

"It's too late. They've seen us," Juanita said, prodding her horse forward as several of the gathering turned to stare grimly at them with haunted eyes.

"Some of them are weeping," Juanita whispered, seeing tears glisten on their cheeks.

"Hello!" Quinn called, trying to sound cheerful. "You folks need any assistance?"

"Only that of God Almighty," one of the men replied. "Why have you followed us? We've no more horror stories to tell. No more ghoulish tales of . . ."

"Mister," Quinn interrupted, "we've no idea what you are talking about. We're on our way east across Nevada and happened to see you folks standing here in the snow. We just wondered if everything was all right."

"Don't you know who we are?"

"Why don't you quit jawin' and just tell us, for cryin' out loud," Hawk demanded.

Juanita's voice was far gentler. *"Are* you in trouble?"

"We're survivors of the Donner Party. We wanted to get up here as early as possible this spring to put things to rest before the damned souvenir hunters arrive."

"What happened?" Juanita asked, dreading the answer.

The men exchanged glances and, finally, one said, "We came all the way from Illinois in a wagon train headed by the Donner brothers. At Fort Bridger they took a new shortcut called the Hastings Cutoff. It was a disaster."

"The Hastings Cutoff don't exist," Hawk said.

"That's right," a man with a frostbitten nose agreed, "but we was told otherwise. Because of that, we got stuck in the Wasatch Range and had to leave goods behind to get over them awful mountains. We'd still have made it into California before winter if it hadn't taken us six days to cross the Nevada desert instead of the two we'd been told back at Fort Bridger.''

"Two days!" Hawk shook his head in amazement. "It would have taken you at least five and probably more, if your stock was used up."

"They were," a smallish man agreed, his mouth pinching down at the corners. "I lost all of my oxen and my wagon. We abandoned three other wagons trying to pull through miles of deep sand east of the Truckee River. Then Custis Crowder skinned us out of our livestock and overcharged us for replacement supplies. We couldn't pay his prices so we sent men over this pass to Sutter's Fort."

"When was this?" Juanita asked.

"Last September. We needed affordable grain and supplies. Captain Sutter treated us right."

"He is a fair man," Hawk agreed. "So what went wrong?"

"An early winter. Hell," the immigrant said bitterly, "we didn't get our supplies from Sutter's Fort until late October and the next week we got buried under a terrible blizzard right where we're standing. It didn't stop snowing 'til early this spring."

The man began to tremble as he tried to finish. "Right here in this clearing we lost more'n forty men, women, and children to cold and hunger. Some of 'em were buried under snow—others wandered off to freeze and save food for their kids."

"And no one could get out for help?" Juanita asked, finding it hard to believe this horrific tale.

"Some tried, but were lost."

Juanita dismounted and handed her reins to Quinn,

feeling dazed. Inez did the same. They couldn't help but join the grieving Donner Party women.

"We was trapped here nearly four months," someone told Quinn and Hawk. "You wouldn't believe the suffering."

Quinn's eyes lifted to the topped trees and he tried to imagine these starving, snowbound men chopping pine tops in a desperate attempt to keep their families alive.

"Enough of this talk! We got bones and bodies to find and bury," another man snorted. "And we don't want no strangers watchin'. No offense, but we'd like you people to be on your way."

Quinn saw Juanita cradle a woman in her arms. "I don't have much money to spare," he said, "but you can have what is left."

"Money can't replace what we've lost. We're finished."

"No man is finished unless he quits," Hawk argued. "Where you headed after the buryin'?"

"We'd planned to buy prime farmland in California, but now we're busted. Some are going back to Illinois— others just haven't been able to decide yet."

"Illinois has already got way too many people," Hawk said with his characteristic bluntness. "It's California that needs more Americans."

"That's what we've heard, but . . ."

"You folks just need time to rest and think about the future," Hawk told them, reaching into his buckskin jacket and removing the last remaining Yellowstone nuggets.

The Donner Party stared, then crowded around. Finally one of them said, "Mister, those are worth a *lot* of money."

"Yep. Enough to buy you some farmland, tools, and supplies so you can get back on your feet."

"We can't take so much!"

"Then consider it a loan should we ever meet again some day in happier times. But this is seed money for California. Not the Oregon Territory—California. And I ask that you folks do whatever you can to make her a part of the United States of America."

"We've been to Sutter's Fort. We know about the Bear Flag Revolution and we all support General Fremont and what our people are fixin' to do."

"Then help 'em when you hear the call to arms," Hawk said, placing the huge nuggets into an immigrant's hand. Without another word, he climbed stiffly back into his saddle and rode away.

For several moments, everyone was in shock. Finally, the one who held the nuggets said in a husky voice, "Who *is* he?"

"His name is Hawk," Quinn answered. "And my friend is a mountain man."

"He's a saint!"

"Isn't there anything I can do to help?" Quinn asked.

"If you meet any souvenir hunters, tell 'em to stay away from what they're now callin' Donner Pass. You tell 'em we'll shoot any souvenir hunters on sight!"

"I'll warn them."

Quinn remounted and rode over to collect Juanita. He saw that the women were gathered around a pile of debris that was just beginning to poke through the melting snow. He recognized charred wagon parts. Strips of leather. Rotting canvas and clothes. Bones of animals . . . or perhaps even people; Quinn didn't want to know.

"We're going to burn whatever will burn," a tall, very

thin woman vowed as she began to douse the remnants with a jar of kerosene. "Going to burn everything before they come to pick through our misery!"

Quinn watched the woman struggle to light the soggy mass. It was just too wet and too cold. The debris wouldn't burn and several women began to sob.

"Juanita. Inez," he called, unable to endure another moment as he reined after Hawk, "let's go!"

Juanita and Inez caught up with them about an hour later; not a word was spoken as they rode down to dry ground in the eastern Sierra foothills and made a warm camp. That evening, Quinn realized that Juanita's jewelry was missing. It made him realize that she had a good heart. Too bad she'd sold herself out for money and married Lucius King. Too bad that he and Hawk had also gotten involved.

The gardener who oversaw Sutter's two-acre rose garden knocked on the door of the hacienda where Chaco, Xavier, and three more vaqueros were quartered. When one of them opened the door, the gardener scurried inside, momentarily blinded in the semi-darkness.

Chaco's once-handsome face was still puffy and discolored from the beating he'd taken from Quinn. His left eye remained nearly swollen shut. Now, he glared one-eyed at the gardener and rasped, "I understand you finally have some news!"

"Si, Señor!" The gardener remembered to remove his sombrero as a sign of his respect. As his vision began to adjust to the dimness, his apprehension increased. The Santa Barbara vaqueros looked tough and unforgiving. "I *do* have some news."

"Then say it!" Chaco demanded. "Have the Americanos arrived at Sutter's Fort?"

"No, Señor, but they have been seen crossing the mountains. Today, the sad ones who were trapped at Donner Pass returned to the fort with a most amazing story."

Chaco's quirt flicked like the tail of an angry cat. "I am not interested in a story! We must find and kill these gringos!"

The gardener cowered. Hope for a generous reward was replaced by fear that he might be beaten if his information was judged unsatisfactory. "The Señora and the Indian girl were seen with the Americanos two days ago at Donner Pass. They are, by now, in the desert across the mountains."

Xavier could see that his brother was about to quirt the frightened man. And to what good purpose? It was not his fault the Americanos had slipped out of California and reached the desert. At least now they would not have to wait through any more long and impatient days. It was time to act.

Xavier offered the trembling gardener a silver coin. "Señor, tell us *everything!*"

It soon became obvious that Sutter's gardener knew very little else except that the old mountain man who had almost killed Señor King had caused much happiness among the Donner survivors.

"He *gave* them two big nuggets?" Xavier asked curiously. His impression of Hawk had been of a poor old man.

"Si!"

"And did the old gringo say where they were going in the desert?"

"Si!" The gardener pointed toward the high, blue-green Sierras. "They go beyond the desert to a place called Yellowstone."

"How far?" Chaco demanded.

"Very, very far, Señor!"

Chaco marched across the tile floor and reached for his big-roweled Spanish spurs. "We must waste no more time! Already, we should have killed the gringos and returned to Santa Barbara with Inez and the Señora."

Xavier pulled his older brother aside. "Chaco, we should send the vaqueros back to the rancho. This is a matter of _family_ honor."

Chaco leaned close. "You should know that, from his bed, Señor King has given me the order to kill the gringos. I have given him my word that they will die slowly. Especially the old one who almost made him less than a man."

"Yes," Xavier said, "the old gringo deserves that."

Chaco whispered, "And so does Juanita—and the Indian girl."

Xavier drew back and stared at his brother's battered face. "Señor King wishes us to _kill_ his wife and girl servant?"

"Yes."

"I . . . I could not do that," Xavier stammered. "Maybe he will change his mind when we bring them before him."

Chaco almost smiled. "Maybe. But you are right about the vaqueros. We do not need help to kill an old man and a boat-builder."

Xavier was not so sure that the men they chased were quite that harmless, but he nodded, still troubled by what he had just learned. Secretly, he had always admired Juanita. Not only was she beautiful, but she had always treated him with respect and even . . . shown him what? Xavier was not sure. All he did know was that Señora King was beautiful and, had she not married the rich American, perhaps . . .

"Xavier," Chaco said, sensing his reluctance, "Juanita is even more dangerous than the gringos. She is a better shot than most men. Remember that she never again could be trusted by Señor Kin."

"My brother, I must tell you the truth—I could not take her life or that of Inez."

"Then I will kill them," Chaco said a moment before he began to give orders, sending the vaqueros back to Santa Barbara.

Xavier was extremely distressed. How could they kill a woman and a girl? Yes, they had attacked Señor King, but had they not themselves been beaten? He had heard that the Señora's face was hurt and that the Indian girl had been whipped until her back was bloody. Surely they did not deserve death for trying to save their own lives.

Xavier knelt and made the sign of the cross, unwilling to believe that the Señora and the child were already doomed.

Chapter Five

Since leaving the Donner Party survivors, Hawk had been following a river down off the Sierras toward an endless panorama of Nevada desert. He and Inez had been chattering for hours, although Juanita could not hear their conversation over the river's pounding.

"Hawk," she called, "What is the name of this river?"

"It's the Truckee."

Juanita followed its course far into the desert where it was swallowed up by shimmering heat waves. "Where does it go?"

"Nowhere. It sinks into sand."

"I had expected to meet California-bound immigrants by now," Quinn called up ahead.

"With all that deep snow in the pass there isn't any way a wagon train could get through," Hawk replied as they picked their way through patches of red-barked manzanita. "But we're likely to meet a lot of impatient immigrants at the Washoe Crossing. Juanita?"

"Yes?"

"There's folks comin' into California primed to fight with Mexico. You look pure Mexican and so I'm warning you that someone might say something you don't want to hear."

Juanita had never told them anything about herself and she saw no reason now to reveal that her father had been an American. But she also was very proud that her mother was Mexican. "Then I will tell the gringos something *they* do not want to hear!" she snapped.

"You kin do what you want but I'd advise you to avoid the Mexican-haters."

Juanita glared at him. "That is strange advice for a man who goes out of his way to get into trouble and who is, *himself,* a Mexican-hater."

Hawk twisted around in his saddle. "Now wait just a damned minute!"

"No, Señor, it is clear that you support General Fremont's plan for a California revolution."

"Damn right I do!"

Juanita clamped her jaw tight and would say no more. Being of mixed blood, she had mixed loyalties. But none of that mattered anymore. She would probably never again see California—if she was lucky enough to escape the wrath of Lucius King.

"Let's put California behind us and think about what we must face up ahead," Quinn suggested. "That desert out there looks endless."

"Way off, I see mountains," Inez whispered. "But they're black."

Hawk nodded. "My eyes ain't good enough to see 'em, but mostly they're brown. Those mountains sure ain't nothin' like the ones we've just crossed."

"Is there water?" Juanita asked.

"There's a river that tastes like mule piss and makes you pucker at both ends. But here and there, you'll find a spring with sweet water. There's wild horses livin' off them springs. Paiute Indians, too. Tough little buggers and techy as teased snakes. They'll steal your horses first so you can't chase 'em anymore. After that, they'll steal your grub."

Juanita counted at least a dozen huge wagon camps grouped at the base of the foothills, waiting to assault the Sierras and reach the dream of California. "And they're impatient to cross these mountains."

"For a fact," Hawk agreed. "Those people will want to know exactly how much snow is in the high country we've just crossed. I'll have to tell 'em to wait at least another month. If they don't, they'll mire down to their axles."

"Where," Juanita asked, "is Crowder's trading post?"

Hawk reined up at the first good lookout point. "Do you see that log cabin away out there where the grass ends and the sage begins?"

"Yes."

"That belongs to Custis Crowder. He claims the first grassland after crossin' some thirty or forty miles of desert hell. He *charges* them immigrants to cross his grass and if even one horse or ox takes a bite, he charges them for that, too."

"Wouldn't it be almost impossible to prevent starving animals from grazing?" Quinn asked.

"Of course it would! And when they do, Crowder is a-countin' the bites and addin' up the toll. He's hired a couple of gunmen just in case there's an argument— which there usually is."

"Why would we or anyone else deal with such a bad man?" Juanita questioned.

"Because Crowder has top-notch animals for sale and trade." Hawk pointed to Quinn's horse. "That one is sound, but he's not fast. If we get jumped by the Paiute or the Blackfeet, we've got to have good horseflesh under us or we're goners. Even our pack animals have to be first rate."

"How will we pay for them?" Quinn asked.

"Crowder owes me," Hawk said, his eyes turning flinty, "and it's time he paid the piper."

They followed the Truckee River down through the foothills, then crossed it and headed east. Along the way, they were stopped again and again by immigrants eager to learn how soon they might be able to best the summit and finally enter California. Each time, Hawk gave the same curt answer.

"It's way too soon. Too much snow and mud. Got to wait another three, maybe even four weeks."

Juanita thought it puzzling that Hawk was so rude, given how much he wanted Americans to enter California and help stage a revolution against Mexican rule. When questions about the Donner Party survivors were asked, they were ignored altogether.

"Mister, have you been to Crowder's tradin' post today?" Hawk asked a Pennsylvania miner on a gray mule.

They were within a mile of the trading post with its sprawling log cabin and rundown collection of barns, corrals, and wagons in various stages of disrepair. Juanita was getting more uneasy by the minute. She could feel the tension building in the mountain man.

"Yeah, Crowder is there, same as usual. Saw him less than an hour ago."

"What about Hank and Ernie?"

"They're there, too." The immigrant's reply carried

a note of bitterness. "They pulled guns on a family from Indiana yesterday. Scared them witless. The wife is still shakin' and cryin'."

The man on the mule spat a dark stream of tobacco, striking a targeted rock. "You don't suppose they'd really have shot her and her man over five dollars, do you?"

"They would have," Hawk replied as he reached up to touch his thatch of wild gray hair. "They'd think nothin' over crackin' a man's skull open for two damn bits!"

Suddenly Juanita realized that Hawk was referring to himself. And just as sure as the sun would rise tomorrow over the barren Nevada mountains, she also knew that the old man meant to get even today.

"Quinn," she said, motioning him off to the side where they could speak in private, "did you see what I just saw in Hawk?"

He shrugged. "What do you mean?"

Juanita lowered his voice. "I mean that *he's* the one whose head was cracked open!"

"Naw!"

"There will be trouble if we go to that trading post. Your friend is looking to get even. If he is killed, what will happen to us?"

Quinn conceded her point. "We could forget Yellowstone."

"Then we must figure out a way to avoid that trading post!"

"That's not going to be easy," Quinn told her. "Once Hawk gets an idea into his head, it's stuck."

"If you go to the trading post you could be killed. Inez and I will stay here with these immigrants where it is safe."

"That makes sense. I still expect you're exaggerating the danger."

"I'm not!" Juanita drew in a deep breath and beat down her rising exasperation. "I am just returning a favor you gave Inez back in Santa Barbara."

"Well, I appreciate that," Quinn told her. "I really do. And the truth is, I was already worried, given what Hawk keeps sayin' about Crowder and his men."

"You should wear a gun."

"I have a pistol and derringer packed up in my bedroll. Do you have a gun?" he asked.

"I have a pepperbox."

Juanita had taken Lucius's six-shot weapon and knew that the barrel revolved each time the trigger was pulled. It was unpredictable, occasionally prone to misfire all six barrels at once and blow off its handler's fingers. But the pepperbox was murderous and, at close range, capable of killing several opponents. Juanita wasn't afraid to use it if Chaco or any of the others turned up and attempted to return them to Santa Barbara.

"Are you packing it?"

"Yes." Juanita reached into her pocket and extracted the pepperbox and offered it to him in silence.

Quinn inspected it carefully. "I'd like to borrow this. A pepperbox will intimidate a man. Make him think twice about starting trouble. My aim right now is to try and *avoid* bloodshed at that trading post."

"Very well. But, if you are killed, I will be angry to lose that gun."

Quinn actually chuckled at her poor attempt to make a joke and ease their tension. "Well, thank you for being so concerned for my welfare, Mrs. King!"

"Be careful," she told him, "and don't get shot in your other foot."

"Not if I can help it!"

Quinn jammed the pepperbox into his pocket, knowing that the very last thing he needed was another damned shootout. They'd been fortunate to escape with their lives back in Santa Barbara and maybe their luck would run out here in Nevada.

"Quinn?"

He reined up. "Yes?"

"If there is trouble, I'm sorry I won't be there to help."

Quinn removed his hat and sleeved his brow. It was warmish and he could feel the heat seeping off the desert. After the past few weeks of riding in pines, it was going to be tough getting used to a desert's heat. He had no idea how he'd do in one-hundred-degree-plus weather. Maybe he'd just wilt like a California flower.

"Juanita, I'll try and keep Hawk under control. And maybe we're wrong about his intentions. After all, the man has a powerful need to get back to Yellowstone and Hocina, whoever she may be."

"Yes, and he's also grown very fond of Inez. Just be careful."

"Oh, I mean to! And your pepperbox will make me look about ten feet tall." Quinn gave her his derringer. "Just in case we . . ."

Juanita did something that even surprised herself; she placed her fingers over his lips. "You'll come back—both of you."

"Sure we will."

Quinn left her and waved at Inez, who was off by the wagon ring playing with some girls. She was dark, they were all blond. It didn't seem to matter to the children.

Too bad it couldn't be that way with adults. He galloped after Hawk.

The mountain man's entire focus was on the trading post just ahead. Quinn thought he could detect some powerful emotion playing games behind Hawk's faded gray eyes. Whatever it was, Quinn was not encouraged. Rather, it gave him a sense of foreboding.

"Something you ought to tell me, old timer?"

"Yeah, I reckon there is," Hawk clipped. "When I left Yellowstone, it was with a lot more gold than you realize. But I was *cheated* out of most of it by Crowder and his friends."

"How?"

"Cards. Like you said, I ain't much good and they got me drunk. Next thing I knew, I was bein' whupped with a club like a damned dog. They beat me bloody and pitched me out the door."

"Losing at cards can make a man say and do things he shouldn't. Besides, Crowder wouldn't have to cheat in order to take your gold."

"But he did!" Hawk cried. "I met two . . . no, *three* fellas that all had the same thing happen to 'em! And one even *saw* Crowder dealin' from the bottom of the deck! So this day I do mean to get rifles, powder, and ball in exchange for my gold."

Quinn didn't understand and he was running out of time. "Why would you want rifles? Why not your gold?"

"I can find more gold," Hawk explained. "But the Sheepeaters need weapons to fight off their Blackfeet enemies." Hawk's face mottled with rage. "If I kin arm my poor friends and train 'em how to shoot straight in a fight, by gawd we'll go after them Blackfeet that has raided, plundered, and taken our Sheepeater women for slaves!''

On a hunch, Quinn asked, ''Would I be wrong to guess that the Blackfeet took someone you love? Someone by the name of Hocina?''

''She's my daughter! They took her when I was on a huntin' party. I tried to get her back but nearly lost my scalp. My wife was a Sheepeater. Her people are near poor as Paiutes and they ain't no match against their enemies. I'm gettin' too old to protect 'em anymore so I got to get rifles and teach 'em how to protect themselves.''

''And rescue your daughter.''

''Yeah.''

''I owe you my life, Hawk, but I'm not ready to bust into that trading post and die.''

''Then don't!'' Hawk twisted around in his saddle to glance at Inez for a moment, then he sawed on his reins, sending his mount off at a gallop toward Crowder's trading post.

Quinn also glanced over to see Inez. She was laughing and playing, face turned up to the sun. Then his eyes shifted to Juanita, who was back on her horse, watching him.

He waved and she waved back. Quinn drummed his heels against his horse's flanks and sent it racing after Hawk. He overtook the old man but they didn't say a word until they entered the yard and then Hawk growled, ''Keep your hand close to your gun—and your powder dry. Let me do the talkin'.''

''What am I supposed to do if . . .''

But Hawk wasn't listening. He had already dismounted and armed himself with a Colt revolver and his Bowie. Juanita had read it right; Hawk was out for

Crowder's scalp and now the old man was bursting into the trading post. Quinn jumped down and yanked the pepperbox from his pocket to the sudden booming of gun and rifle fire.

"Holy Christ!" Quinn swore, leaping onto the porch and hearing a scream.

A man appeared, clutching his belly. His eyes rolled like dice while his distended mouth formed a silent plea for help. As more gunfire thundered inside the cabin, he looked neither right nor left but walked stiffly into the yard, threw up his arms, then crashed onto his face.

Quinn peeked into the cabin but it was so dim he couldn't see anything. "Hawk!"

Two slugs whined through the doorway. Quinn heard Hawk bellow and furniture splinter.

"Hawk, are you alive?"

"Yeah," came a weak voice. "But I been shot. Get Juanita."

Quinn plunged into the interior of the trading post, tripping over a body and tumbling to the floor. "Where are you?"

"Over here, Pilgrim."

Quinn found his friend propped up against a long, rough counter. Hawk was clutching his hip and grimacing in pain. His crotch and right pantsleg were soaked with blood. "They might have got me but I sure got them bastards first!"

"You killed all three?"

"Killed Crowder before they knew what hit 'em. Finished one off with my knife but the other got me before I drilled him."

"He's lying out in the yard," Quinn said, trying to determine how bad Hawk was hit.

"Get the Señora, but don't let Inez see me like this.

The Señora knows more about medicine than the both of us put together."

"Maybe there's a doctor among the immigrants."

"By the time you asked around, I'd be dead."

Quinn started to leave but Hawk added, "Quinn, there's a row of cheap trade whiskey behind the counter. Bring me two bottles."

"One is enough," Quinn said, grabbing a bottle and yanking the cork. "Here!"

Quinn raced out the door and mounted his horse. If Hawk could not be saved, they were going to be in one hell of a bad fix, and Yellowstone might just as well be the moon.

"Hawk has been shot!" Quinn yelled. "He's inside the trading post and he wants you!"

Juanita glanced back at the wagons and saw all the people coming at a run. "Keep Inez away."

"But I can help you with him!"

"You *will* be helping," Juanita called as she swept past.

When she found Hawk he was swilling whiskey and humming one of his many bawdy tunes. "Are you going to die?"

Hawk grimaced. "I don't know, but if I do, I'll go out happy. Mind gettin' me another bottle?

Juanita ignored the request and retrieved his Bowie knife. "I'm going to have to cut away your pants."

"Make sure that's all you cut away."

"Lie down flat!"

Juanita hurried to open a shuttered window. She had seen the dead man outside; now she saw two more lying in pools of blood. Hawk followed her eyes. "They both had it comin'. Especially Crowder."

"Drink your whiskey and be quiet," she ordered, cutting away his bloody pants.

"I'll be happy to do that." His eyes dropped. "How's it look?"

Juanita wiped the wound clean. She could see the bullet hole and dark, welling blood. The slug had punched through Hawk's thick leather belt before entering his hip; an inch one way or the other would have meant the difference between a slow, agonizing death and a scratch.

"I'm going to roll you over onto your side."

"What for?"

"To see if the slug came out the back."

"Maybe it blew out my ass," Hawk cackled obscenely. "You wouldn't see it then, would you, Señora?"

"Shut up!"

She rolled him roughly over and saw that there was no exit wound. Juanita wasn't sure of her next move. She had once seen the vaqueros remove slugs from a man, but he'd died. She also had some experience with Indian medicines and healing.

"I'm going to find a thin-bladed knife and see if I can dig out the slug," Juanita told him.

"I ain't sure I'm willin' to allow you to poke around down there. You might miss and cut off somethin' kind of important."

"Be quiet, old man. I don't want to listen to your bad mouth."

"Okay, but be honest. Am I goin' to die?"

"You're too mean to die," Juanita told him as she went searching for a knife.

When she found one, she brought Hawk another

bottle of whiskey but not until she sampled a big gulp. It tasted terrible but she forced herself to take several more swigs out of fear that she might lose her nerve if the digging went bad.

"Don't get drunk on me, Doc!"

"Hold still," Juanita ordered, handing him the bottle and remembering how it had taken three vaqueros to control their wounded man.

"I'll hold still," he vowed. "But, if the bullet is real deep or buried in bone, then leave her alone. All right?"

"All right."

Juanita took several deep breaths before she again doused the wound and this time gently inserted her knife. As the tip of her blade dipped in the welling blood, she closed her eyes and tried to focus on her fingertips, hoping she would be able to distinguish the feel of bone as opposed to lead.

Hawk began grunting and swearing but Juanita was so focused on the knife that she heard nothing and, when at last steel scraped lead, she *knew* she had located the slug. Withdrawing the blade, Juanita saw that blood marked it almost two inches deep.

"Hocina," Hawk moaned, eyes squeezed tight. "Hocina, I'm comin' home."

"Shhh," Juanita whispered, blade again dipping into the wound like a quill into an inkwell. Only this time, she also inserted her forefinger, sliding it down along the side of the blade until she felt the slug's rough edges. She dug at the lead until it surfaced. With a sigh of relief, the mountain man slumped into unconsciousness.

Quinn burst into the trading post. "Juanita, I couldn't stay outside. Is . . ."

"Hawk is going to live," she told him, "and so the Devil is safe for at least a while longer."

Quinn collapsed to his knees and hugged her tightly, causing Juanita to wonder if he was more relieved about Hawk—or that damned Yellowstone gold.

Chapter Six

"Are we ready to go?" Quinn asked, looking into the buckboard at Hawk, who was wedged between enough rifles, pistols, black powder, and ammunition to start his own private war.

"He is *not* ready," Juanita said, "Hawk is far too weak to travel."

"She's right," Quinn agreed, frowning at the old man. "You've taken a slug in the hip and lost a lot of blood. You're in no shape to go anywhere."

"We *have* to move out," Hawk insisted. "Lucius King's vaqueros might still be on our back trail. I'll do my mendin' in the back of this buckboard. Is everythin' valuable out of that tradin' post?"

"Yes," Quinn answered. "It's completely empty."

"Good! Now let's set a torch to it and head for Yellowstone!"

Juanita had argued that looting the trading post and distributing the bounty among themselves and the immigrants was wrong. "It is a sin to rob the dead," she insisted.

"Well," Hawk had grunted as they carried him to the buckboard, "Crowder and his men have been robbin' the *livin'*. And besides, what would you have us do? Burn up all the goods they've accumulated? Destroy their weapons, wagons, and livestock?"

"Of course not. It is just that I believe no good can come of taking things from the dead."

"Señora, I guarantee that these California-bound immigrants would strongly disagree."

Juanita decided not to point out that Hawk and Quinn had appropriated the best wagon and all of the weapons for themselves before offering the rest to the immigrants.

"Torch the gawdamn place!" Hawk said. "Let it be a lesson to any future vultures expectin' to profit off human misery!"

Quinn nodded and put the torch to the building, turning it into a funeral pyre. Juanita and Inez didn't stick around to watch but pointed their horses toward the desert, expecting that the buckboard would catch up soon.

"I don't see what is so terrible about what they did," Inez blurted after a long silence. "After all, they were very bad men."

"They *were* bad men," Juanita conceded, "but Hawk admitted that it was an *execution*."

"But they cheated Hawk and many others. And they killed people!"

"Then they should have been fairly tried and then hanged. Only then would it have been justice."

"The vaqueros will kill us all if they catch us," Inez said. "Chaco doesn't care about justice."

"Inez, there can often be a very fine line between murder and self-defense. We have a right to protect our lives but not a right to kill anyone out of revenge. And remember, Hawk is not a Christian."

"But Señor King, Chaco, and the others swear that they are Christians. They go to the mission church on Sunday and take communion. Yet, they want to catch and kill us."

"True," Juanita admitted, "but you must not judge a religion or a teaching by its followers. The teachings of Christ are what is important, not the behavior of those who claim to be his followers."

Inez was silent for a while before asking, "Señora, will the desert and Yellowstone Indians believe the same things that my Chumash people believe?"

"I expect not."

"Why?"

"That is a difficult question and one I am not sure how to answer."

"But it is important, is it not?"

"Yes. Inez, there are many peoples in this world and almost as many different beliefs. But how could there be many Gods? Did they all share in the work of making the world? I don't think so. There can only be *one* Creator. Nature is far, far too beautiful and perfect to be born of compromise."

Inez wrinkled her nose. "I don't understand."

"You will someday," Juanita promised. "But for now, let us not talk anymore. I am sad and I am worried."

"About Hawk?"

"About *all* of us."

Juanita could not help but twist around in her saddle and gaze back at the majestic Sierras. Would she ever see her beloved Santa Barbara or even California again?

* * *

Chaco and Xavier stood beside the charred ruins of the trading post and listened while an excited, bare-footed American boy from West Virginia told them about the recent shootout.

"I heard the shots and was one of the first to get here," the boy was saying. "You should have seen all the dead men! The old man just walked into this trading post—bold as brass—and shot everyone through the guts!"

"How long ago?" Chaco snapped with impatience.

"Why, it was . . . only last week! After they was gone, we picked through this place but Ma got real mad because I pretty near ruined my clothes. Got charcoal all over myself. But I found some good things. Some knives and spoons, a belt buckle hammer for Pa and . . ."

Chaco had a very short fuse. Xavier knew his older brother was ready to explode so he stepped between Chaco and the prattling boy. "Was anyone else shot or killed?"

"Sure! The old man took a bullet in the gut, but they thought he'd live. They put him in a buckboard wagon and headed off."

"For where?" Xavier asked, pretty sure he already knew the answer.

The boy pointed eastward into the vast, shimmering Nevada desert. "Most of us are bettin' that the old man will die. They say that the young Mexican woman cut the bullet out of him, but he lost too much blood."

"Did you see the old man after he was shot?"

"Yeah. He was as pale as the salt flats. He looked real bad. Might already be dead but . . ."

"What?" Chaco said, trying hard to act friendly, like Xavier.

"Well, they say that the Indian girl . . . and she was *real* ugly and skinny . . . they say that she had some powerful medicine that would save the old man. People reckon that anyone tough enough to kill Mr. Crowder and all his friends is tough enough to pull through."

"Was the old man conscious when they left?"

"Oh, sure! A bunch of us was hiding behind the trading post, trying to get a peek at the bodies, when we heard the old man say they had to leave. Someone was chasin' 'em."

"That's what they said?" Chaco demanded.

"Yes, sir! I swear that's why they left in such a hurry. That buckboard is going to be rough. I know because we all crossed that same trail. It's a bad desert."

"How far to the next water?" Xavier asked.

"Sixty or seventy miles." The boy smacked his lips and gulped as if he were cottony-mouthed. "My pa lost four oxen crossing this last stretch of hell. The trail is marked by the bones of livestock and broken-down wagons. It ain't a pretty sight. My Ma had to leave . . ."

"Never mind that," Chaco interrupted. "Was the woman or the other man shot, too?"

The boy stuck out his dirty hand. "I guess I've said about enough for what I been paid."

Chaco grabbed him by the sleeve and hauled him up on his toes. The kid opened his mouth wide to scream but Chaco drew his knife, pressing it to the boy's throat.

"Are you loco?" Xavier cried. "Turn him loose!"

"I asked him a question! I want an answer!"

Xavier's fingernails bit deep into Chaco's forearm. "If you cut his throat we'll be shot by these people! Use your head!"

The boy was trembling like a leaf. Tears filled his eyes and he wet his pants. Chaco hurled him aside in disgust and the kid sprinted off, wailing at the top of his voice.

"We'd better get out of here fast," Xavier warned, swinging into his saddle. "We needed extra horses and more information, but now there's not much chance of getting either."

Chaco mounted his prancing horse and saw three armed men appear with the boy. When they raised their rifles, Chaco casually reined his horse toward the desert and showed the Americans his contempt by forcing the animal to a walk.

Xavier couldn't believe his own eyes. He saw a white puff of rifle smoke and heard the whine of slugs passing overhead. "Chaco, come on!" he yelled, spurring his horse into a hard run.

But Chaco rode his prancing horse as if he were showing off for the Santa Barbara señoritas.

As he was racing into the desert, Xavier thought, *If Chaco is shot, I won't go on alone. And, after what we learned here, can he still believe that the two Americans are going to be easy to kill?*

Xavier kept spurring until he was safely beyond rifle range. The he dismounted and loosened his cinch, cursing the day he left beautiful Santa Barbara. He also swore that, if he were not scalped or shot dead by the damned gringos, he would never again leave California.

My Diary
June, 1847

We have almost crossed the Nevada desert without mishap although the Paiutes stole two of our best horses. Fortunately,

Inez's mare was not one of the ones we lost. She calls the mare Lupita, and they talk to each other sometimes.

Hawk is recovering, thanks to powerful medicines given to him by an Indian woman who joined our camp shortly after we reached the stinking Humboldt River. This woman has traveled with us for three days and speaks only a little English and no Spanish. Hawk understands her language and says she is a Shoshone who had disgraced her husband and was sold to the Paiutes, who kept her as a slave. She escaped and was living alone when she found us. Her body is thin and bears many scars from her hardships. Hawk says she was on her way to the mountains and that she does not like this desert and so will travel for a while in our company. I cannot judge Tewa's age, though she cannot be more than thirty.

Also being Indian, Inez has shown a special understanding for the outcast desert Shoshone. She says that Tewa can never rejoin her own people, but wants to return and live among other Shoshone. When she learned that it is our intention to visit the Yellowstone Sheepeater Shoshone, Tewa became very happy and excited.

Quinn Wallace learns quickly and is very strong. Hawk often looks to him with what I believe are questioning eyes, but I cannot read the question or know if Quinn gives him a good answer. He speaks mostly of the Yellowstone gold and so I wonder about his heart. I also am sure that he suffers much from this desert heat.

This is a terrible river. It makes the stomach cramp with the usual results. The cottonwood trees along its low, winding banks that might once have given us shade have all been chopped down by immigrants and used for firewood. We see many animal bones along this river and I think this river acts as a slow poison. We also see at least one or two graves each day and I take the time to pray for their souls.

Game is scarce. Sometimes we see wild burros, mules, and

horses that probably once belonged to someone who took pity on them and turned them free rather than killing in harness. We also see many coyotes and they sing mournfully to us each night. I shoot rabbits for our pot and Inez tries to fish but has caught nothing except frogs, whose legs are delicious. Yesterday, Quinn shot a six-foot-long rattlesnake. Hawk skinned and roasted it over last night's fire. He and Quinn ate it, saying the snake tasted like chicken. Inez had some, too, but I could not bring myself to eat a snake.

We also have scorpions and have to be very careful or they will climb into our blankets and clothes at night. Hawk swears that their sting is not fatal. He also says we should stop complaining about the heat because it gets far worse as summer progresses. He says it gets so hot that the air moves in waves and tricks one's eyes into believing that they see good water. This crossing is long and difficult. We move as fast as possible, always aware that Chaco may be following. If so, he must really want to kill us, for this desert is hellish.

Next day. I rejoice because we finally can see the great salt plains ahead and beyond them the faint outlines of hazy mountains. Hawk says they are at least a hundred miles away but four more days will bring us into pines. After that, it is not so far to Yellowstone country. This afternoon we were hit by what Hawk called a "dust devil". It was tall and whirling, thicker at the top, and it was good that we dismounted and tied our horses then jumped into the back of the wagon and covered our heads because the air became so thick with dust that we could hardly breathe. The frightened horses dragged the buckboard into an arroyo and we almost overturned. It took several hours of hard labor to reach level ground but nothing was broken. Our eyes sting because of alkali powder and every crease in our skin burns.

Only the sight of the far blue mountains makes these days bearable. Now that the end of the desert is near, I find myself

*always looking back, wondering if Lucius's vaqueros are still
on our trail. Hawk does not think so, but he does not know
my husband's black heart.*

Juanita awoke under a thick blanket of stars and stared
up into the eyes of the outcast Shoshone and then at
Inez, who whispered "Wake up! Tewa says we are in
great danger."

"Have you told Hawk and Quinn?"

"Yes. They're getting our horses."

Juanita reached for her pistol and then saw that the
men had already led their hobbled animals away up
from the river and were tethering them to the buckboard. She looked back at Tewa and then to Inez. "Can
she tell us what is this danger?"

"No," Inez said in a low, strained voice, "but Tewa
is afraid it is the Paiutes who have come to take her
back as their slave. She has gone to hide in the brush."

"She should have stayed with us!" Juanita could feel
danger in the surrounding darkness. The night was very
still. No coyotes howled, no birds or animals were flitting
or scurrying through the thick sagebrush. The pinion
and juniper pines that dotted the silent hills appeared
sinister. The moon was a dull silver coin half-shrouded
by clouds.

"Let's go to the wagon and stay together," Juanita
decided, fumbling for her shoes. "If we . . ."

Whatever Juanita was about to say was swallowed by
Tewa's piercing shrieks. They turned to see her being
dragged into the brush.

"Quinn! Hawk!" Juanita cried.

"Don't move!" Hawk bellowed. "Stay low!"

Inez shouted Tewa's name and she cried like a snared
and strangling rabbit.

"Hawk, we *got* to help! We can't let them kill her!"

"Nobody moves!" Hawk bellowed. "What they *really* want is our horses! Not that woman! Quinn, you stand fast, hear me?"

"I hear you."

So they crouched beside the wagon and waited as Tewa's weakening screams tore at their hearts.

"Hawk, what are we going to do?" Quinn demanded. "We can't just let them murder that poor woman."

"We don't do nothin' until the sun comes up. If they don't rush us, we hitch up the wagon and get goin' just as fast as she'll roll."

"We can't just leave Tewa!" Inez protested.

"Watch us," Hawk told her. "What they want us to do is come after her so they can cut us down in the tall brush. But we ain't gonna oblige 'em. No sir! We're just leavin' in a big damned hurry."

Inez slumped down in the dirt, sobbing, but Hawk ignored her. "Pilgrim, if they attack, they'll do it at dawn and from all sides."

"Will they shoot our horses to keep us from getting away?"

"They'd rather take 'em alive. Save 'em a lot of work gettin' the meat back to their people. My guess is they'll demand a horse or two in trade for their slave woman."

"Then give them to her!" Juanita cried.

"Nope," Hawk replied. "If we do that, we'd have to leave the wagon and what-all it carries. That woman ain't worth anywhere near so much."

"She is to Inez and me."

Hawk shook his head. "She's just an outcast whore. Tewa got what she deserved."

"Inez said she was beaten half to death by her Shoshone husband's first wife."

"Maybe she was. Maybe she wasn't," Hawk said, anger creeping into his voice. "But we can't do much to help her anymore. Can't you get that through your head, *Mrs. King!*"

Juanita knew that further argument was pointless so she held Inez's hand and prayed that poor Tewa was still alive. She also prayed that the Paiutes would agree to exchange her for food or supplies rather than all their horses. They could lose one and still have enough to ride and pull the wagon. Tewa had suffered enough in this lifetime.

Dawn finally appeared. A gentle breeze riffled the sage and, out on the distant salt flats, Juanita saw tiny dust devils spinning across a vast alabaster stage like slender ballerinas. As the light intensified, the desert became sharply focused; gleaming shafts of sunlight lanced magically through the creosote brush and spindly sage to halo the thick-topped pinions and junipers. Forcing herself to push aside the approaching threat of death, Juanita took courage in the desert's amazing transformation as every rock, plant, ridge, and arroyo glowed.

"It *is* beautiful," she whispered.

"What?" Quinn asked, looking at her closely.

"This desert."

Quinn surprised her by nodding in grudging agreement. "I was thinking the same thing. In a few minutes, it'll turn into hell's backyard again, but for now it is something, all right."

"Here they come!" Hawk hissed, lifting his rifle. "They're dragging Tewa!"

Inez would have jumped up if Quinn hadn't held her down. "Don't move!" he ordered.

The slave woman was bound hand and foot and being

dragged through the brush. At first glance, Juanita was sure she was dead. But then, she saw Tewa give a weak kick.

There were five Indians, all armed with short, thick bows with arrows nocked on their bowstrings.

"Told you they wanted to trade," Hawk said. "Bastards are in for a big disappointment."

Juanita said through clenched teeth, "No, they are *not!*"

Hawk swung around to look at her. "Señora, we *ain't* givin' them nothin' but a few scraps. No horses. No weapons."

"We'll give them whatever it takes to get the woman back," Juanita heard herself say.

Quinn held up his hand, silencing Hawk. "Let's see what it will take. Tewa's medicine was strong and even you admitted she could be damned useful."

Quinn stood up with his rifle pointed at the Indians and added, "And, from what I can see, Tewa *prefers* our company."

"Dammit!" Hawk cursed. "You people don't know the first thing about Indians."

"Then start dickering," Quinn shot back. "Or step aside and keep me covered."

Juanita hadn't expected Quinn to take a stand for the Shoshone woman. Hadn't expected it at all.

"Aw, hell," Hawk swore. "Everyone stay put and let me do all the palaverin'. Just watch your backside to make sure these sneakin' devils ain't comin' up behind to snatch your hair!"

They watched as Hawk went to meet the Paiutes and began to make sign language. The Indians wore breechclouts and reed sandals. Several had feathers in their hair; they were all slender but well-muscled.

After what seemed like an hour, but probably was less than ten minutes, Hawk returned. "I told 'em the slave woman was worth nothin' to us. Told 'em they could keep her."

"What?" Juanita exclaimed.

"Take it easy," Hawk hissed. "If they think we want her, the dickerin' could go on for days and we just ain't got that kind of time to waste. So all of you start gettin' ready to leave and don't give Tewa a glance. Hear me?"

"But what if they let us go?" Inez cried.

"They won't. Them buggers are smart enough to know Tewa would just run away again and then they'd have to brain her and get nothin' in exchange."

Hawk tossed a kettle into the buckboard. "Do you see the one with the buzzard feathers in his hair? That ugly little bugger with a red bandanna tied around his neck?"

"Yes."

"He's the one demandin' two horses for Tewa. It's a damn good thing I had time to cover up all my weapons and ammunition or they'd really get excited."

"Give the man one horse," Juanita said.

Hawk turned to look at their horses and Inez grabbed him by the arm, crying, "Not my Lupita! They'll eat her!"

Hawk placed his hand on Inez's head. "You're right, little one. The horse I give 'em might get et. Can't say it will or won't but it might. You still think Tewa is worth a good horse?"

"Will they take something else instead?" Inez asked.

"Nope. It'll take at least one horse and some food to get Tewa back."

"Then do it," Inez said, tears beginning to run down

her cheeks. "But don't give them poor Lupita. I love her too much."

Actually, Lupita should have been the horse they gave up because she was the smallest and slowest, but Juanita said, "We can give them the mare Goldie. She's suffering from the heat and limping from a rock bruise."

"That ought to do it," Hawk agreed, watching the Paiutes pointing and gesturing at the horses like excited children. "If they get Goldie they'll be happier than a family of hungry chiggers burrowin' into a wooly buffalo."

So Hawk gave them the limping but pretty mare and a few cans of food in return for Tewa, covered with dirt, blood, and stickers.

"We'll wash her in the river and she can ride in the wagon," Quinn said.

"Forget the washin'," Hawk replied. "That water will burn an open wound. Help her into the wagon, then hitch up the team, saddle your horses, and let's get out of here!"

Juanita was more than ready to leave. The dickering hadn't taken much more than an hour but, in that short span, the air had turned hot and the sun as merciless as these desert Indians.

"Will they leave us alone now?" she asked Hawk in private as they hurried away.

"It all depends on if they can eat Goldie down to her bones and still feel like runnin' on foot to catch up with us again."

Juanita twisted around in her saddle just in time to see the Paiutes cut the mare's throat and drop her thrashing on the hot desert sand. Despite the intense desert heat, she began to shiver uncontrollably.

* * *

Finally! Finally they left the desert and began to ascend pine-covered foothills. The air grew cool and they reveled in the scent of pines.

"Is Yellowstone near?" Quinn asked one evening around their campfire.

"She's still a ways off," Hawk replied, looking almost fit again. "But the worst is past. We got to keep drivin' north until we reach the Snake River, then we follow her right into Yellowstone country."

"How many more days?" Juanita asked.

"No more'n another week . . . or two. Thing of it is, though, the rest of the travel is in mountain country. There'll be more game as we move farther north."

Juanita looked at Tewa, who always sat apart from the rest of them, watching for enemies. She was covered with wounds, very quiet and grim. "Hawk, what about Tewa? We still don't know who here people are."

"That doesn't matter anymore because they'd consider her a walking dead woman. No man of her tribe will want her."

"So what is supposed to become of her?" Juanita cried with exasperation. "Or should we just shoot her?"

"Now just simmer down," Hawk replied. "We gave a horse for the woman and, I'll admit, her medicine is strong."

Tewa's lifted her head and Juanita knew she understood her fate was being decided. "So what will become of her?"

His answer surprised them all. "The fact is, *I'm* the only one that could take her for a wife."

"You'd do that?" Quinn asked with astonishment.

"Dunno yet, but like the Señora said, medicine is

strong." Hawk poked at the fire and chuckled. "Ain't this whole thing somethin', though! Let's see. Quinn, you owe me your life and I owe the Shoshone woman my life. Juanita and Inez owe us *their* lives. Hell, the circle just goes around and around. It doesn't have to end. It's just like the Indians' circle of life and damned if that doesn't please me!"

He looked at Inez and winked. "Girl, don't you see how we're all owin' each other and so tied together? This whole thing has turned out just fine!"

Juanita couldn't believe her ears. "Hawk, are you forgetting that we've left dead men in our wake? And that we are running from enemies trying to kill us?"

"I ain't forgot," Hawk replied. "But I don't think anyone has the gumption, much less the will, to cross all that desert."

"Then you don't know the California vaqueros. There is nothing soft or weak about them. They're brave, hard men to whom honor is everything."

"I ain't worried," Hawk said. He looked across the fire at Quinn with bushy eyebrows raised in question. "You worried, Pilgrim?"

"I'm more worried about not finding gold or getting scalped by the Blackfeet."

"That's smart," Hawk said, nodding in agreement. "I figure there ain't a whole lot of profit in worry, anyhow. I believe everythin' in life is all planned out far in advance, that we're all destined to die when the good Lord says it's time."

He winked at Juanita. " 'Course, I'm sure that ain't the way a Roman Catholic sees it, right, Señora?"

"When we die, all will be revealed," Juanita replied, knowing the old coot was trying to bait her into another argument. Hawk loved to argue. He'd argue about anything but he especially liked to challenge her Christian beliefs.

"You believe in a heaven and a hell, don't you?" Hawk said, eyes mischievous.

"Of course! Santa Barbara was almost like heaven and you've told us we are on our way to Colter's Hell."

Hawk guffawed, appreciating her savvy. "Indeed I have! Them bubblin' mudpots and shootin' geysers are Satan's cookin' pots—they can boil you in a second or two."

Quinn glanced at the women, then back at Hawk. "Hawk, all I want in Yellowstone is gold. But, if you want to play general to a bunch of Sheepherder Indians, that's your choice."

Hawk's grin faded. "Seems like all you care about is gettin' rich."

"I care about more than that," Quinn answered, glancing at Juanita. "But getting rich is near the top of my list."

"So," Juanita asked, "does that mean you'll leave us after Hawk leads you to gold?"

"Nope," he answered. "You and Inez can ride with me. I'll even give you both enough of any gold we find so you can make a fresh start if you want to go off someplace on your own."

"That's very generous of you," Juanita said, trying to understand her deep sense of disappointment.

"Sure is!" Quinn said, looking relieved. "We're not cut out for living in the wilderness among bears and Indians."

"How do you know that?" Hawk asked. "You never tried it yet."

"I never cut off my finger, either, but I still know it's not something I'd enjoy. And, as long as we're clearing the air, Hawk, I think you're playing God if you try to teach the Sheepeaters how to go to war against the Blackfeet."

"What the hell do you mean? The Blackfeet have been preyin' on my Sheepeater people way too long. It's time for justice."

"I can see how you want to get your daughter back," Quinn said, wanting to sound reasonable, "but what if the Sheepeaters don't have the stomach for fighting? What if you lead them off to fight the Blackfeet and they *still* get beaten, maybe the whole bunch slaughtered or enslaved?"

"I won't let that happen," Hawk vowed in a voice that rang with conviction.

"Maybe you won't be able to stop it," Quinn said, gentling his voice. "And maybe that's why you shouldn't interfere."

"Ain't interferin'! I mean to have my daughter back!"

Quinn started to say more but Juanita shook her head, warning him to keep still. The atmosphere was so charged that Quinn figured the best thing to do was get up and take a walk in the moonlight.

Several minutes later, Juanita came to join him. They both silently contemplated the stars until she spoke. "I want to apologize. You aren't responsible for any of us and you did act very honorably back in Santa Barbara. Inez and I are in your debt."

"No, you're not."

"Yes, we are," Juanita insisted.

"If I say you don't owe me anything, then you don't! Why do you want to argue about that?"

"I don't," she told him. "And I won't. Good night, Quinn. And I really do hope you find that 'glory hole' Hawk raves about."

"It's there! Where else would he have gotten such huge nuggets?"

"I don't know," Juanita replied, "and, to be truthful, I don't care."

He grabbed her arm and turned her around. "You say you don't care? I don't believe that for a single minute. You care about money, all right. Otherwise, you'd never have married Lucius King, who was old enough to be your damned father!"

She wanted to slap his handsome face and tell him *why* she had been forced to marry Lucius, but pride was all she had left. Somehow she managed to smile and say, "You are right, Señor Quinn. Now, if you will let go of me, I am tired and need sleep."

"I'm sorry," he blurted, releasing her. "I have no right to judge you."

"Nor have I the right to judge you," she said.

"Juanita . . . can we?"

"No." She raised her chin. "If I am like anyone, it is Tewa."

"I don't believe that!"

"The only difference between us," Juanita said, "is that—once—she fell in love."

She hurried away then, before he could see the flood of tears that burned her eyes.

Chapter Seven

Xavier toed apart a pile of dry horse manure, then inspected the remains of a wind-scattered campfire. He sleeved sweat from his brow, then gazed toward the distant, shimmering alkali flats. He was thinking that it was quite possible he and Chaco would die in this Humboldt hell.

"What can you tell me?" Chaco demanded.

"They are only four or five days ahead of us," Xavier answered, wearily hauling himself into the saddle. "Their wagon is still heavily loaded and they are moving slow."

"Why would the old gringo take so many weapons?"

"Maybe to arm the Yellowstone Indians against us."

"That is probably so. But we learned that most of the weapons are flintlocks. They will be worthless in the hands of savages." Chaco also wiped alkali from his weeping eyes. "Remember, we are only after a carpenter and an old man."

"And Juanita," Xavier reminded his brother. "She will never come back of her own free will and she can shoot."

"She hasn't the stomach for killing."

"I am not so sure. Juanita is strong."

"Bah! She is nothing but a whore turned against her own husband and now she has fallen in with thieves."

Xavier took a deep breath. He was losing patience with this kind of talk and it was clear that Chaco was too hate-filled to listen to reason. "If Juanita is so bad," he ventured, "then we should leave her in the wilderness to suffer. Such a fate would be worse than a quick death."

"Yes," Chaco agreed, "but honor demands they be punished before dying."

Xavier touched the large rowels of his Spanish spurs to his horse. There could be no turning back, no change of heart. This grim quest could only end in death—theirs or those they chased.

The next day they came upon an Indian encampment along a sweeping bend of the river and discovered a band of Paiutes, all painfully thin and wearing tattered skins and ragged immigrant clothing. Their women and children stood huddled against the heat, but scattered into the brush while the men and boys grabbed their bows, arrows, and crude throwing spears.

Chaco would have opened fire if Xavier hadn't grabbed his rifle barrel.

"Wait! These people can tell us about those we hunt."

"Let go of my rifle!"

"Chaco, they are eating a horse!"

"So?"

"It is one of Señor King's carriage horses!"

Chaco lowered his rifle. "Go talk or make sign with them. I will wait."

"Do you think they speak Spanish or English?"

"No, but I have heard that the Paiutes expect payment from the Americanos so they must have some way of communicating."

"They will want *something* in exchange for information."

Chaco's thin lips twisted into a crooked, arrogant smile. "Tell them that, in exchange for information, we give them their lives."

"If I tell them that," Xavier replied, "they would probably kill me."

"In that case," Chaco said, "I will kill a few of them first!"

Before Xavier could react, his brother shot one of the Paiutes in the chest. The Indians screamed and jumped into the brush.

"Fool!" Xavier screamed. "There was no need to do that!"

In response, Chaco reloaded. Xavier cursed and put the spurs to his horse. *Chaco is going to be the death of me,* he told himself. *Sooner or later he will get us both killed.*

With Chaco's rifle fire and the pitiful lament of the Paiutes fading in his ears, Xavier drove his horse through sagebrush until he had passed over a rise and put death and sorrow far behind. He dreaded slowing his horse and facing Chaco's wrath, but there was no choice. As a boy, he had absorbed many brutal beatings from Chaco; however, as a man, he was prepared to defend himself.

* * *

"That's the Oregon Trail followin' the Snake River," Hawk declared the moment they emerged from a rocky canyon to gaze out upon a huge river valley.

Everyone dismounted and stared out at the impressive panorama sliced by a river as broad and shiny as a band of beaten silver. Juanita could identify three separate wagon trains crawling along the north bank of the Snake River.

"How many American wagons reach Oregon each year?"

"Thousands," Hawk answered with pride. "I sure wish more of 'em were goin' into California but, when Oregon fills up, they'll spill south."

"I never imagined that there were so many," Juanita said.

"Yep," Hawk said, watching the wagons inch across the landscape. The Mexicans might as well try to plug up a dam with an acorn as stop 'em."

"Where do they start?" Quinn asked.

"At Independence, Missouri, some fifteen hundred miles east. Me and another fur trapper led a wagon train up the Oregon Trail a few years ago. Took us six months and we had them wagons rollin' every day from sunrise to sunset. We took 'em all the way into the Willamette Valley. Ain't near as pretty as Yellowstone country, but it's kinder on the crops and kids they mean to grow."

"Are things so terrible back East?" Juanita asked Quinn.

"Not terrible at all," he replied. "But the East is filling up and everyone has heard about the good climate and rich soil in Oregon and California. Hardly a day goes by that the newspapers aren't touting a Pacific Coast paradise."

"And that's why you came?"

"I wanted adventure and a change of scenery. And maybe a fresh country where I wasn't always being compared to my father."

"A fresh start is what they're all lookin' for out West," Hawk said. "Each year, immigrants start across the big plains of Nebraska, then follow the Platte River, climb South Pass, and roll on to Fort Kearney. After that, they go to Fort Laramie where my old friend Jim Bridger sells 'em supplies while he feeds 'em fur trappin' stories and eyeballs the pretty young women. I hear Jim is goin' blind. Dammit, there ain't nothin' the same about the West anymore. The buffalo herds are bein' shot out across the big plains country. Beaver are nearly all trapped out. The Indians are either gettin' pacified or pushed into killin'."

Juanita started to tell Hawk that nothing ever stayed the same and that change was part of life, but his troubled expression convinced her to keep silent. Old people always thought their own time was the finest and that recent times were a ruination. Juanita had little doubt that, if she lived long enough, she also would lapse into the same tired litany.

They rode down to the Snake River and then followed it for two days, meeting and trading news with the weary wagon train immigrants. Juanita, Tewa, and Inez thoroughly enjoyed the exchange. They could have continued to meet immigrants but Hawk, wearying of people, had decided to take a short cut through some very difficult, mountainous country.

Juanita squatted down among the rocks to regard

their buckboard's shattered wheel. "Can't it be fixed?" she asked.

"Yeah," Quinn replied, "but it's going to take time."

Hawk and Inez had been feeding ground squirrels but now the old man looked up and shouted, "We don't have time! We've got to leave this damned contraption and travel the rest of the way over these mountains on foot and on horseback." "What about your weapons and ammunition?" Quinn asked. "We can't pack all that."

Hawk bristled. "Got to! We'll pack all the rifles, pistols, and ammunition on the sorrels and follow this river up through the Tetons into Yellowstone on foot."

"You can't walk," Inez argued. "You're still too weak!"

"Then, if you're agreeable, we'll trade off ridin' Lupita."

Inez smiled, and Juanita knew the suggestion met with her approval. Gazing to the north, Juanita asked, "What are the Tetons?"

"The prettiest mountains you'll ever lay eyes upon!"

Hawk grinned wickedly. "I've been told by reliable sources that the word 'teton' is French for breasts! Them mountains stand up like 'em so that seems altogether reasonable."

Juanita blushed with embarrassment and it was all she could do to curb an outburst, which is exactly what the old devil was hoping for. She looked to see if Quinn was also grinning and he was, although he appeared to be trying to hide the fact. Thoroughly disgusted with them both, she swore, "Damn gringos!" before stomping away.

The Tetons were spectacular, as were the lush intermountain valleys that they crossed during the following days. They were jagged spikes that punctured clouds and challenged the heavens. Still mantled with snow, their colors ranged between pale lavender and a rich, robust burgundy.

Even Quinn was awed. "I've never even heard of these great mountains."

"That's because they're considerably north of the Oregon Trail and nobody other than mountain men and Indians come up into this country to hunt. Winters are too hard for farmin' and too cold for women."

Juanita overheard the remark. "I'm sure Indian women come here to live with their husbands," she said. "They probably even bear children in the shadows of these mountains."

" 'Course they do! But I was speakin' of *white and Mexican* women. Indian women are tough. Tewa will do well in this country given half a chance and Inez will take to it like a fish in water. But you won't, Mrs. King."

"You really exasperate me!" Juanita snapped. "You are an impossible old fool. And, as for Tewa, understand that I am not about to allow you to impose your lecherous self on that poor Shoshone woman unless that is her choice."

"What does 'lecherous' mean?" Hawk asked, turning to Quinn.

"It's Juanita's word—ask her."

"It means," Juanita explained, "that you have an evil and perverted mind."

Hawk doubled up, whooping. He laughed until he collapsed and started choking and coughing. His face turned purple and, if it had not been for the fact that they so desperately needed him for a guide, Juanita would have let him choke to death.

Instead, she made a fist and pounded it between his

broad, bony shoulder blades while a fretful Inez hovered nearby and a nervous Quinn watched with concern.

"Dammit, Señora," Hawk complained weakly as he finally sucked in great lungfuls of air, "you shouldn't say such funny things to me. Next time, I might not make it."

"Next time I might not *help* you make it."

"Why don't we get busy unloading the wagon supplies and all those weapons onto the horses?" Quinn suggested. "We've still got a few hours of daylight left."

The reloading of their weapons and supplies took more than an hour, with Quinn and Juanita doing most of the work while Hawk did the supervising.

"You ought to just leave them hammers, saws, drills, and spikes behind," Hawk told Quinn. "You won't need 'em in Yellowstone."

"I've brought them this far. I'll take them the rest of the way."

"You'll live in a cave or a wickiup."

"Like hell I will," Quinn groused. "And if we leave anything, it ought to be some of these old Kentucky rifles. Some appear ready to blow up in a man's face."

Hawk bristled. "They're all in good working order! Crowder and his bunch did know their weaponry. Some of 'em don't look too good, but that don't matter to an Indian. How many are there?"

Quinn was sure Hawk knew the number but he counted the Kentuckys anyway. "Eighteen."

"How many Hawken?"

"Seven, but two are busted."

"I kin fix 'em," Hawk told him. "There's a couple of good Hall rifles and a blunderbuss with a muzzle big enough to stuff in a full-grown chicken. And be careful with that sack of pistols."

The pistols were just as varied as the rifles. There were the popular Kentucky pistols in various calibers along with derringers, pepperboxes like the one he'd borrowed from Juanita, and five big "horse" flintlocks with ten-inch-long barrels.

"We got twenty-six pistols and most all of 'em appear to be in good working order," Quinn reported.

Hawk was delighted at this news. "Hope they serve us better than they did Crowder and his two gunnies."

"You were foolish but very lucky," Juanita told him.

"Lucky?" Hawk asked, cocking one eye.

"That's right."

"I had some luck, sure. But I knew them fellas got drunk every afternoon. A man moves slow when he's suckin' on the bottle."

"I don't want to talk about it," Juanita said, turning away.

"I'm curious," Hawk said, looking to Quinn. "What would you have done if I'd bought it at Crowder's?"

"I expect I'd have taken your map and tried to reach Yellowstone and find the glory hole," Quinn answered.

"You wouldn't have even made it across the Humboldt Desert," Hawk predicted. "Nope. You'd have tried, but quit after a couple of days. Then I expect you'd have lit out for Yerba Buena and tried to catch a ship back to New England so you wouldn't have to face King's manhunters."

"You're wrong," Quinn countered. "I'd have stayed and taken my chances."

"Humph," Hawk grunted, turning his attention to Juanita. "What about you, Señora? Would you have stayed with Quinn?"

"Why are you asking us these questions?"

Instead of answering, Hawk looked to Inez and his

expression softened. "You're a Chumash Indian girl but you could be mistook for a Shoshone or most any other tribe. My Sheepeater people will take you in just the same as if you were naturally born among 'em. They took me in and I don't even look Indian."

"What about Tewa?" the girl asked. "Will they also be kind to her?"

Hawk didn't answer right away. Instead, he studied the slave woman and finally said, "Tewa is going to be all right. That's my promise."

"And what," Juanita said, "if she refuses to be your wife?"

"Then she's free to take another man or leave," Hawk replied. "I'd never hold a woman that wanted to go. I'm old and I'm ugly, but I still got some pride."

"I'm sorry," Juanita told him. "It's just that it has been bothering me and I needed to know."

"I'd have been surprised if you hadn't asked," Hawk said. "Now cut that harness free and bring it along. I never waste good leather and we can use it to lash down those weapons and supplies after you've covered them with canvas. Make sure the powder is double covered. Don't want to take any chances in case we get a hard rain squall. It often does that in this mountain country."

"If Chaco and the others are following," Juanita said, "they are sure to recognize this wagon."

"Well then," Hawk decided, hopping over to Lupita and dragging himself into the saddle, "go ahead and burn it!"

Quinn resented burning their wagon. It had carried them and their belongings clear across the desert up to these Grand Tetons. He felt like a sailor having to destroy a beached ship that had just delivered him to a safe destination. Besides, the wagon was made by a craftsman like himself. Every plank, joint, dowel, and piece of hardware was perfect. Most men wouldn't have cared or even noticed the wagon's exceptional quality, but Quinn did, and it troubled him to burn and abandon it on a rocky, unnamed mountainside in the wilds of Wyoming.

"Gawdammit, put a fire under her!" Hawk swore. "What's gotten into you?"

Juanita read the sadness in Quinn's eyes. She was touched and showed it by building the fire herself. "Don't listen to the old man," she whispered. "This was a fine wagon and it deserves far better."

"Then you understand?"

"Of course, but you surprised me."

"What do you mean?"

Juanita didn't want to tell Quinn that every time she decided he was shallow and greedy, he peeled away a layer, revealing something much finer than she imagined.

"I want to know," he insisted.

"I'll tell you if you tell me what you would have done if Hawk had died back at the trading post."

"You mean about you and Inez?"

"Yes."

He toed the earth, looking uncomfortable. "I suppose I'd have taken you and Inez to the Oregon-bound immigrants and wished you the best of luck."

"And come to Yellowstone alone?"

"That's right."

Juanita tried not to show her disappointment as she set fire to their poor wagon.

* * *

They followed the Snake River until they came upon a forest-ringed lake with an island resting near its wider southern end. "That's the most beautiful lake I've ever seen," Inez said as they let the horses catch their wind. "What is its name?"

"It don't have a name," Hawk said, winking at the Indian girl. "So why don't we call it Lake Inez?"

"Could we?" the girl exclaimed.

"Sure," Hawk said. "If I had some whiskey, I'd even christen her in your sweet name."

Inez was delighted. Her dark eyes glowed with pride and Juanita couldn't help but love Hawk. These Americanos, she thought, could be so rough and cruel, yet also sensitive and tender. The trouble was, you never knew which you would get at any given moment.

"Look," Quinn exclaimed, pointing to the north end of the island. "Moose!"

"My gosh!" Inez cried. "They're so huge!"

There were three, two cows and a calf. They waded into the lake and began swimming toward the shoreline.

"Will the baby get tired and drown?" Inez asked anxiously.

"No," Hawk assured her. "That calf can swim like a beaver. Just look at 'em go."

They watched in fascination as the mature elks swam powerfully to the mainland and emerged with water pouring off their large, sloping shoulders. The calf clambered ashore only a few minutes later and all of them began to graze on reeds and marshy vegetation.

"Wait until you see the size of the bulls," Hawk said, sounding as proud as if he were speaking of his children. "They are so tall you couldn't touch their backbones except on horseback—and they sure wouldn't allow that."

"Are they dangerous?" Juanita asked.

"They can be if they feel threatened," Hawk told her. "And when they're chargin', they ain't easy to stop. Best thing to do is to shoot 'em from a tree or someplace they can't reach you. Damn good eatin'."

"Too beautiful to eat," Inez said.

Hawk shook his head. "Out in this country, you eat whatever it is you can kill and sometimes you eat what *other* animals have killed for you. Now we're finally enterin' the Yellowstone country."

"It can't be any more beautiful than this," Juanita said.

Hawk stroked his beard, then smiled and replied, "Well, we'll just see about that, Señora."

Chapter Eight

"We're gettin' into the heart of the country," Hawk said a few days later as they continued to follow the Snake River north through increasingly spectacular scenery dotted by small lakes and broad, grassy meadows encircled by pines.

It was in one such meadow that they saw their first herd of buffalo. Hawk reached for his Hawken rifle but Juanita protested. "We've got enough meat. Why kill such magnificent animals if we don't need one for food?"

"Because I *always* shoot buffalo! And there ain't nothin' I prize more than the roasted tongue."

"Can't we find buffalo nearer to your Sheepeater people?"

"Yeah, but . . ."

"Then please wait. Our horses are already packing as much as they can carry. Fresh buffalo meat would rot."

"Ah, you're probably right," Hawk agreed, putting his rifle away. "In fact, I once beat hell out of a man for slaughterin' buffalo for nothin' but blood sport. That's the reason the big plains herds are startin' to disappear. Inez, would you like to sneak in for a closer look?"

"No," the Chumash girl replied. "I want to watch them from right here. Especially the babies."

"They're called calves," Hawk said, "and most of these can't be more than a month or two old. Say, look at them big, shaggy old bulls! Ain't they somethin' though?"

"I never knew they grew so big!" Juanita marveled aloud.

"I've seen plenty bigger. Some weigh over a ton."

"Why aren't they afraid of us?" Quinn asked.

"They don't know we're here because they've got bad eyes. We're also downwind so they can't catch our scent. But even if they did, I doubt they'd stampede like they're startin' to do on the Great Plains. They have no fear of man because Sheepeaters don't hunt or raid on horseback. They'd rather walk up in the mountains and hunt sheep and even deer. Them animals are easier to kill and won't trample you to death when they're wounded."

They watched the buffalo for nearly an hour. The huge, powerful beasts were shedding big clots of hair. Sometimes they would amble over to what Hawk called a "waller" and take a dust bath, grunting and moaning with what Juanita supposed was pleasure. But mostly, the herd grazed, little tails switching back and forth at deer flies.

They rode around the herd and, later that afternoon, they came upon a low waterfall and a small but stunning heart-shaped lake. "I don't suppose this lake has a name?" Juanita said.

"No," Hawk said, "it doesn't."

"Then we could name it," Inez suggested.

"Well," Hawk argued, "you could, but I already named it after my daughter, Hocina."

"If the Blackfeet took her as a slave, how can you be sure she is still alive?" Juanita dared to ask.

"If she had been older, they might have killed her. But bein' young, they'll adopt Hocina. She's a beauty and some thievin' Blackfoot will want to take her for his wife."

No one could miss the bitterness in Hawk's voice. Juanita had to wonder if Hawk would lose his own life attempting to rescue a daughter he had not seen in years. And how would he react if she'd become a Blackfoot mother? Given Hawk's extreme malice, he might even attempt to kill not only Hocina's Blackfoot husband, but also his grandchildren. This possibility filled Juanita with dread. She knew nothing about the Indian in this faraway country but was sure Hocina would never allow her children to be killed by anyone . . . even her own father.

"There's another thing that worries me," Hawk went on. "The Blackfeet people have been hit hard by smallpox epidemics. The last one was in 1837. I wasn't in Yellowstone when it happened, but they tell me that almost two out of every three of 'em died of the pox that year."

Juanita wasn't sure she had heard correctly. "Two-thirds of the Blackfeet died in a single year?"

"That's just a guess, but it was a bunch. It would have been even more but the survivors scattered, blamin' evil spirits. They left everythin' they owned and went away, leavin' nothin' but corpses and burnin' lodges. Probably saved them from all gettin' the pox. It didn't improve their natures none, though. There are still way too damn many of 'em and they outnumber the *tukarika* by . . ."

Juanita frowned. "The what?"

"Tukarika," Hawk repeated. "It's a Shoshone word. *Tuka* means sheep. *Rika* means eater. Tukarika. Sheep-eater."

"Will we be able to understand them?"

"Yep, because they have been tradin' with mountain men long enough to speak passable English and even some French."

"I won't have much need to talk to them," Quinn announced. "I plan to find that glory hole, collect all the gold I can pack, and light out of here long before winter."

"Sure, Pilgrim. Get the gold and run out on us."

"Now wait a minute," Quinn protested. "Just because you're bound and determined to wage war on the Black-feet doesn't mean the rest of us share that desire."

"I ain't askin' you to fight," Hawk snapped. "But there's work and trainin' to do for my Indian people before I go off gold huntin' with you."

"Then give me Colter's map and I'll go alone! Dam-mit, Hawk, I'm not waiting around while you play ser-geant to the Sheepeaters. No, sir!"

Hawk started to grab for Quinn but Juanita rushed between them. "This talk can wait! We haven't even gotten to the Sheepeater camps yet. And don't forget about my husband's vaqueros . . . or, for that matter, the possibility of Crowder's friends showing up unex-pectedly."

"They won't come this far," Quinn predicted.

"Don't count on that," Hawk growled. "I don't know

about the Mexicans, but Crowder's kind would cross the desert, especially if they suspicioned there might be some Yellowstone gold.''

"Why would they think that?"

"Because of what I lost to 'em playin' poker. Remember? I was drunk and I might have mentioned my nuggets came from Yellowstone.''

"Damn!" Quinn exclaimed. *"Did you?"*

"Afraid so,'' Hawk confessed. "In fact, I sort of drew 'em an extra map.''

"No!'' Quinn wailed, looking ready to kill the old man.

"Now, take it easy,'' Hawk said, motioning for silence. "They only gave me a couple dollars for it and I told 'em all about the Blackfeet. That pretty well cooled 'em on the idea. Besides, I kilt all three of 'em.''

Quinn wasn't appeased. "Hawk,'' he said, "those huge nuggets aren't easy to forget and those men are bound to have told others—a brother, some curious friends. And they must have spent those gold nuggets or we'd have found them before we torched their trading post. Nuggets that big will always attract attention.''

"Then it's a damn good thing that we brought all their rifles and pistols,'' Hawk bristled. "Maybe my Sheepeaters will help us shoot some of them bastards if they come into this country.''

Quinn groaned and Juanita couldn't blame him. It seemed the more they learned about Hawk and the wreckage of his past, the worse things became.

"I think we should stop worrying about what might never happen,'' Juanita said. "At least until we reach the Sheepeater camps and have time to sort things out.''

"That's a fine idea,'' Hawk pronounced. "Señora, you're real smart. I could tell that right away.''

Hawk would have said more except for the sharp crack of lightning and an icy blast of wind that drove a chill deep into their bones.

"It's gonna squall," the mountain man predicted, forcing his horse into the pines at a fast trot until he dismounted beside a mound of gigantic rocks. "We'll build us a wickiup and camp here for the night! Tie your horses up short! Quinn, start draggin' over some dead and fallen lodgepole pines!"

Juanita could feel the storm rushing in at them as they began to hastily erect an Indian-style shelter. She and Inez helped Quinn drag fallen pines, brush, bark, and even armfuls of pine needles while Hawk and Tewa raised the poles and used leather strips to lash them together at the top. Juanita could see that their wickiup would only be about eight feet in diameter and she couldn't imagine how it could keep the rain or snow from driving in from the top. But after seeing how the Shoshone woman was packing the dirt, bark, and branches tightly into the gaps as high as she could reach, Juanita jumped forward to help. Soon, the wickiup was solid, except for an entrance crack opposite the onrushing storm.

"Check the horses again!" Hawk yelled over the gathering storm. "Help me haul in all our supplies! Weapons first! Inez, bring in some dry wood and pine needles before it gets wet and smokes us out!"

Hawk kept shouting orders as the first icy drops, driven by hard wind, numbed their faces. They were getting drenched when Hawk finally ordered everyone to crowd inside and gather around a rock ring encircling a shallow fire hole. With all their supplies crammed inside, there was hardly enough room to sit, much less stretch out and sleep. Furthermore, when increasingly powerful blasts of wind began to shake the wickiup, Hawk bellowed, "Everybody grab a pole and hold her down tight or we'll all get buried and burned alive!"

Juanita had never felt such a wind! The wickiup, with its poles and thick outer layer, must have weighed hundreds of pounds and it was even protected by the nearby rocks as well as the huge forest. Yet, there were a few times when it actually rocked back and forth and Juanita was certain it would topple and they'd all be crushed.

"Bear your weight on them poles!" Hawk yelled through the swirling smoke. "Hang on tight!"

The wind screeched like a wild animal, relentless and awesome. Juanita heard trees splintering and felt the earth quiver. Surely they were about to die! However, just when it seemed their end was at hand, the forest fell silent except for the sound of a steady rain, some of which managed to slide down through the smoke hole to wet their faces and sizzle against the flames.

"That was a real humdinger!" Hawk declared, folding his arms and looking well satisfied.

"The worst I've ever experienced," Juanita said, finally relaxing. She was squeezed between Quinn and Inez, both of whom smelled plenty rank in the sudden heat of their brave little fire.

"Tewa, get some of that venison roasting," Hawk ordered, licking his lips. "It'll soon be dark."

"I'd best check on the horses to make sure they didn't break lose and run away," Quinn said.

"Good idea," Hawk replied.

It was a struggle for Quinn to extract himself and, after he was gone, Hawk muttered, "All he cares about is gold. You California women don't want to trust that man an inch, much less start to likin' him."

"He's a good man," Juanita defended. "And I think

you know that or you wouldn't have chosen him to come with you to Yellowstone."

"Aw, Quinn is all right—in his own fashion. He's brave and he's a lot tougher than he first appears. It's just that I was hopin' he'd start to realize that there are more important things in this world than money."

"It takes time," Juanita said.

"We might not have much time, Señora. Not if your Mexicans are after us as well as the others."

"They are *not* 'my Mexicans'," Juanita replied in exasperation, "and Quinn won't run out on us when trouble starts. He didn't forsake Inez and me in Santa Barbara and he didn't do it at Mr. Crowder's trading post when you were so bent on revenge."

Hawk poked the fire. Tewa was cutting strips of venison and putting them on sticks for roasting. "You're stickin' up for Quinn all of a sudden," Hawk said. "Why?"

"I am not! But, from what I can gather, you promised him this . . . this 'glory hole' and now you're backing out on taking him to find it. That doesn't seem very honorable."

"There is no honor in the face of rank greed!" Hawk lowered his voice. "My Indian people . . ."

"They're not *your* Indian people," Juanita corrected. "They are the Sheepeaters. People you have befriended."

"That's what I was sayin'—they're *my* people!"

Hawk glared at her with such ferocity that Juanita knew it was futile to argue. When the rain slackened, she climbed outside and went to see if the horses were still tethered.

Quinn was leaning up against a pine, staring into space, well protected from the rain. Juanita stood beside him. "You shouldn't let Hawk get you so upset," she said.

"Oh, yeah? Didn't I just hear you shouting at each other?"

Juanita had to smile. "That's true. He loves baiting us."

"Why?"

"I don't know but he just does. Maybe Hawk enjoys seeing us get angry. Stoking our fires. Perhaps it gives him some kind of pleasure that we can't understand or explain. But it doesn't matter. When we reach the Sheepeaters, you *should* go and find that gold. After you have it, you've nothing to be ashamed about if you leave us all behind."

He started to argue, then realized what she'd just said. Quinn's broad shoulders slumped and he toed the wet pine needles at their feet. "I think he's sorta crazy, Juanita. I know we're being followed and there is big trouble coming at us with your husband's people and them at the trading post and probably the Blackfeet. There'll be a lot of killing ahead and I don't want to be standing in the middle of it."

"Neither do I."

"Then the answer is simple," Quinn told her. "I take a few days to find that glory hole and return with the gold. Then, we saddle our horses and travel southeast as far as we can through his rough country."

Juanita frowned with confusion. "Southeast?"

"That's right." Quinn actually chuckled. "I don't know why it didn't come to me way sooner. If we ride southeast, we can't miss the Oregon Trail, which we can then follow all the way back to St. Louis, Missouri."

"If we could do that, what's there for us?"

"Safety!" Quinn exclaimed, stomping his boot down

hard. "No more crazy mountain man and no more running."

Juanita chose her next words carefully. "I mean, what is in St. Louis for Inez and me?"

The question seemed to confound him. "Why ... why, I'll even give you some of my Yellowstone gold. You two could buy a business or live a life of leisure until you decided what was best for you both."

"I see."

"Juanita," he told her, "if we stay here, someone is probably going to kill us. That much ought to be obvious."

"I'll think about it."

His eyebrows shot up with disbelief. "What is there to think about? I'm offering you and the girl a way out of this trap and some of my gold to boot! Could anything be fairer?"

"No," she told him, "it couldn't. But the idea of leaving ..." She couldn't quite put it into words.

"Leaving what? A crazy old man and a woman banished by her own people?"

"Quinn, that poor Indian woman was a *slave!* Inez and I were slaves, too. Sure, we had it a lot better. But we were still slaves without any freedom save to wander my husband's house and be at his beck and call."

He sighed, then said, "Look. I remember what happened back in Santa Barbara so I'm not judging your past."

"Oh, really?"

He flushed with anger. "Oh, to hell with it! I'm going after that gold and then I'll come back and give you and the girl one last chance to go east with me. If you turn that down, you're not as smart as Hawk thinks. It's your only chance, Juanita. Maybe just as important, it's the only hope for Inez.''

"Thank you," Juanita said very formally. "Like I said before, I'll think on it."

"You and Inez would be a lot better off gold hunting with me. Once we find it, we all keep riding hard for the Oregon Trail."

Juanita nodded, unable to argue with his reasoning. The wind was picking up and she shivered. "The horses are fine?"

"They're not going anywhere," he replied sullenly.

"Then let's rejoin the others and get dry. There's food roasting and I'm hungry."

"Me, too," Quinn said, taking Juanita's arm and leading her into the wind.

They broke camp early the following morning under a cold, dark sky that again threatened rain. Juanita was surprised to see ice on the riverbank. "How can it be so cold when it's well into June?"

"It can snow here all year 'round," Hawk informed them. "That's why my Indian people like to camp within strikin' range of the mud pots and the geysers."

"Are there lots of girls my age?" Inez asked.

"There will be some, but not too many. The last time I was here, the Sheepeater people numbered only a few hundred."

"How much farther to their village?" Quinn asked.

"They don't have a village," Hawk replied. "Leastways, they didn't before. They live in small, scattered family groups. Some prefer to live higher in the mountains and be nearer to the sheep. Others favor the valleys, where it's more protected from the bad weather."

"How much farther?" Quinn repeated.

"We could come upon them—or the Blackfeet—at any time," Hawk replied.

Quinn glanced sideways at Juanita; she tried to smile but failed. "Hawk, maybe one of us should ride ahead" Quinn said. "You know, to be a scout in case we do stumble upon the wrong Indians."

"You're right," Hawk said and began to speak to Tewa, using broken English along with rapid sign language. After a few minutes, the woman nodded and kicked her horse into a gallop.

"Where is she going?" Inez asked.

"She's now our scout," Hawk said. "Believe me, she'll do a better job of it than me with my failin' eyes, or the Pilgrim."

"But she could be captured or killed!" Inez exclaimed.

"Not likely," Hawk said. "I've given her a pistol and she knows how to use it. We'll give her a couple of hours head start. Dismount and rest yourselves and the horses."

They watered their horses and then tied them to the trees, but they did not relax and they did not socialize. They were all thinking of the slave woman and wondering if they'd ever see Tewa alive again.

Chapter Nine

Tewa could feel her heart racing to the beat of her pony's flying hooves. She clenched the pistol Hawk had given her and knew that she soon would come upon a Sheepeater camp resting beside the spirit lake. It had been years since she and her people had first visited this place to trade their arrow points and fishing spears for beautifully tanned sheepskin hides, but Tewa still remembered these friendly people.

She had been a girl then, not much older than Inez, and accompanied by her father and brothers. Despite her youth, many young Sheepeaters had gazed upon Tewa with favor. When an especially handsome young man boldly touched her without permission, Tewa's brothers had challenged him to fight. She recalled how the elders had decided that an apology should be given rather than shedding blood.

Afterward, Tewa had been closely watched, but one night, when the moon was hiding behind the clouds, she had slipped out to visit that same young man. Oh, but that had been a night to remember! It had also been the beginning of a powerful man-hunger leading to Tewa's shame and banishment. Sold into slavery for adultery, the desert Paiutes had beaten and worked Tewa beyond her physical limits. Her body and spirit, always strong, had withered like a thirsty flower in the searing desert sun. In desperation, Tewa had secretly offered herself to someone other than her master in exchange for the promise of eventual freedom, but she had been betrayed. In a fit of rage, her Paiute master beat her almost to death and sooner or later would have finished the job if she had not escaped and been rescued by Hawk. For this, she owed the old mountain man her life, and vowed never again to be unfaithful. In a way she did not herself yet understand, Tewa loved this American and she was already prepared to die for him.

Now, she was returning to this camp a shamed but free woman—Hawk's woman. Tewa could scarcely believe this turn of good fortune. She understood Hawk's Sheepeater wife was dead and that his beloved daughter had been captured by the Blackfeet. And although she would never tell Hawk, Tewa felt certain Hocina was either dead or her spirit had already been consumed by the hated enemies.

Tewa crested a rise and saw the lake. She reined her horse up, her lips forming a trembling smile. After her terrible years as a desert slave, this beauty was almost unreal. She inhaled, feeling a healing presence wash away the shame and heartache of her sad and shameful past.

She walked her horse down to the edge of the lake, knelt beside the still, blue water, and sighed with contentment—until she saw her gaunt reflection. Although she was still young, much of Tewa's once considerable beauty had been burned away by the merciless desert sun. But her spirit remained strong. Long ago, when her mother lived, Tewa remembered hearing that bodies soon grew old and failed but that spirit never died. And so it was, Tewa thought, for I am no longer beautiful but I am stronger now than ever before. My spirit will never die, just as the spirits of my mother and grandmother yet live in this hard world. For surely, without their strength and protection, I would be dead now instead of possessing the honor of being Hawk's only wife.

Tewa rocked back on her haunches and pictured herself killing Blackfeet alongside Hawk. Such a death would be so honorable that her youthful shame would be forever erased. In death, she would become a Sheepeater legend, like Hawk.

Tewa's lips formed a tight line of fresh resolution and she undressed, then waded into the lake to wash herself. For a few minutes, she would lie still and allow water to soak away the stench of the cruel Paiutes and their blistering desert. Yes, she was still thin and weak, but that would soon change.

Eat everything you can, she told herself, and grow strong again to fight well with Hawk!

Tewa's horse nervously tossed its head and snorted. Only then did she notice the three Sheepeater men watching from the shadows of the pines. Stifling the urge to run, Tewa combed her damp hair with broken fingernails and stared with defiance as they began to approach with a freshly killed deer.

"Who are you?" an older man wearing a sheepskin jacket and breeches asked.

"I am Tewa."

"What do you want here?"

"I bring my husband, who you know as Hawk."

The three hunters were surprised, then delighted as their stern expressions changed to happy smiles. They began to chatter like excited children.

"Where is Hawk?" the handsomest one asked.

Tewa turned to the south and pointed. "Hawk brings friends and weapons for his Sheepeater people."

"Who are *your* people?"

"I am *panaiti toyani,*" she replied, using the familiar name for her people, meaning mountain dwellers related to Bannock.

They did not dare to ask Tewa anything more, for it was clear that she was a woman of great importance. Furthermore, she was almost one of their own people. The Bannock and the Shoshone had long been trading partners and friends, commonly united against their powerful enemies.

"Where is your village?" she asked

"That way," the leader said, pointing north.

Tewa nodded to show that she understood. Without saying anything more, she mounted her horse. "Hawk," she solemnly proclaimed.

They nodded with respect. Tewa reigned her horse south to rejoin her husband and only then did she allow herself a secret smile.

"Here she comes!" Inez cried, forcing Lupita into a gallop as they all rushed forward to greet Tewa.

Tewa has changed, Juanita thought, even before they reached her. The Shoshone woman was sitting up proud and straight on her horse with a smile that could not be hidden. What could have happened?

Juanita guessed that Tewa's newfound confidence had everything to do with her status as Hawk's woman. This pleased Juanita because, until now, she had thought that Tewa might have lost the gift of happiness forever.

Tewa explained that the Sheepeater camp was not far away. Encouraged by the prospect of finally ending this long journey, the group pushed forward and were soon immersed in the beauty that surrounded them. Juanita saw deer everywhere as well as elk. A bald eagle floated effortlessly down out of the clouds to tear a crimson-bellied fish from the sky-blue water, then disappeared into the forest that ringed the opposite shoreline.

Riding beside the immense lake made Juanita aware that the heart of Yellowstone was cradled in a vast basin surrounded by range after range of towering mountains. No wonder so few whites had entered this hidden paradise! And now they were entering a valley whose geology almost defied description. Juanita forgot herself as she gazed upon a world unlike any she had ever seen before or could even have imagined.

"There she is!" Hawk crowed. "The biggest geyser basin in Yellowstone. Don't it beat anythin' you folks ever seen before in your lives? And you thought I was spinnin' windies!"

"I can hardly believe my eyes," Quinn said.

"It's a great big hell hole, isn't it?"

"That it is," Quinn replied.

Juanita stared at the unworldly scene that lay before them smoking, groaning, and belching hot gases. She saw dozens of geysers spitting up water and countless blue-green, boiling pools. Mud pots that reminded her of chocolate or caramel burped and bubbled, making

loud, lip-smacking sounds from the bowels of the earth.
Littering the vast thermal field were the bleached bones
of animals and even the chalky white remains of once-
great trees, along with tall mineral fountains that issued
scalding water and brine.

"It's . . . it's somehow very beautiful," she said to Inez,
who had drawn closer. "I never imagined the pools
could be so colorful."

"They are beautiful," the girl agreed. "But scary."

It was true. And while the colors were stunning and
the landscape breathless in its rare savagery, Juanita also
felt intimidated by the underground forces of nature
that, until now, were completely foreign. The earth
seemed angry in this place. She could hear it growl,
hiss, spit, and belch and she tasted something foul on
the wind.

"It's as if we are looking at Satan's doorstep," she
said aloud.

"Well," Quinn responded, "let's just hope he lets us
pass by without inviting us inside."

Suddenly, a huge white dome as big as a cabin begin
to spout a geyser into the sky while making a fearful
sound.

"It's going to blow up!" Inez cried.

"Hold on, child!" Hawk yelled. "We're plenty far
enough away that we won't get scalded. Just relax and
enjoy the show!"

Juanita swore that the earth beneath her feet was
shaking. Their horses began to dance about as a deafening roar and a surging fountain of steam and water
began to climb higher and higher. The noise was fright-
ening and the white steam was caught by the wind,
which carried it like a rooster's tail across the prehistoric
basin. How long the geyser went on belching smoke,

steam, and boiling water into the sky Juanita could not tell for she, like the others, stood mesmerized by the sight until, at last, the earth seemed to weary of its show and the fountain sank back into the dome.

"It'll do that every hour or so," Hawk said proudly. "I have set here from sunup to sundown and watched it erupt thirteen times."

"Always that big?" Inez asked.

"Yep." Hawk made a sweeping motion with his arm. "This here is one of the biggest boilin' fields in Yellowstone, but there are plenty of others. The water is hot enough to boil a fish or a human in seconds."

"I see bleached bones down there," Juanita said.

"Sure, you do! In the winter when it's so cold, buffalo and all other manner of animals come down here to eat the grass around them geysers, pots, and pools. But that ground is dangerous because where you think it's solid, it'll break through and drop you into a kettle. That's what happens to the animals whose bones you see out there. They were grazin' in the wintertime, enjoyin' the green grass where they didn't have to dig down for it. They just stepped a little one wrong way or the other and had the hide boiled off their legs and stomachs. Even if they do manage to crawl out, they die."

"We'll give that place a wide berth," Juanita exclaimed.

"You have to know exactly where to cross," Hawk replied.

"Do you *really* know?" Quinn asked.

"I'd give it a try if I was in a fix," Hawk told them. "But only the Sheepeaters really know where it's safe to move in there. They'll use them pools to boil food in the wintertime and even camp down in all that steam when it gets especially cold or they think there are Blackfeet Indians in Yellowstone.''

"Why couldn't their enemies just follow their trail?'' Juanita asked.

"They might,'' Hawk conceded, "but more than a few have gotten cooked alive. That kind of thing tends to discourage 'em.''

"Hawk, have you ever taken a 'misstep'?'' Inez anxiously asked.

"Not yet. When we ride down closer I'll let you take a close look at those pools. They're ringed with every color you can imagine but mostly come in reds, oranges, greens, and blues. And, in some of 'em, the water is so clear you think you can stare down into 'em more than a hundred feet.''

"What if one of the geysers erupts while we're down closer?'' Quinn wanted to know. "Seems to me we'd be running a big risk of getting scalded.''

"That's right, Pilgrim,'' Hawk admitted, "but wasn't you the one that once told me that life was just one big gamble?''

"Sure,'' Quinn replied, "but I also told you I didn't like being called 'Pilgrim'.''

"Fair enough,'' the mountain man said. "I reckon, since you have come this far, maybe you ain't a 'pilgrim' anymore. I'll call you . . .''

"Quinn. And I'm still not so sure we ought to ride in close to that field.''

"It don't matter to me,'' Hawk told him as he remounted and headed down into the inhospitable looking basin. "But you'll be missin' a handsome sight and all you have to do is to ride single file behind me.''

Juanita was tense and her horse jumpy as they started down. She could feel the heat intensify and she expected that the powdery white earth might give way and swallow them all. But that didn't happen and they skirted the basin, stopping occasionally to tie their horses and tip-toe over to a pool of gurgling water and gaze downward, wondering at its depth and temperature. And even though the air was cool, the intense heat caused them all to sweat profusely.

"What makes it so hot?" Inez asked.

Hawk considered that for a moment, then answered, "The Indians say that middle earth is filled with fire. We call it hell, but I reckon it's all about the same. Only difference is, they don't believe that the Devil is at work downstairs."

"You told them about Satan?" Juanita asked.

"Why, sure! Told 'em about how we believe he is red with a pointy tail and a pitchfork. They thought that was so damned funny they about fell over laughin'."

"You shouldn't make a joke out of Satan," Juanita said.

Hawk scoffed. "To be honest, Juanita, your Bible talk doesn't hold much water for me anymore. I have sort of adopted the Indians' attitude about spirits and the afterlife. Seems to me they view things clearer than most whites and they damn sure don't go around whippin' themselves and feelin' guilty about this and that all the time."

"They don't know any better," Juanita said.

"You might come to change your view after you've been around them awhile," Hawk suggested. "Anyways, I hope you'll listen and learn how they live and view things so different than what we were taught."

"Maybe I'll teach *them*," Juanita declared.

"Ha! Missus King, you do have a lot yet to learn."

Juanita could see that there was no use in talking

about these matters anymore, but she was still angry and upset when they finally reached the modest Sheepeater village. She was disappointed at how small it was, given all of Hawk's bragging these many weeks. What she saw were just a few dozen people moving about some wickiups. The people were mostly old or very young.

Quinn must have been having the same thoughts. "Their camp sure isn't much to look at," he remarked. "Is this really their main village?"

"Yep," Hawk replied. "But you have to remember that it's summer and most of the grown-ups are livin' in the mountains huntin' sheep and goats. Besides, Sheepeaters prefer small, scattered encampments. They've found it safest not to gather except for an occasional celebration. That way, they can't all be surprised by enemies."

Juanita and Inez read each other's disappointment. Maybe they'd been unrealistic to expect a picturesque and busy Indian village, where hordes of happy children were playing instead of this collection of tired wickiups that looked ready to collapse.

"I don't see any horses," Quinn said.

"That's right," Hawk agreed. "Sheepeaters are walkers, sort of like Tewa's people."

Tewa nodded in agreement; her mountain people also preferred walking to riding. It was simpler and, in steep and rocky terrain, even faster. They used packs on dogs to carry much of the camp gear and, if food became very scarce, as a last resort the dogs could be eaten.

When the villagers saw Hawk and his party, they rushed forward with happy greetings. The men and women wore beautifully tanned elk, deer, and even bear and wolf skins. The children were mostly barefoot but all the adults wore moccasins and fringed leggings. A number of women also wore bear claws and bone necklaces. Their hair was long and dropped straight to their shoulders.

Hawk dismounted and all the children vied for his affection. Then he remembered to introduce Inez, who soon replaced the mountain man as the center of attention. There were a few girls her age, but the boys apparently were hunting up in the mountains. Very soon, Inez was giggling and racing away with her new friends to explore the little village.

She's going to take to this much better than I am, Juanita thought, finding it difficult to smile as the village women studied her with interest.

After the reunion, Hawk informed Juanita, "We've been given their biggest wickiups until the hunters return. In the meantime, we can build a few of our own. Quinn, I reckon you can show these people a thing or two about construction."

"Sure, but just remember that I came all this way to find gold nuggets, not go Indian," he reminded the mountain man. "Now I'll unsaddle and pack our horses."

"I want to unload the rifles and pistols," Hawk decided, taking the reins of the pack horses. "I want to show these women and children that things ain't ever goin' to be the same in this country. The days of fearin' Blackfeet are past."

Hawk looked over at Tewa. "Woman, help me spread out everything, includin' the powder and ammunition. Go bring some hides we can lay 'em on."

Tewa's chin lifted with pride because she knew that this was Hawk's way of showing the village that she was his new wife.

"I could help," Quinn offered.

"No, thanks," Hawk grunted.

The villagers became excited when Hawk and Tewa began to display the weaponry. There were squeals of delight from both the children and the women.

"I still think this is all wrong," Juanita whispered to Quinn. "Killing Blackfeet isn't going to bring Hocina back."

"You'll never convince him of that," Quinn said. "Take a look at these people's expressions and you can see that everyone is just as thirsty as Hawk for Blackfeet blood."

"Yes," Juanita reluctantly agreed, "I see what you mean."

When the weapons were finally all laid out, a number of the older people fell to their knees, weeping. Even some of the youngest children had tears in their eyes by the time Hawk was finished. Quinn realized that hatred and bitterness toward the superior Blackfeet ran deep and strong among these gentler people, who now believed their time of revenge was finally close at hand.

"God forgive him and us," Juanita whispered, making the sign of the cross. "Nothing good can possibly come of this."

"Maybe we'll be long gone before it happens," Quinn replied. "All I need to do is find that glory hole and we can leave Yellowstone for a safer world. We don't need to be a part of this madness."

Juanita didn't know what to say about that, so she said nothing and just watched as Hawk made a big show of allowing the villagers to handle all the weapons.

"Hawk," Quinn finally said when he lost patience, "don't you think that's enough? Our horses need to be fed and watered."

"Don't fret about it," Hawk said before he instructed everyone to carry and stack his arsenal in a nearby wickiup.

"Hawk," Juanita said, "we've got a problem."

"What's that?"

"Our wickiups are crawling with lice and fleas because these people allow their dogs to sleep inside them!"

"Señora, you have to remember that these are very *poor* people. They don't have much but they love to share and they're goin' to be insulted if you refuse to live in their houses."

"I'm sorry, but I can't be blamed for not wanting to share their bugs."

Hawk was in no mood for complications. "All right," he snapped, "then sleep under the stars same as we've been doin' since leaving Santa Barbara."

"I will!"

"The thing is," Hawk said, softening his tone, "there just isn't any time to waste buildin' new wickiups. There are too many important things that have to be taken care of first."

"Such as?"

"Such as I need to go off to the mountains and gather up the hunters so I can start trainin' them to use our guns and rifles."

"How long will you be gone?"

"A week. Maybe two."

Juanita shook her head. "Quinn won't sit around here that long."

"He won't have any choice. That map I gave him is useless unless a man is familiar with Yellowstone."

"I don't suppose he knows that," Juanita said, her eyes narrowing suspiciously.

"Nope. But after he rides this country for a week or two, he'll find out and come back."

"What if he blunders into the Blackfeet?"

"He's got a fast horse and can shoot straight. It'll be up to Quinn to save his own hide." Hawk glanced up suddenly, then hurried off, saying, "Here he comes now. Keep him happy, Señora. He likes you a whole lot better'n me."

"Juanita, you are right about those empty wickiups crawling with lice and fleas," Quinn said, scratching vigorously.

"Hawk is leaving to bring in the Sheepeater men so he can start training them to wage war. He says it will take a week to round them up, perhaps longer."

"I was afraid of that."

"I wish you'd wait until he returns before going away. I'm worried that Chaco might arrive when you're both absent."

Quinn shook his head. "Well," he said after a few moments, "I'd never forgive myself if that happened. I'll hang around until Hawk returns."

Juanita threw her arms around Quinn's neck and hugged him tight, surprising them both. She recoiled with embarrassment, saying, "Quinn, I'm sorry. I was just so worried and . . ."

"Don't apologize. I enjoyed it."

"And I'm also ashamed for thinking you were shallow and avaricious."

"What does 'avaricious' mean?"

"It means greedy."

"I'd like to be rich," Quinn admitted, scratching again. "But I do have a conscience and have been known to do a good deed or two. Anyway, I'll get to work on new shelters the first thing tomorrow morning. That all right with you?"

"Of course," Juanita replied. "It will be dark soon and we've had a very long and eventful day."

"We sure have," he agreed. Quinn toed the ground. "I also want to apologize for sometimes being sarcastic."

Juanita started to protest but he raised his hand and added, "I *have* been less than a gentleman. You may not believe it, but before I met Hawk, I was happy. I had a successful boat-building business and I enjoyed living in Santa Barbara."

"But you're not happy anymore?"

"Those Donner Party folks showed me the grim side of frontier life. One mistake in the wilderness and you can be dead."

"Yes, but I sense that you're troubled about something else."

"I'm beginning to wonder if Hawk's gold nuggets even came from Yellowstone. I wonder if Hawk brought me here for reasons that have nothing to do with gold."

"That would be pretty lowdown."

"You bet it would! And one more thing—if you think your husband's men might suddenly appear, then we need to prepare for the worst."

"What did you have in mind?"

"We should camp in those woods yonder," Quinn told her, pointing north beyond the village clearing. "I'll build a couple of wickiups in there and we can take turns standing guard."

Juanita arched her eyebrows. "Do you really think that's necessary?"

"If your husband's vaqueros are marksmen, they could sneak to within rifle range and drill us before we knew what was happening."

"I see your point. To be safe, we'll sleep in the forest."

"Maybe we ought to *live* in the forest until we figure out what our next move might be."

It suddenly occurred to Juanita that Quinn might have an ulterior motive for wanting to get her off alone. But then she thought of all the lice and fleas in the village and decided she would prefer to take her chances with Quinn.

"All right," she heard herself say, "we'll live in the forest for a while."

He grinned. "The thing of it is, Juanita, we just can't be too careful."

I couldn't agree more, Juanita thought, trying to read the real truth in his stunning blue eyes.

Chapter Ten

Hawk tied a pair of rifles across the back of his saddle and checked to make sure his three pistols were securely tucked under his belt. Finding his weapons in good order, he gave Inez a hug. "Child, I'll be back soon. The women here have told me where to find their hunters so I shouldn't be more'n a week. Might even be back in just a few days."

"But what if Chaco and the others come here before you return?"

"The Señora thinks they gave up," Hawk told the Chumash girl. "Besides, Quinn is staying. These people may look harmless, but even the women and children know how to fight. You'll be safe. Make friends and have fun while you can. Life gets tougher as you get older."

Quinn steadied Hawk's horse until he mounted. "You hurry back, old timer. I'm not willing to wait forever to be shown that glory hole and a pocket of gold."

"That will keep a little while longer," Hawk replied. He twisted around in his saddle, looked over the village, and then asked, "Where is Tewa? I thought she'd be here at least to say goodbye."

"She's traveling with you," Juanita said, pointing toward the distant trees. "Tewa is waiting."

Hawk scowled. "I ordered her to stay here just this morning! That woman don't listen worth a damn!"

The mountain man kicked his pony into a brisk trot. When he reached Tewa, he began yelling and ordering her back to the village.

"Dammit, woman," Hawk bellowed, "you're shaming me before my people!"

"Then be quiet," Tewa said with great patience, "and let me follow you into the mountains."

"Why?"

"Because I am your woman. and because I will take better care of you than you would take care of yourself. I have food, and if we meet Blackfeet enemies, I can see and shoot them first because your eyes are no good."

Hawk opened his mouth, then clamped it shut. Finally, he grumped, "You might make the mistake of shootin' my friends instead of the Blackfeet."

"Don't talk foolish. I know Sheepeaters."

"How?"

"They and my people have always traded."

Hawk placed his hands on his saddlehorn and studied his woman closely. "Did any of them recognize you yesterday when we arrived?"

"No."

"Good," he said, with a vigorous nod, "so let's quit talking and find the hunters."

Tewa did not allow herself an outward smile but instead lowered her eyes. "Whatever you say, my husband."

"Ha!" he barked, then set out briskly through the forest.

Tewa could not remember when she had been so happy. All day she and Hawk rode through the Yellowstone wilderness, often fording streams and coming upon geysers or bubbling pools of steaming water. Twice, they surprised elk and deer grazing in small, hidden meadows and once, a huge moose crashed through the slender lodgepoles, knocking them over like so many match sticks.

"I haven't had moose meat in quite a spell," Hawk said, watching the awkward-looking beast bound gracefully over a six-foot-high stack of deadfall. "We ain't got time to shoot and butcher one up now."

Their progress was slowed by the thick forest and fallen trees that, in some places, forced them to take lengthy detours. But always they climbed toward the mountain peaks, Hawk explaining that this was where the hunters would find sheep during these warm summer months. That evening they came upon a beaver pond and made camp.

Hawk went to shoot a beaver while Tewa prepared a fire. His rifle's explosion echoed through the high mountains and he returned with a fat beaver for Tewa to roast over their fire.

"Glad to see they weren't all hunted out before the market for their pelts went to hell," Hawk commented later that evening as they sat cross-legged before the campfire. "There were times when we'd clear out a hundred miles of river. We even trapped the young ones. Never liked to, though."

Tewa cut Hawk strips of hot, juicy beaver tail while she savored ribs layered with delicious fat. Above the crackle of their campfire, she could hear the approaching rumble of thunder in the higher peaks and felt the air grow cold. Her only buckskin dress was ragged, thin, and badly worn. She would have to tend the fire all night in order to keep warm.

Hawk yawned and gazed up at the swarm of bright stars and yawned again. "Well," he said, "I reckon I'm going to go to sleep. Tend the fire a spell."

Tewa watched him cover himself with his buffalo robe. Hawk quickly fell asleep while she added twigs to the fire. The cold night air made her shiver and, hearing thunder grow louder, she decided to join her husband and be warm, too.

"Hey," he protested, waking up with a snort. "What are you doin'?"

"I am your wife and I am cold. My dress is too thin for a chief's woman."

"I'm not a chief."

"You are a leader," Tewa said, seeking the heat of his body and slipping her hands under his buckskins. "You are like a chief to the Sheepeaters."

"What do you *really* want?"

Tewa wondered if she dare reply. She had already acted boldly and spoken more than was proper. But when she felt Hawk relax, she was prompted to confess, "I want a good husband who will father strong sons and daughters."

Hawk drew her closer and his whiskers prickled her cheeks. "Tewa," he replied in a hoarse voice, "I doubt that I could father a child or live long enough for one to grow strong."

"I will help you live long. I'll take care of Hawk."

"Would you fight for me?"

"Yes . . . and die."

For a long while, Hawk held her very still, then he began to move his hands over her body. "I believe you would," he said. "Ain't no doubt in my mind that you have great courage."

"I want a son like Hawk. Will you give me a son?"

She felt his rough old hands slip down to drag up the hem of her dress as he whispered, "I'm going to have one of the Sheepeater women make you a soft, new dress. They tan it using two brains instead of just the usual one, so it's softer on your skin than a breeze comin' through the pines. And we'll sleep on bearskin rugs this winter while our son kicks inside your stomach. How does that sound?"

"Good!"

Hawk laughed and mounted her with sudden urgency. Tewa had known many men but he was . . . different, though he grunted while he thrust at her with his hard body. She helped coax out the warm, precious flow of his seed until he went limp and fell back, wheezing and panting.

"Hawk is still strong," Tewa said, lying close beside him and resting her head on his shoulder. "Hawk gives me a tall, strong son."

"Or maybe a pretty daughter."

"Yes," Tewa said, crossing her legs so she could not lose any of his seed. "Maybe."

Snow dusted the high country that night and there was still frost on the meadow grass when they broke camp. In the early afternoon, near the timberline where spires of rock touched clouds, they found Sheepeater hunters butchering three large mountain goats. When the hunters recognized Hawk, they became very animated, making Tewa even more proud to be his woman.

"I bring you many rifles and pistols," Hawk told them, handing over his own weapons for their inspection. "Now we can kill all our Blackfeet enemies!"

The Sheepeaters hastily finished the butchering and packed the hides and meat. That night they camped with more hunters, and so it went for the next five days until they numbered more than fifty men, all anxious to join Hawk and return to their main villages for guns and rifles.

Tewa walked beside Hawk's mount on their return, proud to be at his side while her own horse packed the enormous hind quarters of a bull moose. Hawk had also shot three elk. These animals, coupled with the mountain sheep that already had been killed, ensured that the people would be fed for several months and that their women could smoke and jerk the meat and prepare it for winter.

"Juanita," Quinn called as he stood beside the new wickiups he had built just inside the forest near the Sheepeater village. "Here comes Hawk leading his subjects like some victorious Roman general returning from war!"

"Tewa, how come you're walking?" Juanita asked with disapproval.

"My horse carries meat but I believe I carry something even more precious . . . in my belly."

Juanita understood her meaning but managed to hide her surprise amid the excitement.

"Well," Quinn said, "it looks as if you've got a mountain of meat but you probably used up most of our ammunition."

"Nope," Hawk answered, "just a few bullets for the moose and elk. The Sheepeater hunters killed the rest with arrows. That's goin' to end, though, once we teach 'em how to handle rifles."

"What do you mean 'we'?" Quinn asked. "I'm not volunteering and I still think it's a mistake."

Hawk's lips formed a hard, disapproving line. "The Blackfeet have owned tradin' rifles for years but they are mostly old fusees and blunderbusses. With the rifles I got from Crowder, we'll be much better armed and, by gawd, we'll find 'em and give 'em a whippin' before the first snow falls!"

Quinn took a step back and was about to make a sharp retort when Tewa crowded between them, blurting, "Quinn, I believe I am carrying Hawk's baby."

"Well . . . well, congratulations," he stammered, wondering how a woman could tell so quickly that she was with child but deciding that Indian women might have their own methods. "That's . . . that's fine!"

Hawk relaxed and even smiled. "I ain't sure whether or not I've planted a seed in her, but I've sure been havin' fun tryin'!"

His cheeks burning, Quinn excused himself, sparking Hawk's ringing laughter.

That night the Sheepeaters feasted on big chunks of moose meat, which they roasted on heavy poles turned over a bonfire. The fire was so intense that it cast its light high up into the canopy of the surrounding forest. The people sang, danced, and laughed. Like everyone else, Quinn ate far too much, but he did not feel like laughing.

"Why have you turned so quiet tonight?" Juanita asked him as the hour grew late and people finally began to wander off to their wickiups.

"You want the truth?"

"Of course."

"All right then," Quinn said. "The truth is that I just can't shake the feeling that something bad is going to happen to us and to these happy people."

"I see."

"And I'm getting a bad feeling that I'll never find any gold in Yellowstone."

"Oh? Would that be so terrible?"

"It wouldn't be good. I've no intention of being a poor man. Living like this isn't my style."

"I see," Juanita said. "But you must know that, even if you found a lot of gold, you'd still have a lifetime of trials and tribulations."

"If you're rich, those trials and tribulations are a whole lot fewer, I'll bet."

"Money doesn't make you happy," Juanita told him with conviction.

"I beg to differ with you."

"Mr. King was very rich, but also very miserable."

"That's because everyone in Santa Barbara knew him to be mean and ruthless. And be honest with me—don't you regret what has happened since we fled Santa Barbara?"

"Some parts of it I do," she confessed. "I hated the Nevada desert and that horrible, foul-tasting Humboldt River. And I have also been worried and afraid since we ran away."

"See?" he told her. "Life isn't as good when you don't have the luxuries."

"Quinn, please let me finish."

"Sorry."

"I have no regrets about losing the past, other than I wish that Inez had found safety among her own Chumash people."

"I'll bet they are all dead," Quinn told her. "Or else they've given up and moved to the towns to live as near slaves and beggars."

Juanita thought his assessment much too harsh. "I don't know about that."

"No matter," Quinn said. "Besides, Inez seems happy with these Sheepeaters. You both can be happy going with me to St. Louis. If we can find that gold Hawk promised, we'll live almost as well as you did at your husband's grand hacienda."

Juanita watched the fire shadows dancing in the treetops. The stars were bright and the moon was as yellow as butter. "Quinn," she suddenly asked, "are you going to teach these people how to use Hawk's new weapons?"

"Nope," he said after a prolonged silence, "because these people are already doing just fine. They're happy. Let's change the subject."

"All right," she said. "What did you think when Tewa said she was carrying Hawk's child?"

"Can a woman ... well, she sure seems happy. Trouble is, Hawk has got to be sixty or seventy years old."

Juanita cocked her head and smiled. "So?"

"Well," Quinn spluttered, "that just seems a bit long in the tooth to be a new father."

"Why?"

"He's old enough to be her grandfather!" Quinn exclaimed. "And how much time will he be able to give to a child?"

"If he gives it life, maybe that's enough."

"That's one way of looking at it," he conceded, "but I think a kid ought to have some time with his real father."

"That's true," Juanita said, pushing herself to her feet, ready to go to sleep. "But Tewa has had a terrible life up to now and a child would bring her great happiness."

Quinn stood, not wanting her to leave. "Juanita, I've decided that tomorrow I'm going off to see if I can use Colter's map to find that glory hole. I was wondering if you might like to go with me."

"I can't."

"Sure," he said, watching her slip out of the firelight to disappear into the forest, leaving him suddenly very alone.

Quinn sat back down beside the fire. "Maybe, if I find that glory hole, she'll change her tune," he said aloud.

But even as he spoke those words, Quinn knew them to be untrue. Juanita King didn't care about money. And he had to admit that that was a fair part of what made her so damned appealing.

Quinn saddled his horse early the next morning in a cold, drizzling rain and peered up at a leaden sky, searching for sunlight but finding none. He wore a heavy coat covered by a rain slicker, but he'd lost his hat. He had not ridden a mile before the rain trickled down his face and the back of his neck into his shirt and then rivered along his spine into his pants. Cold and uncomfortable, Quinn took temporary shelter under a pine and unfolded Colter's treasure map.

He had studied the map so often that he had a good idea that Hawk's long-lost glory hole was less than twenty miles to the north near where three creeks joined a river. Just to the east of this junction was an unusual set of low cliffs composed of fractured black columns. Quinn had never seen such an odd geological feature, but then, neither had he seen any geysers, mud pots, or boiling pools before Yellowstone. If he missed the junction of the streams, Quinn figured it was almost a sure bet he would be able to see the dark, column-like rocks. After that, it was simply a matter of locating the fallen tree and digging out the glory hole where its mighty roots had softened the riverbank.

"I can do this," he muttered, cussing himself for losing his hat.

"Do what, you filthy gringo?" a soft, sinister voice asked from the nearby thickets.

Quinn's heart turned to stone but his hand stabbed for his holstered pistol which, unfortunately, was buried under his coat and rain slicker. By then he felt two rawhide reatas settle over his head and he was being jerked over the back of his saddle to skid across a bed of soggy pine needles.

Quinn tried to tear the reatas loose so he could defend himself but, from the corner of his eye, he saw the blur of Chaco's boot moving toward his eyes. Quinn tried to roll sideways but his mind exploded with searing pain and he spiraled into unconsciousness, only to awaken much later bound hand and foot.

"So," Chaco said, standing over him with a cold smile,

"we meet again. Did you think I would forget and turn back?"

Quinn blinked, trying to clear the blood that still flowed into his eyes. He was sure he had been savagely beaten while unconscious. His ribs felt cracked and maybe even broken.

"We expected you," Quinn said.

"This map," Chaco said, holding it up to his face, "is the place where we find gold."

"There is no gold in Yellowstone."

Chaco slapped his face with the map, drew his knife, and pressed it to Quinn's throat, hissing, "The truth, or I will skin you alive, Gringo!"

When Quinn looked into the man's eyes, he knew that Chaco would do exactly as promised. He swallowed hard and said, "All right, it is a map to gold."

"That's better," Chaco said, running the blade of his knife across Quinn's cheek to create a thin smear of blood. "So you will take us to this gold, eh?"

"I'll try," Quinn said.

Chaco dragged him to his feet and shoved him toward his waiting horse, but when Quinn tried to raise his foot to the stirrup, he groaned from the pain in his ribs. "I need help," he said.

"Xavier, help him into the saddle!"

Xavier was gentle and Quinn could see torment in the younger Mexican's eyes when he helped him mount, whispering, "You had better find the gold, Señor."

"And if it is not there?"

"Then even God could not save you."

"But you can. Juanita said you aren't like your brother. That you have some . . . some decency."

In response, Xavier placed the noose of his reata around Quinn's neck. "Señor Wallace, you are already a dead man but it would be better for you to die fast rather than slow."

"That's it, huh?"

"Yes," Xavier replied, mounting his own horse. "Now, which way?"

"North," Quinn answered, wondering how long he could stay upright in the saddle. He *had* to keep riding just as long as it took to think of some way to save his life, then return and warn Hawk and the Sheepeater village.

Quinn soon lost track of time, but when his horse came to a stop, Chaco quirted him back into wakefulness. "How much farther!" he shouted.

"Long ways," Quinn mumbled. "Couple of days ride."

"You're lying!"

"Let him be!" Xavier cried. "Can't you see he's already half dead? I don't think there is any gold. We should just do what we came for and leave."

"Not without fair payment," Chaco vowed. "After we find the gold, we kill this one and the others, then ride down to Mexico City to live as rich men."

Xavier blinked with surprise. "But . . . but what about Señor King?"

"He is already rich enough," Chaco said. "And he is also a gringo."

"The map," Quinn said, "let me see the map."

"Give it to him," Chaco ordered.

Quinn used a trembling forefinger to trace the map. "We ought to come across a stream that joins this river soon."

"And then?" Chaco demanded.

"Then we will spot some unusual cliffs that look like a wall of cracked pillars."

"Go on!"

Quinn took a deep breath. "And then I'll tell you what else to look for . . . when we work out a deal to set me free."

Chaco raised his quirt and slashed Quinn across the eyes, nearly blinding him. The vaquero drew and cocked his gun but Quinn recovered enough to raise his head and glare at the man, tears streaming down his cheeks.

"Kill me and you can forget about going to Mexico City as rich men. I'm the only hope you have for finding gold. Before you pull that trigger, just think about that, Chaco."

The barrel of Chaco's gun shivered like a dark finger of death but the man finally lowered and holstered the weapon. "All right," he said, "your life for the gold."

"How do I know you'll honor that promise?"

"You don't," Chaco said. "You'll just have to wait and see."

Quinn turned to Xavier. "Give me your word I'll be set free."

"I can't."

"Give it to me!" Quinn shouted. "Swear it to the Virgin Mary or to Jesus or shoot me right here and now and let's be done with it!"

Xavier's eyes turned bleak as he looked to his older brother. For a long moment, Quinn felt his life hanging by a thread, but then Chaco said, "Swear it to him."

"If I swear it by the holy blood of Jesus, it stands!"

"Swear it and let's ride," Chaco replied, grinning wickedly.

"All right," Xavier breathed, "in the name of Mother Mary and holy Jesus, I swear we will turn you loose if you find the gold."

Quinn tried to focus ahead. "Good enough," he muttered, knowing that Chaco still meant to kill him the moment they found the gold but that he now held Xavier bound by his holy oath. It was as much as he could have expected and enough to give him a faint glimmer of hope.

Chapter Eleven

It was late the following afternoon when Quinn finally recognized the black cliffs drawn on Colter's map. They were perhaps a hundred feet tall and three or four times as wide.

"That is it." Quinn told his captors through crushed lips.

Xavier had taken charge of the map and now he held it up, looking around until he pointed north. "And the creek we've been following must turn to the northwest in another mile or two."

"I expect so," Quinn confirmed.

Chaco, as always, was impatient. "Let's ride! I want to find it before dark."

"Can't be far now," Xavier said, "but we should be making camp soon. Perhaps it would be better to wait until tomorrow morning and then . . ."

"No!" Chaco interrupted before spurring his horse

back toward the creek. "We still have another hour of daylight. Plenty of time to find the old man's gold."

They'd removed the noose from around Quinn's neck because it had become troublesome in the thick forest and brush, but his ankles were lashed to his stirrups. If he tried to leap from his saddle, he'd be dragged to death.

Quinn's right eye was swollen almost shut and his side felt as if a spear was being driven deeper into it with every stride of his horse. However, he was at least thinking clearly now, aware that this excursion might end in death despite Xavier's holy promise.

Juanita had been right when she'd told him that Xavier was a far better man than his older brother. If presented even the slightest opportunity, Quinn would attempt to reason with the young vaquero. It was obvious that Xavier feared and perhaps even hated his vengeful brother. Would he possibly stand up against Chaco. Quinn didn't think so.

They were following a wide, swampy meadow when they flushed a magnificent pair of trumpeter swans. Mallard ducks protested from the tules and they saw a moose watching them from the safety of the trees.

"Look," Chaco said, pointing ahead, "that must be the second stream we're looking for!"

Despite the sloppy and treacherous footing, Chaco spurred his horse into a gallop, yelling, "Come on!"

"Xavier, I won't be able to stand a gallop," Quinn warned.

But the younger vaquero slashed his quirt down hard across the rump of Quinn's mount, propelling it forward. To ease his pain, Quinn stood in his stirrups as Xavier drove his mount through the marshland until they reached the intersecting stream where Chaco was anxiously waiting.

"Give me the map!" Chaco demanded, tearing it away from Xavier. "It can't be far ahead!"

Xavier motioned Quinn to follow his brother and they galloped on, the marshy meadow becoming even soupier and swarming with hordes of hungry mosquitos. The insects were relentless but Xavier kept Quinn moving until they reached the second intersecting stream.

"Now where?" Chaco demanded, waving the map at Quinn.

Quinn took a deep breath, feeling mosquitos ravaging his face, hands, and neck. The game was almost over and he had lost faith in Xavier being able to save his life. It was time to take matters into his own hands, no matter how long the odds.

"Well?" Chaco shouted, batting furiously at the mosquitos. "Answer me!"

"Not much farther," Quinn said.

"It had better not be," Chaco warned, "because I am out of patience and you are almost out of time!"

"Let's get out of this place!" Xavier cried, batting furiously at the mosquitos swarming all over their horses and starting to drive them into madness.

Chaco quirted his horse and forced it into a run, still engulfed by a cloud of mosquitos. Forgetting everything else, Xavier followed, leaving Quinn unattended for a moment as he watched the vaqueros furiously whipping their horses toward higher, drier ground. The hooves of their animals threw up big gobs of black mud with sucking sounds. Quinn reined his horse around in the opposite direction and sent it racing back across the marshy ground. He didn't dare look back and fully expected to be overtaken and killed by an enraged

Chaco. But at least this was a chance and he was going to make the very most of it before he died.

"Ya! Ya!" Quinn shouted as his laboring animal finally cleared the swampy ground and plunged into the forest. Quinn ducked a low-hanging tree limb as his horse crashed through heavy brush and somehow cleared a rotting log.

"Ya!" he shouted, pounding the animal's sweaty ribs with his boot heels as he felt his confidence growing with every stride of the animal.

He risked a glance back over his shoulder and his spirits plunged. Both of the vaqueros were behind and closing rapidly. They were magnificent horsemen and better mounted. Quinn almost wept as he kept booting his own valiant animal forward. He expected to be shot—or roped and hanged. Either way, Quinn figured he was a dead man.

But suddenly, he saw a dark form bolt out of the trees into his path. His horse shied so suddenly that Quinn was almost unseated. It was a bear cub, frightened and confused. Quinn heard a roar and the crashing of brush and he realized it was the cub's mother charging to the rescue. Against all reason, Quinn hauled up on his reins and turned his horse back toward the cub. His move caught the vaqueros by surprise just as the grizzly burst into the clearing and attacked.

Her rush was so sudden and ferocious that none of them had any time to react. Quinn's horse began to buck in terror and crashed into Chaco's animal, knocking it over, then stampeded into the thick forest, still bucking and squealing. Quinn clung to his saddle horn, hearing screams and gunfire. His horse might have run until its heart burst but it crashed into some deadfall, catapulting Quinn so violently that both his stirrups were ripped loose. He struck something big and solid and lost consciousness.

Quinn didn't wake up until the next morning when a timid sun filtered through the forest canopy to warm his face. His horse was dead, impaled on a thick branch.

It took him nearly an hour to reach the prior evening's killing ground. Chaco had been mauled to death while Xavier had managed to climb a tree and empty his gun down into the sow, which was also dead. The only thing still moving was the bear cub, whining and fretting beside its mother and licking its body. When Quinn tried to approach the tree and determine if Xavier was still alive, the cub made a fearsome dash at him, and Quinn backed off. The cub wasn't much bigger than a large dog, but it looked to be all fangs and claws.

"All right," he said, "you win. I won't come any closer."

In response, the cub growled and showed its fangs.

"Xavier!"

The vaquero didn't answer. Quinn could see that he was draped in the fork of the tree and looked to be unconscious. Quinn was still debating his next move when he noticed Xavier's horse standing about a quarter mile away, its head drooping low to the ground. Quinn staggered out to Xavier's mount and discovered that the grizzly had raked it deep across the rump.

The animal raised its head when he approached and nickered hopefully. "Easy," Quinn crooned, "we need each other's help."

Quinn gathered the chestnut's braided rawhide reins and started to look for a rock to help him mount. But then his eyes chanced to return to Xavier. *Before I ride away, I should at least put the kid out of his misery. That would be the merciful, Christian thing to do.*

Quinn tied the chestnut to a pine and slipped a rifle from the saddle boot. He approached the tree with the idea of shooting both Xavier and the cub, if necessary. He even took aim on the cub, which began to make hissing noises again, but when its hissing turned to a crying sound, Quinn couldn't bring himself to kill the little bear.

"All right then," he finally said, lowering the rifle. "Let's see how tough you are after you get real hungry."

Quinn walked back to Chaco and pulled a big knife from the vaquero's clenched fist. Its blade was at least ten inches long and covered with hair and dried blood. It was obvious that Chaco had used his knife, probably dealing the mother bear fatal wounds before his brother had finished her off with his pistol at almost point-blank range.

"At least you died fighting," he muttered.

The cub had come out to investigate. Hissing and at the same time making pitiful crying sounds, it circled Quinn and acted half-scared.

"Life is hard," Quinn told the cub, wondering if the little critter stood any chance of survival on its own. Probably not, which was a shame because none of this was the cub's fault, or its mother's. They were just acting in self-defense when he'd stampeded between them.

This disturbed Quinn and pricked his conscience. He realized that fate had not only dealt him a stroke of good fortune, but also of responsibility. He owed the mother bear, and the only way he could come close to repaying her was to save her orphaned cub.

Quinn was trembling from hunger so he made a fire and considered butchering the mother bear—but he just couldn't bring himself to do that when he looked at the cub, which was grieving as surely as any orphan child.

"I'm sorry the way this worked out, little fella," Quinn said. "But now I'm hungry and I suppose you are, too. Difference is, I doubt you'd enjoy roasted bear meat."

Quinn extracted hard-tack, beef jerky, several chilies, and three cans of peaches from Xavier's saddlebags. He used Chaco's knife to open the peaches and he began to toss a few slices to the cub, which ate them greedily.

"Peaches are gone," he said as the sun began to dive into the pine forest, "and I doubt you'd like jerky or chilies."

He was wrong. The cub was so famished that hunger overcame its fear. It ate the chilies right out of Quinn's hand, although it made a lot of noise and kept sticking out its tongue, growling impressively, and displaying its sharp little fangs.

"Hunger makes beggars even of kings," he told the cub before glancing up into the tree at the still-unconscious vaquero. "So, are you going to let me get your mother's killer down from that tree?"

The cub went sniffing around, looking for more food while Quinn tackled the problem of whether or not to try and reach Xavier, who confounded him by continuing to breathe. The problem appeared insoluble, so Quinn went to sleep and didn't wake up until the next morning when the cub roused him by sniffing and licking at his beard. Quinn blindfolded the chestnut, found a suitable log to climb up, and mounted. When he rode back to the tree where Xavier was hanging, the cub followed him closely and licked its lips as it stared up at the unconscious vaquero.

Quinn was able to whip the nervous horse in close to the bent lodgepole and then reach high up, snag Xavier by his gunbelt, and drag him to earth. The vaquero landed so hard on his back that Quinn heard air whoosh out of his lungs. He could just as easily have landed on his head and broken his neck. Quinn was thinking that would have been a whole lot better anyway.

Xavier was in terrible shape and he'd lost a lot of blood. Both of his legs were bent unnaturally and the grizzly had savaged his chest, exposing a glistening white sternum. She'd also bitten a large chunk of meat from Xavier's left shoulder. Given those grievous wounds, Quinn could not imagine how Xavier had still managed to scramble up the tree. Fear must have provided him with inhuman strength. The cub sniffed and snarled at the unconscious vaquero as if it knew that Xavier had finished off its mother.

"You can give him hell all you want," Quinn told the feisty cub, "but he can't hear you."

Quinn doctored Xavier's wounds, even sneaking some of the cow's fat to cover them with. He was so famished by nightfall that he chased off the cub and hurriedly carved some meat off the mother bear which he soon had roasting over his campfire. It was good, but tough, and he ate it until his stomach nearly burst. Then he prepared for sleep with the cub watching him and fretting.

"Your mama wouldn't mind you eating some of her, if it'd keep you alive. After all, she died trying to save you. Come on and have some meat, little fella. Otherwise, you're going to starve to death."

The cub came over and sniffed the meat, then gulped it down.

Quinn smiled. "I'm glad you changed your mind. Your mother would be proud."

Quinn named the cub Lucky on account of how they

both were lucky to have made each other's acquaintance, given their desperate circumstances. He and the cub gorged on roasted bear meat for two days and often heard cougars and wolves in the timber screeching for the rotting bear meat. During that time, Quinn kept applying fresh bear grease to Xavier's awful wounds and waiting for the young vaquero to either live—or die. Finally, Xavier opened his eyes and stared at Quinn and Lucky, then closed them again and slept some more.

To Quinn's complete amazement, Chaco's mauled horse appeared. The poor beast was a terrible sight but the vaquero's saddlebags were still intact. In addition to finding Colter's treasure map, Quinn discovered more peaches, chilies, and a few pounds of dried beans. He boiled the beans in a battered tin cup and then he and the bear cub wolfed them down. But the damnedest part was that the half-starved and lonesome cub actually was beginning to treat Quinn as its new mother! Lucky never left Quinn's side and even tried to lick his face when he fell asleep.

"You're becoming a big nuisance," Quinn grumbled, pushing Lucky away and regarding him with disapproval. "I should have shot and eaten you!"

In response, Lucky just whined and then tried to lick him some more so Quinn gave up trying to discourage his attentions. After all, Lucky did have his engaging moments and he sort of acted like a big puppy, only with lots of teeth and claws.

Xavier, dammit, was going to live; the vaquero was just too tough to give up. So, with great misgivings, Quinn fashioned a travois, hitched it to Xavier's horse, and started back to the Sheepeater camp with Lucky spooking his horses and making himself a real trial.

The gold can wait a while, Quinn decided, *now that I know where to find it.*

Quinn's return, three days later, caused quite a commotion. Hawk had positioned a dozen hunters side by side along a firing line and was trying to teach them to shoot when the camp dogs first saw Quinn and started barking. Then they saw Lucky and their barking intensified. The pack sent the cub streaking through camp, finally taking refuge in a wickiup and sending its former occupants fleeing for their lives.

Back on the firing line, one overly-excited Sheepeater almost exterminated Hawk with his errant blunderbuss. Inez was one of the first to reach Quinn, who was so beat up and disfigured he might not even have been recognized had it not been for his clothing.

"What happened?" the Chumash girl shouted, not waiting for an answer but racing around to the side of the travois to gape with amazement at the semi-conscious vaquero. "It's Xavier! And what's that bear cub doing in that wickiup?"

"He's mine . . . for the time being," Quinn said wearily. "And I wish those damned village dogs would leave him alone. He probably went inside looking for food, or to take a nap."

Juanita put her arm around Quinn and eased him down from Chaco's horse as he grunted, "My ribs are broken on the right side."

"You look like death."

"I've a right to 'cause I've sure seen a lot of it this past week."

"Before I shoot that bear cub, why'd you bring this murderin' Mexican to our camp?" Hawk demanded. "He'd have died soon enough anyway."

"I know," Quinn said, leaning on Juanita for support. "But he's not such a bad one. Juanita was right. It was Chaco that was pure poison."

"One of a litter of snakes is as bad as the next," Hawk growled. "We'll drag his bloody hide out into the forest and let the animals finish what that cub's mother started."

"No!" Juanita cried. "We're Christians, not animals. We'll look after Xavier until he recovers."

"So he can get strong enough to bury a knife in our backs?" Hawk challenged. "Señora, you ought to know better."

"I know Xavier has a good heart," she said, praying that this was true.

"What?" Hawk roared. "This is one of the vipers that have been chasin' us for the last thousand miles with no more on their bloody minds than revenge."

"He's a human being," Juanita said, placing her hands on her hips and not backing down. "And, dammit, we're going to do everything we can to save his life, and if you shoot that bear cub, I'll shoot *you!*"

Quinn patted his gun. "Hawk, that cub is my pet, and if you so much as make him squawk, I'll kill you myself."

Hawk's jaw dropped and he gaped in astonishment. "You come back half dead bringin' the enemy and a damn bear and have the nerve to stand up for 'em!"

"That's right," Quinn said. "So why don't you go back to playing soldier with the Indians and leave the rest alone."

"Well, dammit, then I just will!" the mountain man bellowed, stomping away in a huff.

"Will he really leave them alone?" Juanita asked.

"Yes," Quinn said. "He could tell we meant business."

"I hope so. But what are we going to do with that bear cub?"

"Juanita," Quinn said, "the question you should be asking is, what is the bear cub going to do with us?"

After helping Quinn to his wickiup, she bent down and hugged his neck. "I was so worried about you! I thought sure you'd been killed by the Blackfeet. All of us did. Inez was beside herself and even Hawk was upset."

"Compared to Chaco, I'd have been better off running into the Blackfeet," Quinn told her as she began to inspect his many wounds.

"These are mostly superficial cuts and bruises," Juanita told him a few minutes later, "except for your ribs. They're going to take a while to mend."

"I'm not staying any longer than I have to," he told her. "Just as soon as the pain eases, I'm returning to collect Hawk's gold. I was within a mile or two of that glory hole!"

"It's empty," she said, avoiding his eyes.

Quinn sat up quickly and paid for it with a jolt of pain that made him cry out, "What?"

"After you were gone for several days, Hawk began feeling guilty. He confessed that he had already emptied the glory hole. He says he's been looking for years but hasn't found any more gold in Yellowstone."

"Juanita, I'll kill him!"

"If it makes you feel any better, Hawk feels terrible about lying to you all this time."

"Not as terrible as he'll feel after I get my hands around his scrawny neck!"

"You're in no condition to be threatening anyone," Juanita said, firmly holding him down on her blankets. "But I'm also very sorry that you won't come out of this with gold."

Quinn couldn't believe this cruel turn of events. First the vaqueros almost killed him, and now he had to confront the fact that he'd been tricked into coming all the way out into this wilderness for nothing.

"I should have known," he muttered, fighting off a cloud of despair.

She leaned closer. "Has it really been *all* that terrible?"

"Of course it has!"

"You told me once that you came West seeking adventure. Well, now you've really found it!"

"Sure, but I also told you I came West to get rich. And look at me now. I'm a thousand miles out into the wilderness, I own almost nothing except my clothes, and I'm half dead!"

"No, you're not," Juanita argued. "Xavier is the one half dead. He might never walk again without a limp. You've only lost the tip of your toe. But think of all you've learned since we went on the run."

"I've learned that I like sleeping in a soft feather bed instead of on pine needles in this leaky wickiup."

"If it leaks, it's because you didn't build it well enough yet. Now you can help us all out. Hawk and these people need someone steady who can build things to last more than a season."

"Juanita, listen to me. The whole bunch of them are marching off to war with second-rate guns and rifles that they won't be half-prepared to use. Hawk is headed for a massacre! And after that happens, what will become of the Sheepeater's women and children? And the old people that can't hunt or fend for themselves?''

Juanita shook her head with sadness. "I don't know," she answered. "But what I do know is that we *need* you here."

"This is not my fight. And it's not your fight, either. We don't belong in Yellowstone. We should leave before we get trapped here by winter snow."

"But I can't do that!"

"Why?"

"I've fallen in love with Yellowstone," she confessed. "And I love these people."

"You'll love St. Louis and its people, too!"

"No," Juanita said, shaking her head. "I won't. And they will never need me the way these people need me. I've never been needed before."

He tried to embrace her but she pulled away. Frustrated and in pain, Quinn shouted, "Dammit, woman, *I* need you!"

"I know that," she said, looking away for a moment. "And so I've got a terrible decision to make, don't I?"

"It's an easy one."

"No, it's not, Quinn. I feel very blessed to be here."

He took a deep breath. "Are you going to try to convert these people to Catholicism? Is that what this is all about?"

"No," she said, "it isn't. They have their own religion."

"I'm relieved to hear that," Quinn said. "So, if that isn't the reason for staying, what is?"

"I love Yellowstone and these simple people and so does Inez. She never wants to leave this place."

"Perhaps that will change after a winter."

"Perhaps," Juanita agreed. "We'll just have to wait

and see. And I want you to wait here with us. I want it so bad that I was even afraid to tell you the truth about the gold. I was sure if you learned the truth, you'd leave immediately."

"And I will as soon as I mend these ribs."

When he saw the tears in Juanita's beautiful brown eyes, Quinn reached up and touched her lovely face. "Please listen to me. I also have fallen in love with you. I'd . . . well, I'd like us to go to St. Louis and be married."

She blinked. "But I'm Catholic and still married."

"To hell with that! Your husband is . . ."

Juanita placed her hand over his lips. "According to the Pope, I will *always* be married to Lucius King."

Quinn couldn't believe his ears. "But you tried to kill him with a knife! Remember?"

"Pruning shears," Juanita corrected. "And I've prayed for forgiveness ever since."

"For gawdsakes, he wants you dead! What are you thinking?"

The tears finally began to slide down her cheeks. "I only know that I am a devout Catholic. I've been taught in the ways of the Church and I can't just throw all that aside. It's too big a part of what I am."

"But Lucius King sent men to kill us."

When she just stared at him, tears running down her cheeks, Quinn lowered his voice. "You say you love me and I've told you I love you. Yet, you tell me in almost the very next breath that nothing can come of it because of your church."

She nodded, unable to speak.

"Juanita," he said, "go away and let me sleep. I've had enough of your craziness."

She scrubbed her eyes dry with her forearm and then whispered, "Hell is forever, Quinn."

"Hell is what we create on this earth. Now leave me alone and go see if you can save Xavier so that, on some dark night, he can cut all our throats."

"Xavier will never do that," Juanita promised. "And I'm very sorry about your gold."

"It was never mine," he said bitterly. "And if we hadn't had that fight with your husband and Chaco, I'd never have been driven out of California. But when that happened, I took it as providence that I should come to Yellowstone."

"I'm glad you did. Chaco could have murdered us all. Once again, I owe you my life."

"You're wrong about being still married to Lucius King," Quinn said as she was leaving. "A true union between a man and a woman is forged deep in their hearts, not mouthed in solemn but soon forgotten vows."

"I wish I could agree with you."

"Pray on it, or just think on it long enough, and you will," Quinn said. "Or better yet, watch these Indian people and then tell me they aren't bound together just because they didn't have a minister or priest to sanctify their marriages."

Quinn closed his eyes, not wanting to see Juanita's tears. However, just as she was leaving, he said, "Juanita?"

"Yes?"

"My bear cub is hungry so throw him a few scraps of meat and he'll be your best friend. He's probably upset with all those barking dogs."

"Are you sure he won't attack someone? Maybe a child?"

"Yeah," Quinn said, yawning. "His name is Lucky

and he loves peaches but is also very fond of chilies, beans, and bear meat . . . if it's burned half to a crisp.''

Juanita nodded and went away. Quinn didn't fall asleep for a while because he couldn't decide what upset him the most, Juanita's insistence that she remain faithful to her marriage vows, or the fact that there was no Yellowstone gold and he'd been suckered by Hawk.

Both were hard blows to take, but Quinn guessed that the one that kept Juanita from becoming his woman, his wife, was the hardest he'd ever known.

Chapter Twelve

After tossing some meat into the wickiup for Lucky, Juanita hurried to Xavier's side. The vaquero was ringed by the Sheepeater children, whose faces reflected a mixture of curiosity and horror. Juanita thought it likely that they had never seen anyone so badly wounded and still breathing.

"Go away for now," she ordered the staring children. "Inez, you, too!"

The others ran back to their houses, but Inez hesitated. "Señora, if he lives, will Xavier still want to kill us?"

"That's a good question. Why don't you ask him for yourself?"

Inez leaned over Xavier. "Quinn saved you from a bear and neither the Señora nor I would ever want to hurt you. So why do you want to kill us?"

Xavier wet his lips with the tip of his tongue. This question was very important so he focused on his words and answered, "Inez, if I live, I swear that I will *never* hurt any of you!"

"Swear to Jesus?"

"Yes," Xavier gasped. "I swear to Jesus and to the blessed Mother Mary."

This satisfied Inez, who went away happy. Juanita beckoned Tewa over to help her clean the wounds and set the broken bones. The Shoshone woman was impassive and Juanita guessed this was due to the harsh things her husband had told her about Xavier and Chaco.

"First," Juanita began, "we need to clean out the wounds with those medicines that you used on Hawk. Then we will bandage and set his broken legs."

"Señora," Xavier whispered, "I do not think that I will live. Please leave me alone to die in peace."

"Be still!" Juanita scolded. "You can bite on a stick if you feel the need to scream. This will not take long."

"I am evil and bound for hell and damnation."

"No," Juanita said, "your brother Chaco was evil. You were just weak and stupid."

"My brother is dead. I must pray very hard for him."

"All right, then," Juanita said, "but pray to yourself in silence."

Tewa brought her special Shoshone medicines of crushed leaves, seeds, insects, dried berries, and flowers mixed with grease to form lotions that would fight the expected infections. A close examination revealed that Xavier's chest wound was not as serious as first thought, but that the horrible bite in his shoulder could wither that limb or cause blood poisoning and death.

"The fangs went deep here," Juanita said as she washed away crusted blood and torn, useless shreds of flesh. "Xavier, can you feel anything in this arm?"

Xavier managed to wriggle his fingers, two of which

had been almost bitten off during his desperate struggle for life.

"Good," Juanita said with relief as she continued to extract the dead flesh and corruption. "I see mangled tendons and muscles. Perhaps you might lose the use of this arm."

"With only one arm, I could not be a vaquero," Xavier told her with desolation in his eyes.

Forcing roughness into her voice, she replied, "Life has greatly changed since I tried to kill my husband and ran away from Santa Barbara with Inez. But many of the changes are good."

"Not for me. But you must know that it was never my intention to kill," Xavier confessed. "I would not have allowed it to happen."

"Quinn tells me that Chaco almost beat him to death and you just watched."

Xavier closed his eyes. "I was prepared to fight Chaco after we found the gold. I would have tried to save the gringo. I swear it!"

"I want to believe you."

"I would give everything if you believed me, Señora!"

Juanita *did* believe him, but her anger was real and forgiveness did not come easy. "Quinn saved your life and now it is my turn to see that it is not lost to sickness. If you heal, you owe us everything, Xavier."

"Just tell me what I could do!"

"I don't know yet," she admitted, glancing aside at Tewa. "But you and Chaco have caused us great hardship and the price will be high."

Xavier inhaled raggedly. "Perhaps the old gringo or the younger one will always wish me dead."

"No," she answered with certainty. "There has

already been too much hatred and death. Forgiveness is necessary—and loyalty."

"My first loyalty is to God, Jesus, and Mary and then to those who have saved my sinful life."

"I will hold you to that pledge."

"If you wish, I will write it in my blood."

Juanita almost smiled because Xavier was so fervent. "No," she said, "you cannot spare another drop."

"But later . . . if I live to serve you."

"We can talk of that another time, Xavier. For now, pray in silence."

"Si, Señora." Xavier extracted a rosary from his pants, closed his eyes, and began to count beads and offer blessings.

Tewa prepared her Shoshone medicines while Juanita used warm water to peel away Xavier's shredded, blood-caked shirt. What was left of it was stuck to his body. When she was finally able to remove all the cloth, she washed Xavier's torso and then let Tewa apply her medicines. Each wound was then covered with sheepskin and, where possible, bound with strips of buckskin.

"He has lost much blood," Tewa said as they removed the vaquero's breeches and leggings.

This was the part that Juanita almost dreaded. If even one of Xavier's legbones protruded through flesh, he would probably contract gangrene and die of infection.

To her great relief, Juanita discovered that Xavier's right leg was a simple fracture that would require nothing more than setting the bones and a good splinting. His left had been dislocated at the knee by a powerful swipe of the grizzly's paw.

"I am not sure what to do about this," Juanita said to Tewa. "Do you know?"

The former slave woman whispered, "We will need

at least three men to hold him still while we fix this knee."

Juanita understood that the dislocation was so severe that it would be extremely difficult and painful to pop it back into the knee socket.

"I will be right back," she said, hurrying off toward the lake where Hawk and the Sheepeaters were practicing loading weapons.

"I need help," she told the mountain man who sat cross-legged, glaring at her. "Xavier's leg is dislocated."

"To hell with him," Hawk grunted. "Can't you see I'm teaching these men to clean and load their weapons? Dammit, woman, I told Tewa to stay away from that vaquero—you can bet I'll give her hell when I see her next!"

Juanita lost her composure. She reached down, grabbed a loaded pepperbox, took aim, and fired it directly between the mountain man's legs. The weapon boomed and a shower of dirt, burning powder, and wadding sprayed into Hawk's face.

"Jesus Christ!" he screamed, leaping off the ground and slapping at his crotch and shirtfront. "Have you gone crazy? If all them barrels had exploded at once, I'd only be half a man!"

Juanita pointed the smoking pistol at him. "I want three of your strongest men to help us with Xavier and I want them right now!"

"You'd shoot me . . . for that murderin' Mexican?"

"Yes, because if you refuse me, you're every bit as heartless."

Hawk stared down at the smoking powder burns front-ing his breeches and shirt. "Look what you just did to me!"

"I want three strong men for a few minutes."

Juanita got her help and Xavier mercifully lost consciousness getting his knee wrenched back into alignment.

Two weeks later, Quinn, Juanita, Xavier, and Lucky sat watching Hawk train about thirty bored-looking Sheepeaters to fire their assorted weapons. The old mountain man had positioned them in an imaginary skirmish line about twenty yards above the lake. He'd carved a human-shaped target out of a log and propped it up with a pole jammed in the mud.

"They haven't hit it even once so far," Juanita said, "and they've probably wasted a hundred rounds."

Quinn yawned in the lazy afternoon sunshine. His wounds had almost healed except for his ribs, which still ached. Xavier was in much worse shape. They'd carried him out on a crude stretcher.

"All right," Hawk yelled, "for the last time! You need to point the barrel of your weapon right at the target like you would a spear. It ain't that hard! Now everyone move up and keep movin' until I yell 'fire'."

The Indians dutifully marched forward, and when they were close to the target, Hawk bellowed, "Fire!"

The concerted thunder of rifles and pistols was deafening. Lucky yelped and shot off into the forest while an immense white cloud billowed lazily across the shoreline. The target was completely invisible until a gentle offshore breeze cleared away the gunsmoke to reveal the unmarked target.

"Gawd-dam-it!" Hawk screamed, jumping up and down like a kid throwing a man-sized tantrum. "Every last damned one of you missed him!"

The mountain man was so incensed that he drew a

Patterson Colt from his belt, ran up, and blew off the wooden head of the target with five shots. The riddled head sailed twelve or fifteen feet out onto the still-roiling lake.

"This is insane," Quinn snorted with disgust.

Juanita agreed. "Nothing good can come of this madness."

Even Xavier dared to add, "I have never seen anything like this in my life. These Indians should stick to spears, bows, and arrows."

"All of you just shut up!" Hawk screeched, waving his empty pistol, "or I'll blow all your heads off, too!"

"Don't be childish," Juanita said. "Have you thought of going to see the Blackfeet and trading a few horses for your daughter, then making a lasting treaty?"

"A treaty? They'd hang my scalp on a pole!"

"He's right," Quinn said. "The Blackfeet have been fighting whites since they first met up with Lewis and Clark. They'd never accept a treaty."

"That may be true," Juanita said, "but something has to be done or this is going to turn into a disaster."

She climbed to her feet and headed off. "I'd better find a piece of meat and retrieve Lucky," she said.

"Better make sure Hawk's shooting gallery is done for the day," Quinn suggested.

When Juanita was gone, Xavier said, "I hear Lucky chewed up another dog."

"Afraid so," Quinn admitted. "I thought that cub had already whipped all the bad ones, but I guess there was one more that needed a fighting lesson."

"What will become of him?"

"He'll get a lot bigger."

"Of course," Xavier said, "but I mean after you leave for St. Louis."

"I don't know."

"I do," Xavier said, "someone will shoot him."

"I'm afraid you might be right about that," Quinn said. "And that would be a shame because he likes people and might even fight off a grizzly should it attack one of us."

"Maybe you should take him way into the mountains and leave him behind," Xavier suggested.

"Lucky isn't nearly big enough to fend for himself. He'd get eaten or he'd starve. He needs at least two years of growing before he can survive. Even Hawk admitted that."

"Then you should stay in Yellowstone."

"For a bear?" Quinn shook his head. "No sir! I don't want anything bad to happen to him but he's just a bear."

"Juanita says that Lucky considers *you* his mother."

Quinn chuckled. "I expect he does. But I can't live for a bear."

"Then do it for a beautiful woman who loves you—and a people who need you to help them when the Blackfeet return to Yellowstone."

"Has Juanita really told you she loves me?"

"Yes."

"I wish she hadn't done that." Quinn scowled. "Did she also tell you that she still considers herself married to Lucius King and that your Catholic religion will never allow her to remarry?"

"What if Don Lucius were dead?" Xavier quietly suggested.

Quinn had been gazing at the lake but now his head snapped around. "Are you saying that you'd return to Santa Barbara and kill Lucius King so Juanita's conscience would be clear enough to marry me?"

"Si!"

"Xavier," Quinn said, "you're not a killer."

"Perhaps not, but I am not opposed to telling a small lie . . . if it will right a big wrong."

Quinn didn't follow his reasoning. "What do you mean?"

"I will go away awhile, then return to inform Señora that Don Lucius died from the wounds suffered when he was shot and gelded by Hawk." Xavier showed his perfect white teeth. "So what do you say about that?"

"It wouldn't work. Hawk admitted that he didn't really castrate King. He only scared him half to death to teach him a lesson."

"Ah, yes, but Don Lucius was bleeding very badly when you left him lying in the street. Also, he is not young like us and his health was poor. I would tell the Señora that her evil husband got blood poisoning and finally died."

"You're serious, aren't you?"

"Very much so."

Quinn could not hide his astonishment. "You'd actually do that for me?"

"You saved my life." Xavier grinned like an innocent boy, then his expression changed. "But there is another reason."

"Which is?"

"I love the Señora," Xavier admitted. "And, if you are foolish enough to leave this paradise forever, then I will tell the lie anyway and ask her to marry me."

Xavier's expression left no doubt as to his sincerity. "Why are you telling me this?" Quinn finally stammered.

"Because honor prevents me from letting you leave

this place without knowing the feelings I have for the Señora deep in my heart.''

Quinn didn't know how to respond to this frank confession although he'd noticed how the vaquero's expression changed whenever he looked at Juanita and thought that no one was watching. Quinn climbed to his feet. "I'd better go help Juanita find Lucky,'' he said.

"Adios.''

The vaquero closed his eyes again and breathed as deeply as he could without dredging up fresh pain. Xavier felt much, much better now that he had decided to be completely honest with the gringo. What this had proved was that he really was an honorable man incapable of hiding love deep in the silence of his lonely heart.

Two more difficult weeks passed before Hawk announced that the Sheepeaters were ready to battle their hated Blackfeet enemies. Tewa, not known for her displays of emotion, came to Juanita and Quinn. "These people are not ready to fight the Blackfeet!'' she cried.

"We know that,'' Quinn said, scratching Lucky's belly while the cub chewed a bone. "But what can be done? These people will follow him into battle, ready or not.''

"He will be killed! They will all die!''

Quinn looked at Juanita and saw that she was just as upset as Hawk's woman, but also at a loss for a solution. He turned back to Tewa. "What do you want me to do?''

"Go talk to him,'' Tewa begged, fighting off tears. "Hawk is too brave. He has even forbidden *me* to fight at his side because he knows the Sheepeater people will be defeated. Make him stay here, please!''

Quinn doubted that anything short of cutting off one of Hawk's legs would change the mountain man's mind. "Tewa," he asked, "how much of Hawk's vengeance has to do with his daughter, Hocina?"

"What do you mean?"

"Does he want revenge for her, or for the Sheep-eaters?"

Tewa was slow to form a reply. "Hocina," she said, "is always in Hawk's mind. Sometimes he calls out her name at night."

"We also have heard him do that," Juanita said. "Hawk is tortured by the loss of his daughter. But how long has it been since she was taken captive by the Blackfeet?"

"At least four summers."

"After four years," Quinn said, "Hocina is probably either a Blackfoot at heart—or dead. Getting the Sheep-eaters killed on a raid is not going to bring her back."

"Then tell him this!"

"I have. It's obvious that these people will never be good fighters. They are afraid of Blackfeet and only want peace."

"Quinn," Juanita said, "please try again to reason with Hawk."

"Okay, but it will just make him angrier and more determined."

Tewa prepared to leave. "Don't tell my husband that I spoke to you."

"I won't."

When Quinn went to see Hawk, their conversation went just about as he'd predicted.

"Don't tell me about Injun warfare!" the mountain man shouted. "I know we can catch some of the Black-feet by surprise and kill 'em!"

"All right," Quinn replied, "but what happens afterward when the entire Blackfeet nation realizes they've been routed by less than fifty inexperienced fighters?"

Hawk's eyes narrowed with cunning. "Then, by gawd, we'll draw 'em into this country, set a big trap, and kill some more!"

"No, you won't," Quinn argued, "because by then you'll be low on ammunition and these people will scatter like frightened quail. The Blackfeet will storm into Yellowstone determined to murder every Sheepeater in this main village or any other."

Hawk looked ready to burst with anger. "Well, dammit, what do you care? You're ridin' off to St. Louis so you don't risk your precious scalp."

Quinn was fresh out of patience. "Hawk," he warned, "if you weren't just a crazy old coot, I'd knock out your teeth!"

"Try it and I'll break your *other* ribs!" Hawk blustered, raising his fists and shuffling his feet in ridiculous pantomime of a bare-knuckles fighter.

Quinn backed down, but not out of fear. Even convalescing, he was more than a match for the old mountaineer. But fighting wasn't going to help anything.

"Listen," he said. "We both know that the *real* reason you're in such a heat to get to the Blackfeet is so you can rescue Hocina."

"No, it ain't!"

"Yes, it is!"

"Get away from me," Hawk growled, actually placing his hand on the bone handle of his hunting knife.

Quinn grabbed Hawk by the back of his shirt, spun him around, and punched him right in the nose. The nose cracked and blood gushed down to cover Hawk's mouth and beard.

"Damn you!" Hawk bellowed, drawing his knife and brandishing it in Quinn's face. "I'm goin' to carve out your gizzard!"

"For what, telling you the truth? That you're willing to get all these peaceful mountain Indians murdered because of Hocina?"

Hawk stood quivering, the knife poised between them, but Quinn didn't flinch or say another word until the old man finally lowered his blade.

"Gawdammit!" Hawk shouted in anguish, "I *loved* my daughter more than life! Loved her like I never loved another livin' thing and now she's a Blackfeet slave woman! You saw Tewa when we first took her from the Paiutes. You know that an Indian slave woman is livin' in hell!"

"Then let's steal her back," Quinn said, totally surprised by his own words because the idea had never entered his mind before. "Let's find Hocina and bring her back to Yellowstone."

"We wouldn't have a chance."

Quinn's eyebrows shot up in question. "Hawk, we'd have a lot better chance than your peaceful Sheepeaters would of surviving hundreds of avenging Blackfeet!"

"Yeah," Hawk conceded, "we probably would."

"Then let's do it. We can leave tomorrow. We'll take extra horses as relays and bring your daughter back to Yellowstone."

"They'll come lookin' for her."

"Maybe so," Quinn said, "but by then the first snows will be falling and we can shake them off our trail."

"All right," Hawk decided. "We'll do it!"

In a rare sober gesture, Hawk hugged Quinn until he wanted to scream because of his still-mending ribs.

But, somehow, Quinn bore the pain long enough to extract himself from the crushing bear hug.

"Do that again," Quinn wheezed, "and *all* my ribs will be cracked."

"Sorry," Hawk said, wiping his eyes dry before he hurried away.

Chapter Thirteen

Juanita rocked back and forth on her knees in the doorway of Quinn's wickiup and wailed, "I can't believe you've offered to join in this madness with Hawk! You're *both* going to get scalped by the Blackfeet if you try to find Hocina."

"No, we won't," Quinn argued, trying to think of a logical reason why not while pushing a loudly protesting Lucky out the door and yelling, "Git now! Go find something of your own to eat!"

The bear cub wasn't happy, but when Quinn grabbed a handy switch, it ran off squealing, probably to torment and steal bones from the camp dogs.

Juanita crawled inside the wickiup. "Tewa says the Blackfeet have many large villages and Hawk doesn't even know which one has his daughter."

"I admit that what we plan to do is dangerous," Quinn said, knowing how foolish he must sound, "but we can . . . well, hide outside their villages and watch for her.''

Juanita raised her hands in a gesture of futility. "Why did you agree to do this?"

"If I tell you," he said from his blankets, "will you calm down?"

"All right, tell me."

"The truth is that Hawk has promised to find me another glory hole—but only if I help him find Hocina."

Juanita stared, then realized he was making a joke. She wanted to laugh. She wanted to cry. Most of all, she wanted to throw her arms around Quinn's neck and beg him not to commit what would be tantamount to suicide.

"Oh, dammit," she cried, leaning forward to hug him tightly, "you're impossible!"

"Is that why we're in love?" he asked, trying to sound light-hearted.

"I don't know," Juanita admitted, turning serious, "but I can't bear the idea of you being killed by Indians."

"I'm not going to get killed," he promised. "The Santa Barbara horses are faster and stronger than any Indian pony and we'll take extras as relays. If we get lucky, we'll snatch Hocina and outrun our pursuers."

"What if they track you back here?"

"I expect they'll try. But we can lay ambushes and easily keep ahead. We'll lead them anywhere but back here to Yellowstone. That way, even if we fail, no harm will come to these gentle people."

Juanita marveled at how simple Quinn could make

all of this craziness sound. In truth, he was going to ride hundreds of miles north, attempt to find one particular Blackfeet village, then rescue a young woman who might not even want to be rescued. The whole idea was sheer madness.

"Quinn, what if I never see you again?"

He expelled a deep breath. "I believe you will, Juanita. And remind yourself that, given all the long odds we've already faced and all the obstacles we've overcome, I think we've done amazingly well to still be alive. Don't you?"

"Yes, but . . ."

He pressed a forefinger to her lips. "Why be so pessimistic? Hawk and I are both marksmen and we have the horses to get us out of any trouble. I honestly like our chances."

Juanita didn't want to cry so she hugged Quinn's neck and kissed his mouth, whispering, "Quinn, just love me!"

"Are you sure?" he asked, remembering how, just a few days before, she'd told him she still respected her marriage vows.

"More sure than I've ever been of anything in my life."

Quinn's lovemaking was so intensely satisfying that Juanita found herself gasping, biting his neck, and raking his muscular back until they both stiffened, holding their breaths and spiraling into ecstasy like wind-whipped leaves madly whirling up to heaven.

They did not emerge from his wickiup the rest of that day or night and few words were spoken. Whenever thoughts of sin and damnation crept into Juanita's mind, she savagely beat them back and urged Quinn to love her into heaven again.

The next morning, they parted and Juanita went off in the woods alone to compose herself for what might be their final goodbye.

Hawk was also having trouble saying goodbye to Tewa. "Gawdammit, you're not comin' with us because it's too damned dangerous!"

"I *will* come," the Shoshone woman insisted. "You can beat me but I *will* come to fight beside you against the Blackfeet."

"We're not going to fight 'em," Hawk argued. "We're just goin' to steal my daughter from 'em. How many times do I have to explain it?"

Tewa wasn't listening. "I will stand proud and straight before my husband Hawk and welcome death with honor."

Hawk was obviously embarrassed by all the attention they were receiving. "Tewa, you're about the *stubbornest* woman I *ever* married! And I'll come back to you," Hawk promised, climbing on his horse and grabbing the lead rope to their string of relays that carried their supplies and a few extra Hawken rifles, just in case they did need to ambush the pursuing Blackfeet from long range.

Quinn saw Juanita at the edge of the woods and knew she had been crying. He handed his reins to a boy and led her back into camp. In front of everyone, he took Juanita into his arms and kissed her, then used the edge of his thumb to wipe away her tears.

"This is now my woman!" he shouted, giving her another big hug and kiss. "And I am her new husband!"

Everyone knew that this was a very solemn occasion

and one fraught with danger, but even so, many of the people laughed and some of the children clapped their hands with appreciation. Juanita put her arm around Quinn's waist, laid her head on his shoulder for a moment, then walked away without shaming him with her fears. She would not allow herself to think about the sin of adultery. She was prepared to pay the consequences—in this life and the next. She loved Quinn and was achingly proud of him for risking his life for Hocina and everyone in this peaceful Sheepeater village.

When Juanita reached their wickiup, she turned and impulsively shouted, "I *am* Quinn's woman!"

"Damned if she isn't," Quinn said, grinning from ear to ear as he hugged Inez and then mounted his horse. Out of the corner of his eye, Quinn saw Tewa throw a saddle on Xavier's fine chestnut.

Hawk's Shoshone woman is coming, he thought. *We can no more stop her than we could stop the sun from rising tomorrow morning. It would be useless to even try. So let her shadow us until Hawk accepts the inevitable. Besides, the more I think about it, the more I realize that Tewa might even save our lives. She's Indian and a rugged survivor. It's possible she will be the only one who will return to this village alive.*

Quinn didn't wave goodbye to Juanita. It would have been too painful. But he did see his bear cub drag an elk leg bone over to Xavier and settle in for a tasty meal. From his litter, the vaquero called, "I can't walk yet, but I can still shoot. Don't worry, Juanita will be safe."

"We'll never lead the Blackfeet back here," Quinn promised the handsome young Mexican. "Get well soon, Xavier, because everyone is getting tired of carrying you around on that damned litter!"

For a moment, the vaquero didn't realize that Quinn was teasing him, but then they both laughed. In the short time that Quinn had known Xavier, he had come to like and respect the vaquero because he never complained and was excellent company. "Adios, Xavier. Don't flirt so much with my woman."

"It would do me no good!"

"And take care of Lucky!"

Xavier made the mistake of petting the hungry cub. It took a swipe at his hand and snarled over the bone it had probably whipped a pack of dogs to get. Xavier recoiled and shouted, "Lucky does not need anyone to protect him!"

Quinn figured that was true enough. He put his horse into a lope after Hawk. They would put in long days and short nights but both had agreed that they must not overwork their horses. Instead, they would try to keep them in good condition for what might prove to be a race for their lives.

That first night out, Tewa slept alone and apart. They watched the twinkle of her campfire as she cooked her solitary dinner.

"She's probably eating a whole lot better than we are," Quinn complained as they chewed dried moose meat, tougher than rawhide.

"Yeah," Hawk agreed in a subdued voice, "she probably is."

"Like it or not," Quinn said, "she's coming with us. What's the matter with you, anyway?"

Instead of getting angry as expected, the mountain man leaned back on his buffalo robe, laced his fingers behind his head and gazed up at the stars.

"Truth is," he said finally, "I've gotten real attached to Tewa. I know she's easily young enough to be my daughter and that I'm actin' like an old fool, but she's a damned fine wife and I just don't want her to get killed or fall into the hands of the Blackfeet like happened with Hocina."

"I understand."

"But you still want us to use her, knowin' full well the odds that she might get caught or killed."

"Never mind," Quinn said. "Just forget what I said. I'm going to sleep."

"Go ahead. I don't give a damn."

"Well, I will then! But what I was trying to say is that Tewa is going to come—one way or another. You can't stop her so we might as well have her on our side."

"I'll consider it," Hawk replied as Quinn drifted off to sleep.

They awoke at dawn to the welcome sight of Tewa roasting venison at their campfire. Quinn expected another fight but Hawk just grinned and acted as if everything was according to his liking. Tewa tenderized her deer meat with herbs and it sure was a lot tastier than the previous night's moose meat.

Later that morning, Quinn heard squawking and saw a wedge-shaped flight of what he was sure were big pelicans heading west. When he asked Hawk about them, the mountain man said, "Yep, they're pelicans. Round about this time of year you'll see 'em headin' for the Pacific Ocean. You'll also see Sandhill Cranes on their way to winterin' down around Santa Fe and even as far south as Old Mexico."

"Winter *is* coming," Quinn said, still feeling the night chill in the air.

"You bet it is. We'll cross some high country up ahead and the aspen will already be turnin' colors. To me, autumn aspen are as pretty as a sunset or a young woman like Tewa.''

She overheard that, blushed, and got very busy.

"We could get caught in snow?'' Quinn asked.

"You bet!''

"How far north will we have to go to find the Black-feet—if they don't find us first?''

"A couple hundred miles.''

"That's not so far.''

"It can be in this rough country," Hawk warned, looking back at Tewa, who was listening intently. "The good news is if we get caught in a blizzard, it'll wipe out all our tracks. The bad news is we must cross the Continental Divide—the snow up there can bury a man and his horse.''

Quinn chewed on while he listened to the bugling of a bull elk. His eerie trumpeting call floated over the mountains and the long, colorful valleys chocked with aspen groves. Quinn guessed the lonesome sound carried for miles and miles. "Hawk," he asked, "why is he calling?''

"He's announcin' his arrival to the lowlands, tellin' everyone to get out of his way and that he needs some ground of his own to winter upon.''

"Is that right?''

"Sure, and you'll also see mule deer as well as Bighorn Sheep all comin' down to the valleys because the snows get too deep up in the higher country.''

Quinn's eyes were irresistibly drawn to the big mountains. "Those same snows that could block our return into Yellowstone?''

"That's right, and we're goin' to need some luck to find Hocina and return across 'em before they close.''

When they passed the black columnar cliffs near

where Quinn had once almost died, he rode over to see if there were still any physical remains of Chaco and Lucky's mother.

"I guess I should have buried him," Quinn said, staring down at Chaco's bones. "It would have been the proper thing."

"Why bother with such nonsense?" Hawk said with disgust. "That one is in hell and so it don't much matter what happens to his bones. Why, maybe the only good thing Chaco Diaz ever did was to die here and feed our Yellowstone critters."

Hawk rode over to the grizzly sow's desiccated remains and dismounted. He toed the equally ravaged skeleton. "Too bad we couldn't have saved her hide. Grizzly make mighty fine winter robes."

Tewa used her knife to cut the claws away from what remained of each foot.

"What's she do that for?" Quinn asked.

"Grizzly claws and eagle feathers are considered powerful medicine by all Indian peoples," Hawk explained. "She'll make a necklace for herself."

"For *you,*" Tewa corrected.

Hawk beamed and they continued north into wild country that was new to Quinn. The deep and swift river they followed was joined by another just as impressive. For two days, the landscape alternated between vast strands of lodgepole forest and lush meadows where the grass was so tall it bent like wheat and teemed with birds, insects, raccoons, muskrats, beaver, and mink.

"In another month, most of these marsh and meadow birds will be long gone," Hawk announced. "A few ducks and the Canada geese will winter but they keep to the middle of the bigger lakes and are impossible to shoot and retrieve."

"What about beaver?" Quinn asked, noting one of their recent dams. "You told me that all you early trappers completely hunted them out."

"We missed a few," Hawk said, "and I'm glad. Hate to see them all disappear but I wish I had a few traps to set. At this time of year the beaver pelts are prime."

"No time for that," Quinn said, his eyes locked on a pass higher than the timberline. "Do we have to ride over that?"

"Sure do! And some more that are even higher."

Late in the afternoon they descended a crooked canyon, following a well-worn game trail. A frigid wind burned their faces as ominous thunderheads collected over distant peaks, leading Quinn to believe they probably ought to make camp.

"There's one hell of a geyser basin just up ahead a mile or two," Hawk called, snatches of his rough voice whipping back to them on icy gusts. "There's some rocks we can find shelter under and pools just hot enough for bathin'."

"I'm not going to take a bath in this weather!" Quinn shouted.

"Suit yourself. But my woman and I are gonna enjoy one. Might as well join us!"

When they topped a rise and Quinn saw this field of geysers, pools, and mud pots, he changed his mind. Steaming and flowing across a quarter mile of hillside, they created mineral formations that reminded Quinn of caramel-flavored taffy or hot butter and molasses. Here and there delicate travertine terraces supported immense boiling pools delicately frosted with sugary icing. Quinn supposed that, for untold centuries, these limestone pools had bled downward to form long, dagger-shaped stalactites. Where the stalactites were thickest, the mineral deposits created intricate chocolate and licorice clusters. Each little pool of boiling water contributed to the torrent that bounced and foamed its way into the cold, rushing river far below. Soft, billowy steam clouds floated upward, then bent and ran with a capricious north wind.

"We'll camp down where the hot water joins this freezin' river," Hawk announced. "There's where we'll find rock overhangs in case we get hit with a rain squall. There's good fishin' so we'll feast tonight. Tewa tells me she's good with a fish spear."

Quinn had often watched the quick Sheepherder boys spear big trout in the Yellowstone lake. The boys would sit crouched for hours on rocks and their aim was deadly. Now, Tewa used Hawk's knife to sharpen a pole and she wasted no time in collecting their dinner as bugs began to dart across the water, bringing the fish close to the surface.

"This pool is teeming with trout!" Quinn exclaimed, squatting on his heels and watching the fish swarm.

"Beats anythin' I ever seen," Hawk said. "The hot water tumblin' down into this river must carry a lot of fish food. Anyway, they're so thick you can almost hook 'em in the gills with your fingers."

That evening they devoured fish until they could eat no more; then Tewa smoked the rest and wrapped them in green leaves.

"The meat will keep for many days," the Shoshone woman told them as she packed the fish for travel and then peeled out of her clothes to join her husband in the steamy water.

Quinn was dubious about joining the pair until Hawk began to tease him. Shamed by his silliness and feeling the bite of the wind, Quinn succumbed. It was a good decision, for the geyser-fed water was like a bath and they soaked until well after dark.

"We'll sleep right up close to the bank and stay warm as babes unless it starts to rain," Hawk said. "If that happens, I know of a little cave just under some nearby rocks."

Tewa wasn't at all embarrassed by her nakedness. She had filled out considerably and Quinn couldn't help but notice that the Shoshone woman was quite comely.

Drowsy and weak from the long, hot soak, Quinn rolled into his blankets and slept until lightning split the night and a hard, freezing rain began to rattle through the canyon. Thunder shook the walls, rebounding across the high rocks like cannonballs.

"Grab a horse or two and keep your powder dry!" Hawk shouted, untying their animals and dragging them off into a darkness so absolute that even Tewa had trouble following.

Fortunately, the riverside cave was very close and they had everything packed inside in less than ten minutes. Shaking and chilled, they discounted the threat of being fried alive by a bolt of lightning and dived back into the steaming river for warmth.

They slept very late the following morning.

"There's fresh snow on that mountain yonder," Hawk said as they saddled their horses and prepared to cross a high pass. "Don't look very deep, though."

"The chance that it *will* be deep when we want to come back in a hurry worries me," Quinn said. "We're not going to get ourselves trapped, are we?"

"Who can say?" Hawk replied with a shrug. "But, if we can't get through this pass, neither can the Blackfeet."

"If they trap us, they'd have no reason."

"Stop worryin' so much," Hawk replied.

Quinn wasn't comforted, but they set their minds to getting over the pass. They did it by nightfall although it took a lot out of their horses.

"It'll be easier tomorrow," Hawk promised as they hunkered down in more rocks and ate smoked fish while watching a shimmering blanket of bright stars.

They kept moving north the next two days and chanced upon a small hunting party of Crow Indians whose extra horses were laden with freshly killed buffalo.

"These people can be trusted," Hawk explained to calm Quinn. "The Crow hate the Blackfeet almost as much as I do."

Quinn thought the Crow were a handsome race, taller than California or desert Indians and quite reserved. They talked with Hawk for about an hour, using their hands as much as words. Hawk traded them an excellent knife for some buffalo meat and it wasn't until he returned after dark that Quinn and Tewa realized he had some exciting news.

"They've seen Hocina!" he exclaimed. "They say she's living in a winter camp not more than twenty miles north beside a big river!"

It was all that Tewa and Quinn could do that evening to calm the old mountain man down, arguing that it would be a mistake to push their horses to exhaustion just before all their speed and strength might be required for escape.

"I can't believe our good fortune!" Hawk kept repeating. "The Crow stole some Blackfeet horses from that camp about a month ago. But first they'd spent a couple of days staking the village out and that's when they saw my Hocina.''

"If her mother was a Sheepeater Indian, how could they be certain?" Quinn asked, voicing the question that had been bothering him ever since they'd left Yellowstone. He didn't want to come right out and use the word, but Hocina was a half-breed.

"I described her."

"But you haven't seen you daughter in four years."

"That don't matter. Hocina looks one hell of a lot different from any Blackfeet!"

Quinn dared not even glance at Tewa, but he sensed that she shared his grave misgivings. Putting their lives in jeopardy, only to discover at a critical moment that there had been a case of mistaken identity, would prove disastrous. To die attempting a noble deed was tragic enough, but to die foolishly was altogether unthinkable.

"Hawk," Quinn blurted, "Tewa and I are both willing to risk our lives to rescue your daughter but you *have* to promise me that we'll sneak up on that camp and watch it long enough to be dead sure we've really found Hocina."

"I'll know my girl the moment I see her," Hawk vowed. "And after that, you can help or not. But I won't wait more'n one dark night to sneak into that camp and deliver her from a livin' hell."

"All right," Quinn said, trying to calm the old man down. "We're with you. We just want to make sure."

"Well, so do I!" Hawk raged. "Do you think I've come this far to throw our lives away by mistake?"

"No," Quinn replied, "I don't."

"Then let's get a few hours sleep and move out long before sunrise."

Quinn smothered his misgivings but promised himself he wasn't going to let go of their fastest horse or their straightest-shooting rifle until he was back in Juanita's loving arms.

Chapter Fourteen

They had been riding hard since long before dawn and Quinn could feel the shuddering, stumbling weariness of their horses. *We're running them into the ground. What is Hawk thinking?*

"Hawk, hold up!" Quinn shouted angrily when it became clear they were not stopping for a midday rest.

The mountain man reluctantly reined their horses down from a fast trot, shouting, "What's the matter? One of your horses goin' lame?"

"Not yet," Quinn replied, "but they're going to, if you don't slow down and give them rest. This is a good place to stop."

Quinn dismounted, aware that Hawk was seething. This was an ideal place to rest until darkness allowed them to move in closer to the Blackfeet encampment that the Crows had described. It was low and out of the wind with deep grass and a fine stream to slake their thirsts.

"Get back on your horse!" Hawk ordered.

"Nope," Quinn replied. "Hawk, it's been a long time since we ate and rested. I'm played out and so are these horses. And, if that isn't good enough, so are you and Tewa."

But Hawk shook his head. "We're pushin' on until we see that Blackfeet camp!"

"Or they see us." Quinn began to unsaddle his horse. "Hawk, I'm not going anywhere for a while and neither should you."

"We can rest tonight," Hawk spat, sawing on his reins and forcing his exhausted mount back into a trot, leaving not only Quinn but Tewa behind.

"I must go with him," Tewa said.

"Yeah, but try to make him understand that we can't steal Hocina away from the Blackfeet on played-out horses!"

Tewa glanced toward her husband, then back to Quinn. She turned a palm up to the overcast sky to indicate that there was nothing she could do—nothing either of them could do to slow Hawk down. Then she sent her horse racing after the mountain man.

"Damn!" Quinn swore, caught in a dilemma. He decided to hobble his own horse and the pair that he was leading, allowing them to drink and graze. If things went sour up ahead, three fresh horses might be their salvation.

"Someone has to use their head," he groused as he loosened his cinch and then hobbled the animals. When he was finished, Quinn rummaged around in his pack and found the pemmican that one of the Sheepeater women had prepared. It was as tough as a boot heel and he wished like hell he had some of Tewa's smoked trout or that buffalo meat that Hawk had traded from the Snake Indians. The pemmican was so hard that Quinn soaked it in the river for fifteen minutes, then chewed it until his jaw muscles ached.

His hunger satisfied, Quinn stretched out and yawned, feeling his body ache from too many long days in the saddle. He was almost too tired to sleep and had to work hard to push the rioting fears from his mind by admiring the way air and sunlight combined to dapple the stream's glistening surface.

His eyes burned and his head throbbed, reminding him that he had hardly gotten any sleep the previous night, thanks to Hawk's impatience. And who could blame him? No one, but that didn't mean he had the right to jeopardize everyone's lives.

Quinn unbuckled his holster and placed it at his side, then prepared to take a good, long nap. He would catch up with Hawk and Tewa this evening and his mind would be fresh when it came time to decide how they were going to steal Hocina.

This whole thing is crazy, he thought. *White men trying to sneak into an Indian camp and free a half-breed girl. What if she's not even there? Or doesn't want to leave?*

Those possibilities were too dreadful to contemplate so Quinn returned his mental focus to the comforting murmur of wind caressing tall grass and the relaxing gurgle of flowing water.

"There it is!" Hawk whooped just before sunset. "That's got to be the low white bluff the Snakes told me about. The Blackfeet village must be just ahead!"

Tewa didn't know what to say or do. All afternoon

she had been glancing over her shoulder, hoping that Quinn and their extra horses would appear on the southern horizon. But they hadn't and Tewa knew that was a bad omen. If Quinn had suddenly lost his nerve and decided to return to Yellowstone with the extra horses, there was no possibility of rescuing Hocina.

"Hawk," she called, galloping to his side. "We *must* stop and rest until dark."

Hawk ignored her, whipping the horses onward to a ridge where he dismounted. Then he flattened his body against the earth. "There it is!" he said, giggling like a child. "Hocina's Blackfeet village!"

Tewa couldn't help herself. She began to tremble because she had never before seen such a huge encampment. There were so many tepees that they reminded her of a forest of white trees. The Blackfeet horse herd numbered in the hundreds. No wonder the Sheepeaters were so afraid of these people!

"It's a damned big camp," Hawk said. "Bigger than any I ever saw before, even among the Sioux and Cheyenne."

"They number more than the leaves on a tree," Tewa answered. "More than the hairs on a dog."

"Maybe not that many," Hawk told her, "but I'll bet there are more'n a thousand camped there beside that river. The buffalo huntin' must still be real good in this country."

"How will you ever see your daughter among so many?"

"I'm countin' on you to help me with that. And, maybe it's time we got a little lucky and find that her tepee is near this edge of the camp."

Tewa didn't trust herself to speak. It seemed to her

that they would never be able to identify Hocina among such great numbers.

"Come on," he said, backing down to their horses, then hobbling them with nothing more than the ridge between themselves and all those enemies. "It's gonna work out."

"What if they come this way and see us?"

Hawk just shrugged. "We can't be thinkin' about the bad things that could happen. We got to think about the good things, too!"

"But . . ."

"We'll unsaddle and rest their backs," Hawk interrupted. "Then we'll go back up there and find Hocina."

"But if we don't, that might mean that the Crow were mistaken."

"Oh, no," Hawk said, wagging his head back and forth. "They described her, all right. Even told me she was livin' near the river."

He tousled her black hair. "It's goin' to be all right. You can stay here tonight and I'll creep down there and bring Hocina out by myself."

"We must wait for Quinn and our extra horses," Tewa insisted.

"He'll be along."

"But what if he ran away?"

Hawk scratched at his beard. "If Quinn got scared and lit out I can't say as I'd hold it against him. After all, I lied through my teeth about the Yellowstone gold. I lied because I was afraid I wasn't man enough to get this job done alone."

"You are *not* alone."

"No, I'm not," he agreed. "But I wouldn't blame you for leavin' right now."

"Never!" Tewa spat.

"All right," he said in a voice husky with emotion, "but maybe it would be best if you stayed here with the horses when I sneak into that village tonight."

"No, because you don't see very good."

"Yeah," he admitted, "but I'm still a man to be reckoned with in a bad fight."

"My husband, let's wait a day or two so our horses can be as rested as the Blackfeet horses," Tewa begged. "What good would it do Hocina if we brought her out and then the enemy ran us down because our horses had no strength?"

"I'll think about it," he answered, unable to meet her eyes. "Let's stop jawin' and use what little daylight we have left to try and spot Hocina."

Tewa followed Hawk back to the ridge where her keen eyes could watch the village. If Hocina was down there, she would be seen unless time and the enemy had changed her so much that she was now one with the Blackfeet. If that were so, Tewa thought, Hocina would be better off left alone among these enemy people.

Quinn didn't awaken until the sun was almost down. As soon as he realized he'd slept all afternoon, he gathered his horses and swung into the saddle. It was easy to follow the trail of bent grass left by Hawk and Tewa's horses. Rested now, but fretful that he might be too late to help, Quinn pushed ahead at a gallop, often standing in his stirrups to scan the horizon. Sunset blooded the grass and golden insects took wing before his onrushing horses, only to be devoured in his wake by birds and hungry bats. An owl sailed silently across the grassy trail, then angled sharply away as the sun

melted into the spine of rugged, snow-capped peaks.
The rising moon kept sliding in and out of the clouds.

It was long after midnight when he finally saw a speck
of fire on the horizon and realized he must be very near
the Blackfeet camp. Quinn slowed his horses and stood
tall in his stirrups, searching for but not spotting Hawk
and Tewa. This rolling prairie had either swallowed
his friends or they had already been captured by the
Blackfeet.

Unsure of his next move, Quinn decided there was
nothing he could do until morning. He headed for
higher ground where a large stand of trees stood silhouetted against the starry sky. And that's when his horse
pricked up its ears and whinnied a greeting to its lost
companions.

Quinn couldn't pile out of his saddle fast enough to
stop the animal from whinnying a second time. Even
worse, the sound was repeated from the trees.

"Dammit, Quinn, why don't we just fire off a couple
shots and let the Blackfeet know we've arrived?"

Quinn hurried forward, his heart thumping against
the inside of his ribcage. He fully expected to hear a
cry of alarm from the nearby Blackfeet village.

"What are you tryin' to do to us?" Hawk demanded.

"It's all your fault," Quinn shot back. "If you'd have
waited like I asked, none of this would have happened!"

Hawk turned to the Shoshone woman. "You better
find a high spot and watch for trouble headin' out of
the village."

Tewa disappeared, leaving Quinn to wonder why he
hadn't let this fool get himself scalped. *Maybe*, he
thought, *I'm really doing this for Tewa, who doesn't deserve
to die any more than I do.*

They managed to get the horses reunited without any

more commotion. Then Hawk led Quinn up to the rise where Tewa sat with her arms wrapped around her knees, studying the distant village.

"Lord help us," Quinn whispered, seeing the huge Indian encampment for the first time. "It *is* big!"

"I've never seen one bigger," Hawk agreed. "But, in a way, that will make it easier to get into their camp."

"How do you figure that?"

"The more of 'em there are, the less suspicious I'll seem movin' among 'em."

Quinn saw the logic in that and nodded. He gazed at the village a while longer and said, "I don't suppose you've seen your daughter yet?"

"No, it was gettin' too dark by the time we arrived and had our first look-see," Hawk replied before he explained how they were going to hide for a few days while they kept surveillance on the village, trying to identify Hocina. "I sure hope we get lucky and she's stayin' on this side of that village instead of in the middle."

"What if she isn't?" Quinn had to ask.

"Won't make any difference," Hawk allowed. "We're goin' to bring her out just the same."

"Do you have a plan?"

"Now that *you're* here," Hawk replied, "the plan just got better. Tewa and I will go in for my daughter, then you'll come poundin' in through that big horse herd, stampedin' 'em into the middle of the village. We jump on the extra horses you're leadin' and ride like hell while they waste time tryin' to catch and sort out their ponies in the dark."

"That's it?" Quinn asked. "That's your *best* plan?"

"It's my *only* plan," Hawk snapped defensively. "You got a better one?"

"Yeah," Quinn said, unable to curb his anger. "Why don't we make it real simple and just shoot ourselves right now? Because if that's your plan, we're dead anyway."

"No, we're not," Hawk growled. "When you scatter all them Injun ponies through the camp, people will be screamin' and dashin' back and forth like rabbits. The warriors will be afraid to shoot in the dark and the dust and the thunder because they might kill one of their own by mistake."

Hawk sounded so reasonable and confident that Quinn almost believed the man. "But won't there be Indians guarding all those horses?"

"Probably," Hawk admitted. "Plains Indians love nothin' better than to steal each other's horses. It's a game for 'em, so yes, they might have a few guards hidin' in the middle of their pony herd. But you can stampede 'em right over the top of them guards and trample 'em to death."

"I see," Quinn said, struggling to sound calm. "And then, somehow, in the dust and the dark and the thunder, I'm supposed to find and then supply you, Tewa, and your daughter with extra horses?"

"Naw," Hawk said, "just bring a couple extras. We can leave our relays in these trees, then pick 'em up on our way south."

"That's brilliant," Quinn deadpanned.

"Yep, it's gonna work."

Quinn gave up. Tewa had at least managed to convince Hawk that they needed to rest their horses. Maybe they'd never spot Hocina in the village and call off this farce or eventually come up with a far better plan. Perhaps Tewa could enter the camp at dusk. Being a full-blooded Indian, she'd have the best hope of moving unnoticed among the Blackfeet and searching out Hocina. Once that was accomplished, Tewa could sneak the girl out and they could escape with their lives with a full night's head start riding rested horses. Quinn figured they'd need every minute they could muster, considering how many furious Blackfeet would be on their trail.

All the next morning and early afternoon, they hid in tall grass about a half mile to the southwest and surveyed the Blackfeet village. To Quinn, it was a revelation to learn that these were a happy and fun-loving people. The women spent a lot of time preparing meals, scraping and tanning buffalo hides while the children played using small leather balls in a game of skill that was fast and frantic. The children also swam in the nearby river while the older boys fished, rode their ponies, wrestled, and did a lot of talking and flirting with the older girls. To Quinn's way of thinking, they pretty much acted like the friends he'd grown up with.

The Blackfeet men smoked and visited, although a hunting party rode out in the afternoon, probably after buffalo or to guard their territory against enemies. Fortunately, they rode northeast.

"I knew they'd either ride north or east," Hawk said, "because their main worry is the Sioux, an even bigger and stronger people who are also expert horsemen."

"Given the numbers and ferocity of these Blackfeet," Quinn replied, "it's hard to imagine that any other tribe could come into this country and seriously threaten them."

"You haven't seen the Sioux or Cheyenne in action, but mark my words, they are more than a match for these Blackfeet. Indians are always warrin' among themselves—it all has to do with territory and huntin' grounds. The better the huntin', the harder they have to fight to hang onto it."

"When you think about what's happened in America," Quinn said, "it's not much different. The Spanish all but destroyed the California Indians and they in turn were kicked out by the Mexicans who are now being threatened by us Americans."

"And what about the Russians up at Fort Ross and Sitka?" Hawk asked.

"I don't know what will happen to them," Quinn replied. "But if history teaches us a lesson, it's that stronger peoples always enslave or kill weaker ones."

"That's the way I read it," Hawk told him. "I doubt it was much different even back in the East."

"No doubt about it," Quinn said. "After the Pilgrims landed at Plymouth Rock, everything went downhill in a hurry for all the Indians east of the Mississippi River."

"I met a Cherokee once," Hawk said with a frown. "He owned a plantation in Georgia before I met him but then all his people were made to walk clear to the Oklahoma Territory. He said about half of 'em died on what he called 'The Trail of Tears'. It sounded damned wrong to me."

"It *was* wrong," Quinn said. "I'm afraid that the history of every living thing from mankind down to the lowest insects confirms that the strong always either enslave or kill off the weak. It happened all over Europe and everywhere else in the world."

"Well," Hawk muttered, "these gawdamn Blackfeet are *still* strong but we're goin' to whittle 'em down to size with all the guns I brought."

"These people have rifles," Quinn reminded his friend. "Quite a few of them."

"Yeah, but they are mostly old trade rifles that don't shoot straight. I'll give 'em credit for bein' fighters, though."

"That's probably because they understand that they have to be in order to survive," Quinn said, watching a mother and her three small children at play.

"All this talk is givin' me indigestion," Hawk said after a long silence. "Why don't we just shut up and see if we can spot Hocina so we can rescue her tonight."

"Not tonight," Quinn said. "Our horses need at least another rest day."

"If I see my girl today, I'm goin' to get her *tonight,*" Hawk vowed. "And by damn, don't you dare try to stop me!"

Quinn knew better than to argue the point. Hawk was going to do what Hawk was going to do when it came to rescuing his daughter. To take issue with the timing would just cause friction between them at a time when cooperation was vital to their common survival. Still, maybe the man could be reasoned with if he didn't feel challenged.

"All right, since it's obvious you place no value on your life or mine, what about Tewa's?"

"What's she got to do with this?"

"Her horse is just as worn out as ours. If the Blackfeet come after us, she'll also be killed—or worse."

Quinn could see that he'd touched a nerve in the mountain man. After a few moments, Hawk said, "All right, we'll rest the horses at least another day no matter when we spot Hocina."

"Fair enough," Quinn said. "I'll hold you to that."

The afternoon passed slowly and then they all saw a young woman emerge from a tepee cradling a baby in her arms. She looked distinctly different from the other women, being somewhat taller and lighter complected with long, flowing hair that burned with an auburn cast.

"That's her!" Hawk cried. "That's my girl!"

Quinn and Tewa had to grab the mountain man and pin him down, fearing he would leap up and be seen by someone in the village.

"But . . . but she's got a little bugger in her arms!"

"She's a Blackfoot mother," Tewa said quietly.

Hawk's chin began to tremble. He covered his face with his liver-blotched hands and moaned, "Oh, dammit!"

"It is not so terrible," Tewa said. "You are a grandfather and the child . . ."

"Don't say anythin' more!" Hawk shouted.

"Hawk, control yourself or we'll be found and killed," Quinn cried.

"A baby!" Hawk groaned.

"Tewa," Quinn asked, "do you know if she has a husband?"

"Yes, I saw him go off with the hunting party," Tewa answered. "He came out of that same tepee."

Apparently, Hawk's mind was recovering from shock because he blurted, "Kid or not, I'm goin' down there to see my girl!"

"Hawk," Quinn said, "with a babe in her arms, Hocina might decide not to come back to Yellowstone with us."

"She'll come!"

"But what if she doesn't want to leave her husband and put her baby's life at risk?"

Hawk's face mottled with rage. "She's *comin'*, with or without the kid!"

We're as good as dead, Quinn thought as he retreated to check on their horses and tried to fend off an overpowering sense of despair. *Hell, we* are *dead.*

Chapter Fifteen

Tewa could feel her husband's growing anxiety as they waited for the Blackfeet village to go to sleep. Even though she was afraid of what the night would bring, she took comfort from the fact that Hocina's tepee was favorably located at this end of the village and close to the river where it would be easy to reach.

"My husband," she began as the Blackfeet campfires dimmed and the silhouettes faded into their tepees, "we can go follow the river almost to your daughter's door."

"Yeah," he answered, "but I think we can just wiggle through this grass down to about fifty yards from her tepee and then rush for it. Be a lot quicker."

"No!" Tewa had never before spoken to her husband in that tone of voice and it shocked her. Hawk, too, because he stared.

"Why not?"

"There are dogs between us that way," Tewa said. "They would see us coming across open ground."

"And probably pay us no mind. It's a big village and they can't remember the sight and smell of everyone."

"If they began to bark, or came at us, we would be seen by the guards and never reach Hocina. Would you take that chance to save only a little time?"

"No," Hawk muttered, "I guess not."

"My husband," Tewa said, "do you remember that burned tree that we passed by the river?"

"Yeah, why?"

"Your face and hands need blackening."

"All right. Let's get movin'."

"What about Quinn?"

Hawk spat into the dirt. "He's already made it clear he wants no part of goin' down into that village so we'll leave him behind."

"He *must* be told," Tewa insisted. "He is our friend. If we are caught, he could take the extra horses and still get away."

"Yeah," Hawk snapped, "and he'll probably run scared all the way back to Yellowstone, draggin' the Blackfeet right along on his tail. It'd be better if he were caught and killed."

Tewa disagreed. There was a time when Quinn might have done that, but not after falling in love with Juanita. Now, he would think about her instead of himself and lead any pursuing Blackfeet away from Yellowstone. But it would be a waste of precious time trying to convince Hawk of this, so she said nothing. Instead, she began to walk in silence, making a wide detour around the village and finally arriving at the river. After that, it took only a short while before she located the lightning-struck tree.

Hawk was getting upset. "Dammit, we're wastin' too much time!" he complained. "We're goin' to need a big head start."

Tewa listened as she rubbed the blackened bark and then smeared her face, hair, and beard of her husband. But he was still too light so she said, "Rub against this tree like a scratching bear."

"Huh?"

"Your clothes are too pale."

"Oh, yeah." Hawk did a pretty good imitation of a bear and was soon blacked from head to foot. "Now, let's not waste any more time."

Tewa took a deep breath. She was glad he could not see how scared she was. Scared, but determined to see this to the end. She started up the river toward the camp, thinking hard about how many tepees she would have to pass before she reached Hocina's. Seven, if she had counted correctly.

"Tewa?" he whispered.

She stopped and turned, hearing his heavy breathing and realizing she had been moving very fast and he was tiring.

"Here," he said, giving her his favorite pistol. "I guess I better tell you it'll go hard if we are captured alive."

"Yes, I know."

"I won't let that happen to myself," he told her. "I'd go down fightin' but when there was no hope, well, I'd . . . I'd shoot myself in the head before I'd allow them to capture and torture me. I know what they can do and it'd be easier to die of a quick bullet."

"If you die, I will die," she said, seeing no point in saying anything more or allowing herself to think of their child that she carried.

"Yeah, that'd be the best for you." He touched her

cheek. "But we ain't goin' to die so let's not talk of that. Instead, let's go see my daughter. You can see better, so take the lead," Hawk ordered.

It seemed to take them forever to reach the edge of the camp. Tewa was most worried about dogs barking at them in the night and arousing these people. She waited perhaps five minutes, her eyes locked on Hocina's tepee, trying to imagine how the young woman would react.

"Hawk," she whispered, "let me go in alone."

"Are you crazy?"

"Shhh, not so loud. Hocina will be badly frightened if a man awakens her."

"I'm her father!"

"I think it would be better for me to talk to her first."

"No," he said. "I've been waitin' far too long for this to pass on it now."

Tewa understood and accepted this. She stood up in the starlight and began to walk beside the river, counting tepees and trying to still the fear building up inside her like a great storm. When she reached number seven, she paused.

"Is this it?" Hawk whispered.

Instead of answering, Tewa walked up to the entrance of the tepee, ducked her head, and passed inside.

A small fire ring still glowed from Hocina's cooking. It gave enough light so Tewa could see the sleeping young woman and her baby. Having already decided what she would do, Tewa knelt beside her, said a quick prayer, and then clamped her hand firmly over Hocina's mouth.

The young woman jolted into wakefulness. When her

eyes flew open and she saw Tewa and a man she had not yet recognized, she tried to scream and fight.

Tewa smothered Hocina with her weight. The girl was strong but Tewa was even stronger. The baby, though not yet awake, began to whimper.

"Hocina," Tewa whispered, "do not be afraid. My name is Tewa and I have brought your father so we can take you back to Yellowstone and the Sheepeater people."

Hocina froze but did not relax.

Hawk pushed in close, hissing, "We finally came for you. But we got to be quiet and get out of this camp. There are horses waitin' for us."

Hocina reached up and grabbed Tewa's wrist, then tore her hand away. She was breathing hard but said, "Father!"

He hugged her tightly. "I been waitin' for this a long, long time. Now get up and grab what you need. We can't wait any longer."

Just then the baby began to cry and Hocina rolled over a little and puts its mouth to her breast. "Father, I can't leave my daughter."

"You're goin' to have to," he said, rushing his words and actually trying to push the infant's mouth away from Hocina's breast. "We can't take the kid. It'd start cryin' and . . . and it'd be too hard on it. Now . . . make her shut up and go back to sleep so we can leave."

"No," Hocina cried. "I can't do that!"

"It'd die for sure," Hawk pleaded. "Darlin', someone else can raise her up. You don't belong here!"

Hocina hugged her child so tightly that it seemed to be smothered. "Go away. Both of you! I have a husband. They treat me good now. I have . . ."

"Gawdammit!" Hawk hissed. "You're comin' with

me! That's a Blackfoot baby and he'd never be welcome among your mother's people!''

"I won't leave her!"

Aroused by the alarm in Hocina's voice, a dog began to bark. Hocina tried to drag Hawk outside but failed. "We have to go!" Tewa begged. "She isn't coming with us!"

"Sure she is!" Hawk exclaimed, grabbing his daughter by the shoulders and shaking her. "Hocina, you don't belong here! You're my daughter. Your mother was a Sheepeater!"

The baby began to cry. Hocina forgot Hawk and snatched it up in her arms, cradling it protectively as she glared at her father. "Go away!" she ordered. "Both of you!"

Hawk rocked back on his heels. He shook himself as if trying pull out of a bad dream then hissed, "I ain't goin' to leave you. I came too far!"

The dogs began to bark louder. Tewa heard an angry voice answered by another voice even angrier. "Please," she begged, "we have to go. The camp is waking!"

"Hocina, I'm your father so don't act crazy!"

Tewa heard more voices. "Hawk!" she pleaded, grabbing his arm and trying to drag him back outside. "There is no more time!"

But Hawk didn't hear her. "Hocina, why are you actin' like this? Is it because of this baby?"

Hocina scooted away from him, trying to put the fire ring between them as her baby began to wail.

"Answer me!"

"I'm a Blackfoot now," Hocina declared. "A mother and a wife. Father, you're the one that's crazy! Leave now while you can!"

Instead, Hawk lunged across the fire ring, tore the

squalling baby from Hocina, and shook it like a dog might a rat. Then, he raised the screaming infant overhead, eyes wild with outrage as he stared down into the campfire.

"No!" Hocina cried as she and Tewa both threw themselves at Hawk, bowling him over.

Tewa grabbed a fistful of Hawk's hair and managed to drag and wrestle him outside where Blackfeet were milling about in bewilderment, shouting to be heard over the barking of excited dogs.

"Hawk," she pleaded, "stay close and run away with me!"

But Hawk turned and would have plunged back inside the tepee except that a warrior appeared and buried his knife into Hawk's chest a moment before Tewa could react to save him. Hawk staggered but managed to drag his pistol out and shoot the Blackfoot at almost point-blank range. The explosion knocked the young Indian into the tepee. Hocina shrieked and confusion turned to chaos.

"Hawk!" Tewa cried, grabbing him and staggering down to the riverside, where he collapsed. "Oh, my husband!"

"Listen to me, Tewa."

She bent close, willing herself to hear his dying words over excited shouts and the frenzied barking of dogs.

"Save yourself and our baby. Do it for me. Run!"

Hawk tried to say more but couldn't as his body convulsed in death a moment before he entered the Spirit World.

"Goodbye, my husband," she whispered. "I would not leave you for myself, but only for the life of our child."

Taking his knife, Tewa jumped to her feet and waded

out into the river, then sank down so that only the top of her head was visible above the current. The water was very cold, and as the current spun her around, Tewa saw silhouettes of warriors dashing about in the village. She wondered what would become of Hocina and her baby, for the Blackfeet would recognize Hawk as her father. They would also see Tewa's tracks and know that her husband had not entered their village alone. And they would begin the hunt even before the first light of day.

They will see my tracks leading into the water and ride hard downriver to catch me when I try to float past, she realized. If I stay too long in this water, I will either die of the cold or be captured at dawn. Somehow, I must find a way to live and give birth to Hawk's son.

The moon was behind clouds and Tewa prayed for a storm to give her some chance of hiding without leaving tracks. For the next hour, she allowed the swift current to carry her along until she could not stand the cold and feared that it would kill the life in her womb. When she washed up on a sandbar, Tewa left the river and worked her way through some trees to open ground. Then, physically numb but clearheaded, she put the North Star at her back and began to run downriver. If her baby lived, Tewa would name him Eagle because he would have the proud blood of Bannock, Shoshone, and Hawk coursing through his veins. Such a child would surely become great, if only she could find a way to save him from the Blackfeet.

When Quinn saw Hawk and Tewa leave, he knew they were heading into the Blackfeet village despite the earlier decision to wait a few days to give their horses rest. Now, there was no time to rest or stampede the Blackfeet horse herd. Cussing in anger, Quinn saddled his horses and tied their extra mounts in a running lead line before heading for the river just south of the encampment. That was the only possible escape route that Hawk and Tewa could choose after grabbing Hocina.

Quinn rode hard to position himself a few miles south of the village. Then he heard barking dogs and the confused shouting of the Blackfeet men. Finally, he heard a gunshot, followed by shouts and cries. Something had gone terribly wrong. In all likelihood, Tewa and Hawk were both already dead but he could not be certain of that. Berating himself for his own stupid bravery, Quinn advanced upriver, hoping to intercept Hawk and Tewa before they were overtaken by the Blackfeet.

"Tewa!" he shouted over and over until he saw her running for her life along the riverbank.

Quinn charged forward and almost ran Tewa down. His horses were so excited that he lost a few precious minutes trying to get them under control.

"Over here!" he yelled just as a pair of warriors burst out of the trees and sprinted after Tewa.

The Blackfeet were much faster than Tewa so they narrowed the gap in a hurry. Quinn fumbled under his heavy coat for a gun while Tewa staggered toward the waiting horses, unaware that she was about to be caught from behind.

Quinn's first shot was wild but it had the desired effect. His second shot also missed and the flashes from his muzzle gave the Blackfeet a target. Quinn cried out in pain as an arrow struck him in the thigh. He fired again, knocking over one of the Blackfeet and sending

the other racing for cover. It gave Tewa enough time
to reach the horses.

"Let's go!" he shouted, snapping the arrow shaft,
then wheeling his horse around and forcing it into a
hard run.

How bad am I shot, he wondered, *risking a glance down
at the broken shaft protruding from his leg. Is that gunfire or
thunder? God, I hope it's thunder!*

A jagged bolt of lightning split the night sky and
Quinn heard thunder booming down south. He reined
his horse toward the sound and kept it running hard,
hoping they could reach the approaching storm and
use it to cover their tracks.

Tewa shouted, "We have to keep riding until we are
in the storm! Then we must split up!"

Quinn understood because they had often discussed
what they would do if they were pursued by the Blackfeet. It was agreed that they would not lead their enemies
back down into the Yellowstone country, no matter how
desperate their circumstances. Instead, Hawk and Hocina would ride west while Tewa and Quinn headed
southeast; they would only return to Yellowstone in the
most roundabout fashion.

Another hour passed before the storm slammed into
them. Hard and cold, the wind drove sleet directly into
their faces.

Tewa took the lead because Quinn had no idea where
they were or even in which direction they were headed.
The stars had disappeared, and it was all Quinn could
do to hang on.

"We're changing horses!" Tewa shouted into the
whistling wind as she helped Quinn dismount, then led
him to a fresh horse and nearly lifted him back into a
saddle.

"What happened back there?" he yelled.

"Hawk is dead."

"And Hocina?"

"She is dead, too."

Quinn was not really surprised. After all, Hocina had been with those people for years. She would have had to become one of them or else remain a slave, and slaves didn't last long. Hocina must have been desirable enough to attract a husband. It had probably been her only salvation.

"They're coming," Tewa shouted, "but I have been changing directions and the rain is washing out our tracks."

"Have we any chance of escape?"

Tewa didn't give him a direct answer. Instead, she used her knife to cut the shaft away so it barely protruded from his flesh. "We must ride faster now."

A clap of thunder shook the earth. Quinn's horse shied sideways, almost unseating him. "Tewa, I don't think I can get through the night without rest. I'm losing too much blood."

Tewa leaned close. "You *can* do this," she told him. "And you *must* do this or we will be caught."

Quinn didn't remember much more of what happened that long, bitter night but, somehow, he stayed upright in the saddle and the worst of the storm passed by daybreak. Tewa found a hiding place and helped Quinn out of the saddle and over to the shelter of a stand of trees.

She cut away part of his pants, then studied the wound for a minute before she gave him a stick. "Bite hard and make no noise."

"What are you going to do?"

"Cut out the arrowhead."

"Now wait a minute!"

"If I do not cut it out, the leg will poison and you will die."

Quinn took a deep breath, then forced a smile. "You had better give me a damned big stick or I'll bite it in half."

As she extracted the large stone arrowhead, Quinn bit down hard on the stick. When that brought no relief, he spat it out, buried his face into the crook of his arm, and screamed until the cutting was done. After that, he must have passed out for a while. When he opened his eyes the sky was clearing and Tewa made him eat some smoked fish.

"Where are we?" he asked, looking around and seeing nothing but rolling grasslands dotted with rocky outcroppings and an occasional stand of trees like the one they were using for protection.

She pointed, saying, "That way is Sioux hunting grounds or maybe Cheyenne, bad enemies of Blackfeet."

"I get it. You came this way thinking the Blackfeet will be afraid to follow."

"They will follow," Tewa warned, then added, "but maybe not very far."

"But how can they follow our washed-out tracks?"

Tewa must not have thought the question worthy of an answer because she brought out more fish, saying, "Eat."

"I didn't realize you were so bossy," Quinn said. "Maybe you were tougher on Hawk than I thought."

Tewa went off to check on their horses. When she returned, she said, "No Blackfeet . . . yet."

"Then how about a little fire?" They were both wet

and chilled and Quinn's teeth were rattling like dice in a cup. "I'm freezing."

"Eat more fish."

"You eat the rest of that damned fish! What else is in the saddlebags?"

Tewa brought him some jerked venison, which Quinn managed to gag down. For about an hour, they sat apart, listening to the distant rumble of the vanishing storm and gazing out into a broad valley. Far away, they saw a herd of grazing buffalo. Quinn wasn't certain but thought they were migrating south, just as he ought to be doing. If they kept moving south, they would intercept the Oregon Trail. They could easily follow it back to the Snake River, which would lead them into Yellowstone.

He explained this to Tewa, who paid him no attention but kept staring back in the direction they'd just come. Exasperated and weak, Quinn shouted, "Dammit, Tewa, we *could* do that!"

When Tewa didn't answer, Quinn snapped, "Maybe you don't want to go back to the Sheepeater people. Is that it?"

"If I live, I will go back and raise Hawk's son among those people," Tewa told him in a sad voice.

"What happened back there?" Quinn gently asked. "Did Hawk at least get to see and talk to Hocina before he died?"

"Yes."

"And?"

Tewa was slow to reply but she finally looked at Quinn and said, "Hocina knew her baby would die if she came with us so she stayed. My husband would not listen to her or leave in peace. The camp awakened and he was killed."

Quinn didn't ask any more questions and he didn't complain when Tewa told him it was time to get back on their horses. It was then that he noticed his horses' hooves had been bound with leather. "Why did you do that?"

Tewa pointed northwest. "I'll ride that way, you ride south toward the Oregon Trail."

"I can't make it alone."

"You are still strong."

"You're trying to hide my tracks and draw off the Blackfeet so I can make it but dammit, Tewa, I won't stand for that. We're in this together."

In reply, Tewa handed him two guns and two rifles. "Blackfeet are coming so ride fast now."

Quinn opened his mouth to ask how in the hell she could be so sure about the Blackfeet, but Tewa was already reining her horse westward toward high, snowy mountains that appeared to be at least a hundred miles away.

Feeling lost and forsaken, Quinn watched her with the idea that he should follow. But then Tewa stopped, turned back, and waved at Quinn, motioning him to hurry south.

"Until we meet again," Quinn said, shaking his head back and forth before he set his sights on a high, spiked peak far to the south. He would ride as far as his strength would allow, then he would rest.

Chapter Sixteen

Quinn couldn't exactly say how he *knew* he was being tracked by the Blackfeet, but the feeling was strong enough to keep him upright in the saddle. Where was he? How far away was help? A hundred miles? A thousand? Quinn had no earthly idea as that first lonely day passed. He must have looked over his shoulder at least every five minutes, always expecting to see Indians. Weak and anxious about falling off his horse and reopening his leg wound, Quinn somehow stayed in the saddle through a second long night, asleep more often than awake.

With an iron will and determination that surprised himself, Quinn fixed on the idea that if he rode long and far enough, he was bound to reach the Oregon Trail and eventually chance upon someone who would help him. Then he could return to Yellowstone and his beloved Juanita. His strength was ebbing and so, when he saw a thick stand of aspen, Quinn crawled off his horse, wondering if he would have the strength to climb back on after resting. He was shocked at how weak and unsteady he'd become and realized he could go no farther without food and sleep.

With great difficulty, he hobbled his horses, then managed to swallow a few bites of fish before he fell asleep sitting up with his back against a tree. He began to dream that he and Juanita were dancing at a lavish Santa Barbara fandango, the kind that the fun-loving Mexican people would enjoy for many days and nights with games, dances, and feasting. Juanita was dressed in red with her hair up in curls; he wore tight-fitting pants and a bolero jacket with colorful stitching. They were having a wonderful time until Lucius King and Chaco arrived and a reata settled around Quinn's neck. His breath was choked off and he was dragged off the dance floor while Juanita screamed and tried to save his life. Quinn struggled, trying desperately to reach his knife. He could feel his heart growing larger and larger and then he awakened, thrashing and choking on the Montana earth, his body drenched in icy sweat.

He ran his fingers across his eyes and tried to slow his breathing. "What is wrong with me?" he gasped. "Am I seeing my death in a dream?"

It was sunset and with it came the cold. Quinn longed for Juanita's warmth but instead considered making a fire of buffalo chips. After long and agonizing deliberations, he rejected the idea as too dangerous and drifted back to sleep until he was again awakened by the full light of morning.

His fever had broken and the sky was indigo blue with magnificent white clouds rising like puffs of geyser steam. Quinn's horses had wandered to the top of a nearby hill and stood fully exposed to any watching Blackfeet.

"Damn," he muttered, hobbling as fast as he could up the hill and then leading them back down into the aspen grove through leaves that were an explosion of fall colors. Feeling a sense of impending danger that intensified by the minute, Quinn ate quickly, then located a convenient rock and mounted his fastest relay animal.

"Let's go," he said, pointing the sorrel south but often twisting around to gaze fretfully at his backtrail. Well-rested and fed, his horses seemed eager to leave this unforgiving and lonely country.

The morning warmed and the sun felt good on his flesh, finally drying his clothes. Quinn felt much refreshed and when he inspected his leg wound, he saw no sign of infection. For the first time, he began to believe that he would be all right and that the relentless Blackfeet weren't still on his backtrail. Pronghorn antelope dotted the hillsides and he considered trying to shoot one because of his need for fresh meat, but these animals were small and extremely wary—so wary that they quickly moved out of rifle range. To the east, a hawk soared effortlessly in ever-widening circles until it suddenly disappeared behind a hill. It did not reappear as long as Quinn watched for it and he was sure it was feasting well.

Quinn had never seen anything quite so vast as these gently rolling plains. Although the earth was littered with buffalo chips and pocked with their wallows, he saw none and wondered if they had all been hunted out.

Every time he looked back, Quinn worried about the Shoshone woman and tried to imagine what a nightmarish scene it must have been when Hawk confronted his long-lost daughter, only to be rejected and then killed. What a waste of time and effort. And why . . . why had he even agreed to come, knowing beforehand the likely disastrous outcome? Oh, yes, he remembered—he had come so Hawk would not insist on bringing the Sheepeater men north. Well, at least there was some small comfort in knowing he'd saved those peaceable people from the same fiasco he and Tewa had suffered.

At high noon, Quinn spotted a jutting, rocky hill and angled his horses in that direction, deciding it would afford him an excellent view of his backtrail. He wanted to know if Indians were following. If they were not, he would rest and eat more often.

The hill was at least a hundred feet tall. Treeless and pocked with rocks at its crown, it gave him a panoramic view in every direction. Quinn dismounted, clinging to his saddlehorn. Very slowly, he pivoted about and saw nothing move. Not even the hawk he had left a few miles behind.

He leaned his cheek against his saddle, wishing he and Tewa had not separated. Where was she right now? Had the Shoshone woman drawn off the pursuing Blackfeet to save his life or had they divided, some coming after him as well? Taking no chances, Quinn reloaded his weapons just to make sure his powder was dry.

Where are you, my Blackfeet enemies? he wondered. *Are you somewhere close now, watching me? Perhaps even circling around in front so I suddenly blunder into your midst, close enough so you can see terror fill my eyes as you attack? I warn you that will not happen and I'll give you no satisfaction. Instead, I will give you a long chase and bullets so that your women will wail and you will long curse me, even after you take my scalp.*

Later that afternoon Quinn came upon a big herd of buffalo scattered across a valley. When he rode close enough to see their eyes, he let his horses graze while he studied the huge, placid beasts. A thought occurred to him: if Hawk were present, the old mountain man would drag out his buffalo rifle and shoot a cow, then butcher and roast her meat over a buffalo chip fire. Quinn salivated for fresh meat and he did possess a rifle powerful enough to drop one of the animals but he was loath to do so—until he noticed a lame calf. It was limping badly and Quinn wondered if it had been wounded by a wolf or perhaps in a stampede caused by recent storms.

Drawing a Hawken rifle out of its scabbard, he shot the calf, knocking its frail body sideways into that of its mother. The startled herd jolted into a run, heads down and rocking side by side as they lumbered across the valley floor. Their tails were raised, their little black eyes like orbs of polished obsidian. To Quinn's amazement, the herd circled to return to this valley. Several of the cows came to investigate the dead calf, heads down, nostrils flaring, apparently trying to understand or locate the danger.

Quinn found it troubling that God had created such powerful and impressive creatures yet had denied them decent eyesight. Hawk had told him that buffalo possessed an excellent sense of smell but were practically blind and Quinn had just seen this to be true. If he were a buffalo hunter, he would be able to kill dozens of the beasts easily.

When the cows lost interest in the dead calf and finally wandered away, Quinn was able to ride in and butcher enough tender meat to last him several days. But the effort left him weak and shaky, so he gathered a mound of chips and got a fire going. Squatting on his heels with his horse grazing nearby, Quinn sat in the middle of the valley gorging himself on half-raw buffalo meat, willing to take the chance that no Blackfeet had heard his rifle shot.

Quinn feasted until his stomach was ready to burst, then cooked an additional ten or fifteen pounds of meat and stuffed it hot and greasy into his saddlebags. Feeling much stronger, he again rode to high ground and carefully studied his backtrail. No sign of pursuit, but Hawk had warned him that a white man never saw Indians until they were almost on top of him with blood in their eyes. Quinn believed it. The Indians knew this country well and were accomplished hunters and horse thieves, while he was still just an incompetent "pilgrim."

Quinn tightened the cinches on both horses and rechecked his guns and rifles. He was worried, but no longer desperate. If attacked, he guessed he would try to kill a few before he gave the Blackfeet a memorable chase that he felt he could win. Rested and much stronger, Quinn rode through sundown and into darkness, pushing his horses along at a steady trot that Hawk had told him would eat up long miles without unduly taxing them. The fair weather held that night, and by daybreak Quinn felt sure he had ridden a good sixty or seventy miles in the last twenty-four hours. When he added that to what he had traveled since saving Tewa, Quinn guessed he'd come at least two hundred miles all on his own. That gave him a fair sense of pride.

With eyes burning again from lack of sleep the following afternoon, Quinn yearned to make a camp but his anxiety about being followed kept him moving steadily south. He changed horses frequently and tried to keep himself awake by singing old California songs and dreaming of Juanita and how he would one day show her St. Louis and take her to meet his family.

Afterward, they could decide where to spend the rest of their lives together. It didn't matter, as long as it wasn't back in the middle of the Nevada desert. If he never saw a desert or that awful Humboldt River again, that would be way too soon.

"Hate the damned desert," he muttered over and over. "Hate it. Hate it. Hate it!"

Quinn's mind was so starved for sleep late that afternoon that he began to hallucinate and see wagons crossing the prairie. Three Conestogas, as a matter of fact.

He squeezed his eyes tight, making a face; then he opened them again and stared. Yep, Conestogas and they were crossing his direction maybe five or six miles to the south. Were they an illusion? The unraveling of an overtaxed mind? Quinn made a fist and hammered his forehead hard enough to rock himself back in the saddle but the wagons kept traveling east in a tight little line.

"East?" he muttered. "Wagons don't go east! Quinn Wallace, get a grip on yourself!"

But the wagons *were* moving east. And, as the minutes passed, Quinn began to distinguish drivers and several outriders. The wagons were being pulled by eight-mule teams. He raised his finger and counted. "Yep. Eight animals to each team, all right."

Quinn was so exhausted that it took another mile of trotting along before the full impact of this discovery hit him. "By jingo!" he exclaimed. "I've made it!"

Quinn pushed his horses into an easy gallop, determined to overtake the wagons before dark. He was terrified that if he didn't, they would vanish and never be found again. He became so focused on the Conestogas that he did not see the horde of onrushing Blackfeet until they were streaking over the hills, determined to prevent him from reaching the wagons.

He heard their rifles and, a moment later, his horse faltered. Quinn leaned forward, willing it to regain its stride, but the animal had gone stony-legged and began to crumple in its front quarters. Quinn grabbed his lead rope and kicked out of his stirrups an instant before the animal dropped. Somehow, he managed to land on his feet, keeping his relay horse under control and then remounting.

"Yahhhh!" he shouted, driving his horses toward the distant wagons, which were beginning to circle. "Yahhhh!"

The Indians were determined to cut Quinn off from the wagons. Sweat iced his body and he forced himself to ignore the Blackfeet and concentrate on riding like a vaquero. The problem was that one of his relay horses kept hauling back on its lead rope, forcing Quinn to turn it loose.

How far to the wagons? Two miles? No, farther.

Quinn leaned over his mount's withers, fingers lacing into the animal's mane as he tried to ignore the screams and rifle shots. He could hear lead slugs whistling overhead and his arm was almost jerked out of his shoulder when his last relay horse was hit and fell, cartwheeling like a broken toy. Quinn squeezed a last, desperate burst of speed out of his mount, praying that it had the heart and stamina to reach the wagons.

Bullets and even a few arrows crisscrossed his path like a swarm of angry hornets. Quinn wanted to grab his pistol and return fire but knew he'd never hit anything. Over the pounding of hooves and his heart, he heard the Indians' yells change and that was when he first realized that he had come between them to the intersecting point and they could not stop him unless they shot his horse.

"Yahhhh!" he screamed, slamming his bootheels into the flanks of his winded animal as he raced toward the little cluster of wagons. He dared to glance back over his shoulder and saw that he was widening the gap between himself and the Blackfeet ponies.

When Quinn was within a hundred yards of the wagons, a half-dozen men jumped up and took aim and opened fire, drowning out the angry, frustrated howls of the Blackfeet.

"Whoa!" Quinn shouted, struggling to bring his mount under control. But the crazed animal had the bit clenched between its teeth, so Quinn bailed off the horse, struck the prairie rolling, and fainted, still fifty feet from the wagon circle.

"Get up, dammit!" a mule skinner yelled, desperately trying to rouse Quinn back into consciousness. "Get up and help us fight!"

Quinn was yanked to his feet and propelled back into the wagon ring. Someone shoved a rifle into his fists and bellowed, "You brought 'em, now help us kill 'em!"

"All right," Quinn mumbled, feeling blood leak out of his just-reopened leg wound. "All right!"

Everyone was shouting and firing. One of the wagoners slapped his forehead and pitched forward dead before he struck the ground. Another took an arrow in the chest and raised to his toes, his young face going slack with shock as more Blackfeet bullets spun him around until he crashed headfirst through a wagon wheel. Quinn couldn't get his eyes to focus. Hearing the desperation in the men around him as their numbers were decimated, he fired blindly, sucking in the sharp, acrid gunsmoke and trying to stay conscious.

"Watch out!" someone cried. "They're circling behind us!"

Quinn twisted to his left and a pair of Indians sailed through the widest opening between the wagons. He fired instinctively and a warrior sporting a beaver hat and red suspenders was flipped backward over the rump of his pony. The other warrior sailed back over them, his horse racing like the wind. Someone shot him in the back and the Indian landed on his feet, took a couple of ragged steps, and then went down for keeps.

Just as suddenly as it had begun, the attack ended and the Blackfeet retreated in mass with a few of the more daring galloping back to retrieve their dead and wounded.

"Save your lead!" one of the teamsters shouted. "Someone check on Matt!"

"He's finished."

"What about Perkins?"

"He's dead, too!"

"Gawdammit! How many of us are left standing?"

"I'm hit but standing," a bearded man in a red flannel shirt yelled. "That makes four of us. No, five including this sonofabitch that brought 'em down on us!"

"Help me," someone called from beyond the ring of wagons. "I'm hit!"

"It's Ben!"

Like everyone else, Quinn turned to see Ben, who must have run outside the circle earlier to catch one of the loose horses that had stampeded. Now the man was wounded in both legs and struggling to crawl back to the wagons. "I'll get him," a red-shirted man growled.

Their leader shouted, "No! Look at 'em waitin' to drill the first one that goes out there after Ben. You'd never make it."

"But, Zeke, we got to help him!"

Quinn tried to stand. "I'll go."

"With that bad leg you wouldn't get ten feet," Zeke said. "Look sharp and you'll see we aren't the only ones can shoot a Hawken."

One of the Blackfeet had dismounted and was flattened on the grassy slope of the nearest hill. He was on higher ground and they could see that he had two Hawken rifles. With remarkable coolness, the Indian marksman took aim on Ben.

"Zeke, that Indian is gonna drill him!"

"Someone give me a big rifle!" Zeke shouted.

"None still loaded!"

"Then load one!"

Quinn saw a white puff of gunsmoke escape the Indian's Hawken, then he heard its voice an instant before Ben wailed and began to flop around on the grass, demented with pain.

"Hurry," Zeke ordered, keeping his eyes fixed on the Indian instead of his dying friend.

It seemed to take forever for someone to get the Hawken loaded and meanwhile, the Blackfoot sharpshooter leisurely collected his second weapon while one of his companions reloaded the first.

"Kill that bastard!" one of the mule skinners screamed in frustration.

Zeke took aim and fired only a fraction of a second before the Blackfoot marksman, but that was time enough. The warrior appeared to lay his head down on the grass and sleep but there was no doubt he was dead. His companion snatched up a Hawken and became so incensed that he ran down the hill, screaming in a rage. "Shoot him," Zeke ordered when the Blackfoot was in range. A rifle barked and the Indian fell wounded. He shot the dying Ben and was himself shot to death.

"Hold your fire!" Zeke shouted. "I think it's over."

"What makes you think that?" someone asked.

The Blackfeet had retreated beyond even the Hawken's deadly range. Zeke said, "Because they've lost the stomach for more fighting."

"Then we whipped 'em!"

"No," Zeke said, "we killed a few of them and they killed a few of us. It's a draw and we'd better hope to God that they go away because we haven't enough men left to hold off another full charge and save our scalps."

"Never saw an Indian who could shoot Hawkens like that," the man in the red shirt said, gazing out at Ben and shaking his head with sadness.

"Me neither," Zeke answered, turning his eyes on Quinn and growling, "Mister, you cost us three good men."

"Sorry," was all Quinn could think of to say. "I'm real damned sorry."

"Yeah," Zeke said. "Well, I guess you were just trying to keep your hair like anyone would do."

"What are we going to do now?" one of the wagoners asked.

"We wait and hope they ride off and we never see 'em again."

"Then what?"

"We bury our dead," Zeke told him. "Then we move on before another bunch decides to try us on for size."

Quinn said, "I've got to get back to the Yellowstone country."

"Then you do it alone," Zeke replied. "Because we're

bringing wagons back from Oregon so we can form wagon trains going west again next Spring.''

"I got a woman in Yellowstone," Quinn told him, knowing that loss of blood and his near-escape from death was making him sound idiotic. "She needs me."

Zeke stared at him for a minute, then asked, "Is she a Sheepeater woman?"

"No, Mexican woman."

"Ain't no Mexicans in the Yellowstone country. Too cold for them southern people. They'd never make it through a winter. Don't matter what she is, though. We're headin' for St. Louis and you can either come along or get scalped. Makes no difference to me, so suit yourself."

"That's not much of a choice."

"That's right," Zeke said, "and this ain't been a very good day, either. So what's it going to be?"

"St. Louis," Quinn heard himself answer.

"Glad to hear Ben and the others didn't die for a total fool," Zeke grunted before he went to help patch up his wounded men.

Chapter Seventeen

Tewa hadn't wanted to leave Quinn on his own and strike off in a westerly direction while he rode south. With his leg wound and mounting fever, she doubted that he would get very far before the Blackfeet discovered their tracks beyond the path of the rainstorm. But there was nothing else she could have done for Quinn except to get herself killed. This way, perhaps she could at least draw off most of their pursuers and give Quinn a small chance.

That was why Tewa had not bothered to cover her horse's hooves or hide her own trail. They would find her either way, so all that mattered was to ride far and fast, hoping she could reach the mountains and then lose the Blackfeet in the rivers, forests, and rocks. Either that, or happen upon a large hunting party of Crow, Bannock, or perhaps even the fearless Nez Perce Indians she had always admired, with their beautiful spotted horses.

Tewa was relaying and running the legs off her California horses. She knew she would soon have to slow her pace or she would kill the animals. At midday, she came upon a long, grassy plateau with no hills, trees, or rocky outcroppings for ten miles in any direction. Tired and nervous about being exposed on high ground for so long, Tewa kept her horses moving at a gallop, often looking over her shoulder and expecting to see the enemy.

However, the real enemy proved not to be Blackfeet, but prairie dogs. While Tewa was glancing over her shoulder, her weary mount stomped its hoof down into one of the holes and broke its foreleg. It happened so fast that Tewa barely had time to kick out of her stirrups. One moment she was looking backward for the enemy, the next she was being hurled over her mount's head to strike the earth so hard that she lost consciousness.

Tewa awoke late in the afternoon with a piercing, dagger-like pain in her head. She opened and closed her eyes several times, but her vision remained so flawed that the distant mountains were canted oddly to one side. She touched her ringing ears and discovered they were packed with dried blood. There was blood on her face, too, drying into big scabs.

Twice, she tried to stand but fell over as if she were old and weak. *What is wrong with me?* she asked herself while gazing about for her relay horses.

Then she remembered the sickening sound of her mount's foreleg cracking like a dry tree limb. Tears sprang into Tewa's eyes and she shook her head back and forth, hoping to clear both her befuddled mind and vision. Instead, the pain between her ears intensified until she gasped and collapsed.

Hours later, she revived again and this time she swiveled around on her haunches until she saw horses. The one she had been riding was still down, head weaving back and forth, eyes floating in an ocean of pain. The other two animals were grazing several hundred yards away. When Tewa began to crawl toward the fallen horse, one of the extra animals spooked and snorted, trotting off to roll its eyes at her with suspicion. Tewa hardly noticed. All her concentration was focused on retrieving her rifle in order to end the suffering of her injured horse, then catching at least one of the others and leaving this plateau as quickly as possible.

The first task was actually the most difficult because her rifle was trapped under the thrashing horse. She had to use her pistol, placing the barrel directly against the poor animal's skull. The shot splattered her with blood. Tewa recoiled and the horse sighed, expelling its final breath. Reloading the pistol and removing her saddlebags took the last of Tewa's remaining strength.

Maybe the horses will run away at the smell of fresh blood. Without horses, I might as well kill myself and rob the Blackfeet of whatever pleasure they would gain from my torture.

Tewa wished there were a stream close by so she could wash, but since there was not, she began to clean herself with clumps of dry autumn grass and the good earth that clung stubbornly to their roots. When she was too tired to do that anymore, Tewa scolded herself for wasting so much time. The Blackfeet could appear any moment!

Catching a horse was even more difficult than expected. The larger of the two sorrels was easy enough, but the smaller mare did not want to be caught, so Tewa gave up and somehow climbed onto the gelding. It was gentler and more sensible, but lacked the mare's speed and stamina.

"If you stay here, the Blackfeet will catch and maybe roast you tonight," Tewa warned the skittish mare. "So I think you had better stick with me and your old friend."

To Tewa's surprise, the mare followed. Tewa could no longer ride at the gallop. The awful pounding in her head would not stand for it and besides, with her vision playing bad tricks, how could she see any more prairie dog colonies? She had little choice but to ride at a walk for the rest of that day and most of the night. An hour before dawn, she fell asleep and would have landed on her head again had she not caught herself just in time and clung to the saddle.

"I must sleep for awhile," Tewa said to herself. "It does not matter if I am caught and tortured. I *must* rest." She did not hobble the matched sorrels, trusting them not to wander far.

Tewa slept longer than she had anticipated. The sun was well up on the eastern horizon when she opened her eyes. Her head no longer throbbed quite so much and her vision was improving. When she looked at the horses, their legs were straight, as they should be, instead of canted sideways at the knees. But some fuzziness persisted and the mountains that she had been using as a beacon seemed much farther away than Tewa remembered.

She sat up slowly, not wishing her head to spin and ache again. She rubbed her stomach, wondering if Hawk's child still lived. Tewa believed that it would, just as long as she was able to stay alive. She cradled her temples in her hands and offered Shoshone prayers that she would be able to reach those mountains or find help among Blackfeet enemies.

It is time. Time to get on the gelding and ride. But I have not eaten in a full day. Maybe I will eat in the saddle. But

my throat is too dry and what I need is water. Then I will
find water. Because of my prayers, water will be waiting for
me just up ahead. Long before I reach the mountains.

Tewa's faith in protective spirits and prayer was strong,
but she had often seen Juanita praying on her bended
knees and wondered if that made one's prayers even
stronger. On the chance that it did, Tewa added a few
more prayers on her knees, asking the Great Spirit to
protect her from the Blackfeet.

Prayers finished, she pulled up a large clump of grass
and waved it at the faithful gelding. The animal trotted
over to eat from Tewa's hand and then let her remount.
This was a good-hearted horse, Tewa told herself as she
started off again toward the mountains. And the mare?
She was not so good, but Tewa would be grateful for
her exceptional speed and stamina if she had to race
for her life.

She finally crossed the huge, exposed plateau to drop
down into a river basin. An hour later, she shot a porcupine out of a tree. Because she was weak and worried
about a smoke trail, Tewa butchered and ravenously ate
the animal's slippery organs raw. The meat was layered
with fat because the porcupine had been preparing itself
for a long winter. Tewa knew that this fatty meat would
keep her strong enough to reach the mountains. After
that, her survival would be entirely dependent on the
elements. If hit by a blizzard, she would probably die.
If not, she might be able to leave the Blackfeet far
behind.

A thousand times that afternoon, Tewa squinted, trying to get her eyes to focus. After each blink, she could
see clearly for a few moments and then she'd twist
around in her saddle and study her backtrail, always
expecting to see mounted warriors rising up out of the

earth like devil spirits. Her ears still rang and she was not hearing well, but she felt that time would improve these shortcomings.

She rode steadily for the next three days, alternating the gait of her horses between a walk and a jog, never stopping for more than a few hours at a time to rest. Besides her fear of the Blackfeet, Tewa fretted that she would gallop blindly into another prairie dog colony and lose a second horse. To avoid this, she concentrated very hard on the terrain and pinned all her hopes on reaching the sanctuary of the mountains.

Like the gentle Sheepeaters, Tewa's people had favored the mountains over the terrible desert or these grassy, rolling plains. And now, with a westward wind strong in her face, Tewa could smell the sweet, fragrant pines. It helped to clear her senses. Her vision was improving and the clanging in her ears was beginning to fade.

When I reach the mountains, I will finally have the advantage instead of the Blackfeet.

At sundown the following day, Tewa saw the winking light of a very large campfire beside the tall, green mountains. Her heart turned cold and she drew rein, trying hard to penetrate the great distance.

Friend or enemy?

It might be either. This was still Blackfeet country although Tewa thought she was just as likely to see Crow, Nez Perce, or even her Bannock peoples enjoying their last buffalo hunt before the deep snows of the coming winter.

What should I do?

Concentration still required great effort. She needed to get out of the wind, then eat and sleep for a few hours. Under the cover of darkness, she would ride to the mountains to hide and watch these people. If these were enemies, she would make a large detour around them in the night before vanishing into the forest and climbing the high passes to disappear. But if these were friends, then she could tell them her story and they might decide she was worthy of their help and protection.

It took her another hour to find shelter in a low place near a stream where there was good water and grass for her hungry horses. The sun plunged into the mountains as Tewa loosened her cinch and hobbled the horses, unwilling to risk having them climb up on a hill where they might be seen by an encampment now only a few miles distant. After eating the last of the porcupine meat and a skinny muskrat she was able to trap, then stone, Tewa quickly fell asleep.

To her surprise and consternation, she did not awaken until late the following morning. Jumping to her feet, she hurried to higher ground and spied a hunting party coming in her direction. She fell back with a moan; they looked like Blackfeet and were less than two miles distant! If they were indeed Blackfeet, and there was another band chasing her, she was trapped. Should she bolt out of this low hiding place and run?

Not yet, an inner voice said. *First be certain they are Blackfeet. Also, they might change directions and not see you down here. So stay hidden but be ready to run.*

Tewa dashed to her horses. She saddled the mare and, just before she climbed into her saddle, said a hurried prayer. She checked her weapons, deciding she would kill herself before she would again become a Blackfeet slave.

Now all she could do was sit on the mare and wait.

Both of her horses were nervous and impatient. Tewa dismounted and began stroking their soft muzzles. She talked to them in her most soothing voice and prayed that she would not be discovered.

After a long, long time, Tewa crept back to the higher ground and saw that several of the hunters were riding spotted horses and they had veered south. There were about twenty in the party, heavily armed with rifles, bows, and long, feathered lances.

Nez Perce, she thought with relief.

Tewa's first impulse was to allow the hunting party to pass and then ride to their mountainside village and take her chances. But then she realized that these hunters might encounter her own Blackfeet pursuers and be slaughtered. If that happened, she would be the cause of their death. She rode out into full view, then fired one of Hawk's weapons.

The Nez Perce spun their handsome horses around, and when they spotted her, they charged forward. Tewa was determined not to show fear although she could not be certain what kind of treatment she would receive. If they were like the Nez Perce that she had met in the past, and that Hawk had always spoken of as being friendly, then she was in no danger. But who could say? Tewa knew her horses and weapons were valuable and would be a temptation.

"Who are you?" were the first words uttered by a tall, hatchet-faced man with prominent silver streaks in his flowing hair.

"I am Hawk's woman," Tewa replied in a strong voice. "Do you know of him?"

The leader nodded. "How do we know what you say is true?"

"I carry his child," she said, patting her stomach.

"He was killed only a few days ago by the Blackfeet on a big river."

The Nez Perce leader made a circular motion to indicate he wanted to know where this occurred.

Tewa pointed to the east. "I believe they are following me to avenge their dead."

The warriors digested this startling information and said nothing as they studied the quality of Tewa's horses, saddles, packs, and weapons. Although they did not say so, Tewa was sure they were impressed, not only because she was Hawk's woman, but because of these fine possessions.

After a respectful silence, Tewa added, "My husband said all Nez Perce were brave and strong warriors and that their hearts were good. He said they did not fear Blackfeet and would not turn me away."

These words were also digested in silence but, finally, the leader, who was riding an especially handsome spotted stallion, said, "There are Flathead living among our people now. We are all enemies of the Blackfeet."

He made a sign that told Tewa that he wished to know the name of her people.

"Shoshone and Bannock. Like the Flathead and the Nez Perce, we live, hunt, and stand against our enemies as one people. We, too, have fought the Blackfeet."

Apparently, Tewa's words not only were accepted, but also well-received because the leader dismounted and gave his stallion to another warrior. He walked all around the sorrels, inspecting the horses with the critical eye of an expert. "Where are these Blackfeet enemies?"

"I have not seen them because my horses are very swift. But I know in my heart that they are close."

The leader turned to his followers and began to speak

rapidly in his own tongue so that Tewa did not under-stand. After several minutes of lively argument, ten horsemen were dispatched to the east. These scouts rode away at a fast gallop, whooping as if they were going off on a lark instead of risking their lives.

"If the Blackfeet are close, they will be seen," the leader said as if it were not important. Removing an eagle feather from his lance, he extended it to Tewa. "Go to village."

Tewa knew she should not question this man, espe-cially in front of the others but she had to ask, "Where are you going?"

The man pointed south where a storm was gathering. "Hunt buffalo."

Tewa wanted to say he needed to be preparing for a bad fight. Instead, she made herself nod with agreement, knowing that even the slightest hint of argu-ment from a woman would be considered an insult. A cold wind was beginning to blow, pushed in the face of a storm. The temperature was falling and Tewa won-dered if it would snow.

She shivered. "I feel the evil Blackfeet spirits coming like the storm."

"My woman's name is Pokashia," he told her.

Tewa knew that this conversation was finished. It was time to pay tribute to this leader, so she gave him one of her best pistols and said, "Hawk was proud to call your people good friends and good fighters."

They left Tewa and she watched them ride directly into the storm to hunt buffalo as if they had not heard or believed her warning. And maybe there was no Blackfeet danger. After all, she had not actually seen them pursu-ing her and they might have turned back long ago or gone after Quinn. But, based on what Hawk had told

her, Tewa felt sure Blackfeet would never allow an
enemy to enter their camp and kill one of their people
without seeking swift and terrible revenge.

With the icy wind beginning to gust, Tewa hurried to
the village beside the mountains. There were many dogs,
children, and old people and it took her only a short
time to locate Pokashia. She was much younger than
her husband and quite attractive. The woman fed Tewa
and then, noting the dried blood on her face and her
marrow-deep weariness, invited her to lie down on buffalo robes and sleep.

"I cannot rest," she told them, feeling the tepee shake
and the poles protest under an especially strong gust
of wind. "I grieve too much for Hawk."

"He was brave and honorable. You should be more
proud than sad."

"I *am* proud," Tewa said, again rubbing her belly. "I
carry his child."

Pokashia smiled. "Then you are also honored."

"Your husband did not act very . . . interested in what
I had to say about Blackfeet. He said he was going
hunting."

"Hunting for Blackfeet," she replied. "It is not honorable to act as if you were a rabbit fearing a coyote,
eh?"

"No, but . . ."

"We are many. Even the women and our old ones
are still good fighters. The Blackfeet would not attack
in a storm, for that would be bad medicine. If they come
after the storm, we will kill them all."

Pokashia said this with such conviction that Tewa's
fears were quieted. "Have you fought them before?"

In reply, the woman showed her a long stick decorated
with many scalps. "Sleep well now," she said.

When Tewa lay down, Pokashia began to chant and shake the scalp stick as if she were counting coup against the Blackfeet. Tewa was fascinated by the waving scalp locks. Her eyes soon grew heavy and her mind drifted away, listening to Pokashia and imagining the dying wails of Blackfeet carried on the rising wind.

Chapter Eighteen

"Tewa, wake up!" Pokashia urged late that night during the height of the snowstorm.

Tewa jolted into wakefulness. Because Pokashia had fed the fire well, their tepee was warm and its buffalo hide walls glowed with firelight. Tewa heard the high, whining wind and tried to clear sleep from her mind. "What is wrong?"

"My husband just told me our scouts found the Blackfeet camp. It is not far away."

Now Tewa was fully awake. "Where?"

Pokashia pointed to the north. "They are hiding in the forest. Waiting to attack."

"How many?"

"More than our people," Pokashia replied, her pretty face stricken with worry. "There will be a bad fight and many will die at sunrise tomorrow."

Tewa reached for Hawk's weapons. "I led these enemies to your village so now I must help fight them. Where are your men?"

"They are making preparations for battle. My husband and the others have decided to trick the Blackfeet into thinking we are lazy because of the storm. That is why the women, children, and old ones must hide in the trees when we are attacked."

"In this storm?" Tewa listened to the howl of the freezing wind. She could not imagine how they would survive.

"We will stay in our tepees until just before dawn and then go off before the Blackfeet come," Pokashia explained. "If the battle goes badly, we will all join the fight."

Two Bears rushed into the tepee draped in a buffalo robe dusted with snow. He glanced at Tewa and she would not have been surprised if he had spoken to her with anger. Instead, the Nez Perce leader began to make his battle preparations. "The snow will be red with Blackfeet blood tomorrow," he said.

"Two Bears," Tewa dared to say, "I must fight beside you in the morning."

"No."

"But I must! These people killed Hawk and my spirit cannot rest until I have avenged his death." Tewa showed him Hawk's weapons and said, "I ask for this honor as a friend."

The Nez Perce leader studied Tewa, then her weapons. "Are you ready to die?"

"Yes."

Two Bears glanced at Pokashia, then said, "I am told you carry Hawk's child."

"This is true. But Little Hawk will give me great power so I can kill many Blackfeet. I feel him strong inside, eager to avenge the death of his father. Two Bears, I have strong medicine."

"To deny her would be bad medicine," Pokashia said when her husband looked to her. "Tewa will fight like a warrior—and remember, the Blackfeet are many more than we."

"You may fight," Two Bears said as he finished his hurried preparations. "Pokashia, help take the old and the young ones to shelter up to the cave in the rocks."

"If the battle goes badly," Pokashia said, "the strong among us will come down from the mountainside to fight."

"We will kill them all," Two Bears said with conviction. "The Blackfeet are foolish in their pride. When they come into this village at dawn, they will expect to kill us in our sleep. But *they* will be the ones to die!"

Tewa did not refuse the robe that was offered. She listened as Two Bears explained to his wife how the extra buffalo robes and blankets were to be rolled up so they would appear to be sleeping people when the Blackfeet burst inside, bent on murder.

"They will shoot blindly into the darkness of our tepees, expecting to kill us in our sleep. But, when all their guns are empty, *we* will do the killing."

"It will be a great victory for all The People," Pokashia said, eyes shining with pride.

"Come, Hawk Woman," he said, going outside into the storm.

It was all that Tewa could do to keep up with the Nez Perce leader as he and the other warriors made their last-minute preparations. Tewa was numb with cold when Two Bears finally decided that the women, the old, and the children should leave the village and go into hiding. They would have no fire in the terrible pre-dawn hours before the attack. Even worse, they would not know until after the last dying screams and gunshots whether their husbands, fathers, and brothers had won a great victory, or had been slaughtered by the Blackfeet enemies.

Had the night sky been clear, Tewa could have judged the time left until the expected attack, but with the blowing snow, time lost all meaning. There was only freezing cold and suffering until at last she took her place just inside the forest and just beyond the nearly-empty village.

"A few have volunteered to stay as bait in our trap," Two Bears explained as they began the final waiting hours.

Tewa had never been so cold, and although she was afraid of what this day would bring, she was also glad when the first light began to reveal the silhouetted tepees below. As if holding its breath in anticipation of the battle about to be waged, the wind died and the sky began to clear.

"It is a good day to die," Two Bears whispered.

"Yes," Tewa agreed, "but a much better day to win a great victory."

Two Bears almost smiled at those words and Tewa realized she'd lost her fear. She could see more than seventy heavily armed Nez Perce warriors crouched in the snow, ready to spring the trap that would bring them victory. Down in the village the first of those who had agreed to stay as bait emerged. The woman trudged away to do her business and returned with an armful of firewood. Soon, a few other women appeared and did the same. Smoke curled from the tops of the tepees, and from Tewa's hiding place just inside the forest, it looked as if everything was perfectly normal.

The snow had continued to fall long enough to cover the tracks of the Nez Perce warriors now waiting in ambush, and as the light slowly intensified, Tewa saw that Two Bears and the other warriors were looking north, each waiting to be the first to see the stalking enemy.

Where are they? Tewa wondered, *seeing nothing to the north except snow-covered plains. Where are they?*

Suddenly, Tewa detected movement. Just a white, moving mist at first, then figures. They emerged as distinctly human, covered with snow and fast-approaching along the base of these mountains. Like themselves, the Blackfeet were nearly invisible and every one of them carried a rifle. They seemed so like ghost spirits that Tewa's heart began to race and she began to chant an old childhood song learned during her early and happy days among the Shoshone.

When the Blackfeet were within rifle range of the village, they crouched, watching. Tewa's eyes moved back and forth between the enemy and the women who were gathering wood and making preparations for the first meal of the day. She felt strange, as if she were herself a spirit looking down on this peaceful, silent, snowy world about to be filled with screams, howls, and death.

Do those women down in the village realize they are being watched like wild game about to be shot? And, if they do, how calm they appear.

The Blackfeet sprang to their feet and charged across the last hundred yards of open ground. The snow was not deep and they ran fast and silent, their rifles up and ready to fire. Tewa's nose ran and her eyes burned from the cold but her skin was damp with perspiration.

The Blackfeet made no sound until they plunged into the Nez Perce village. Then, one of them threw back his head and let out a shrill, eerie wail that cut through the frozen air like a knife blade and made Tewa's hair stand on end.

Blackfeet warriors dove into every tepee, screaming and firing their weapons. But then, just as suddenly as the sounds began, there was a moment of stunned silence.

"Ah-yiiii!" Two Bears wailed, leaping to his feet and charging down toward his village, a wall of heavily armed Nez Perce warriors close behind.

As planned and expected, the Blackfeet were caught completely by surprise. Having just emptied their weapons, they were helpless against the Nez Perce guns and rifles. The Blackfeet had been so confident that they had not brought their bows and arrows and now there was no time to reload. Dozens died in the first Nez Perce volley. Those that survived had nothing to fight with except their knives and war clubs, but they did so with such savagery that they almost broke through the wave of Nez Perce to freedom.

Finally, also out of bullets, the Nez Perce used their traditional weapons. Arrows hummed through the frigid air. As brave and hard-fighting as the Blackfeet survivors were, they had no choice but to give ground against the now superior Nez Perce. Fighting, screaming, and dying, they sold their lives dearly.

Tewa saw Two Bears fall wounded and rushed to his side. When a Blackfoot screamed and jumped at her with his knife, she shot him through the head and then snatched a pepperbox from under her coat and killed two more of the enemy. She stayed with Two Bears until he was out of danger and then she charged forward, screaming and shooting, consumed by an overpowering need to avenge Hawk.

The slaughter did not last long. Very soon, the blood of friends, but far more enemies, stained the snow. Strong hands lifted Tewa high and her praises were shouted at the bright morning sun.

"Look at Hawk Woman! She who has killed three of the enemy and saved Two Bears. She who lured the enemy to this place where their bones will be picked clean by the wolves and the ravens, then washed away by melting snows. Look at Hawk Woman!"

Only then did Tewa realize she'd been knifed several times. She must have lost consciousness soon afterward, for she did not awaken until another night had passed and she again heard her name being praised by Two Bears.

"She truly has strong medicine," the wounded but recovering Two Bears was telling Pokashia as she cooked their meals. "Hawk Woman is great among our peoples."

Tewa did not open her eyes. Instead, her hand slipped under the buffalo robe and she felt the stirrings of Little Hawk. *It is good now and we will live in peace and with honor knowing we have made Hawk proud.*

The victorious Nez Perce soon broke camp, believing it would be wrong to remain so close to death. They would travel west over the mountains before another storm made the crossing impossible. Once over the mountains, they would return to their traditional hunting grounds and rejoin the rest of their nation, bearing the scalps of many Blackfeet enemies as well as a large supply of buffalo meat for winter.

"But I must now return to the Yellowstone country," Tewa argued with Pokashia. "To *my* people, the Sheep-eaters!"

"You cannot," the Nez Perce woman replied. "It is too far and the mountains too high with all their passes now filled with snow. You must wait until after Little Hawk is born next spring. Then, we will return you to the Sheepeaters."

Tewa continued to argue, remembering Juanita, Inez, and all the others who would be worried about them when they did not return from their disastrous quest to rescue Hocina.

"Shhh," the Nez Perce woman finally told her. "You have tempted Death long enough. Now, rest and embrace Life."

"Yes," Tewa replied. "For Little Hawk."

"And for you—the great Hawk Woman!"

And so Tewa complained no more as she was helped onto one of her horses to begin her journey over the mountains to a place where she had never been, but among a people whose hearts she had won.

It was a good winter for Tewa. She and Pokashia became close friends and she learned a great deal about the Nez Perce people, whom she found to be generous and peace-loving.

"Many years ago, before the whites, our people lived mostly along what the whites call the Snake River and we caught and ate salmon," Pokashia said. "Later, when Hawk and many other trappers came into our country, we treated them as friends, even asking the whites to send us teachers, thinking they would be strong medicine."

"Were they?" Tewa asked.

"Some were good. They came and founded a mission.

There was trouble then and sadness. The mission is no more.''

Tewa wondered about this but did not ask, for it was clear that Pokashia was saddened by the subject. "And what about now?''

"We are friends with the whites, although it is sometimes difficult. We bring fresh horses to trade with those who come down the Oregon Trail. Sometimes there is trouble, but we know that we cannot fight the whites. This is a lesson we and our Flathead friends have learned from watching other Indian peoples. But we no longer ask for white teachers or want another mission. Our ways are better.''

Tewa had to agree, and as she watched these people and waited for her baby to be born, it seemed that the Nez Perce had adopted the best of the white man's ways but somehow managed to retain much of their own culture and customs. Yes, they now hunted with rifles, but they also continued to do so with bows and arrows. Rifles, Two Bears was quick to point out, could run out of ammunition or misfire. Arrows never failed the hunter. If the Nez Perce had any real fear, it was that their lands would be taken away by the whites some day. Never mind that they had signed many treaties, and many promises had been made; they had seen treaties broken too often among other Indian peoples.

"This is our land. The land where our ancestors' spirits roam and their bones feed the grass and the trees,'' Pokashia told Tewa. "As you know, to The People, the land is sacred. It never can be taken away, never given. It *belongs* to the people who have been born, loved, lived, hunted, or died. The whites cannot understand this. They each want to take a little piece of the land for themselves until it has been cut up like so many little pieces of meat and then devoured to nothing. This is not our way."

"Nor is it the way of the Shoshone, Bannock, or Sheepeater peoples," Tewa explained. "But I understand what you say and I have seen this happen before."

Pokashia leaned forward earnestly. "Will the Sheepeater people fight for their land?"

"No," Tewa said. "They are too few."

"Numbers should not matter in these things," Pokashia said. "Take away The People's land and you kill their spirits. Do not the Sheepeater people understand this?"

"I don't know," Tewa admitted. "I have not been among them long enough to read their hearts."

"If they give up their lands to the whites, they will have no hearts left!"

Tewa nodded, and seeing how troubled this conversation was making Pokashia, she decided to speak of it no more.

Little Hawk was born the following spring—strong, loud, and happy. Tewa found much happiness in this son of Hawk; it was with great sadness that she prepared to leave her new friends and return to the Sheepeater people.

"Goodbye, Pokashia," she said, hugging the woman and then many others before she climbed into the saddle and was given her baby.

"Come back to visit someday!" Pokashia called.

"I will," Tewa promised.

Though he was one of the chiefs, Two Bears had insisted that he personally deliver Tewa and Little Hawk back to the Sheepeater people in Yellowstone. Because of the threat of Blackfeet, twenty warriors were to accompany them over the long trail east. The trip would take several weeks and the country was difficult and dangerous.

They crossed the Oregon Trail and were saddened to see that it was already bringing the first wagon trains westward in a trickle that soon would become a torrent.

"Too many whites coming through these lands," Two Bears lamented. "No more like Hawk."

"No," Tewa said, recalling how the desert Paiutes had also hated the growing tide of emigrants that had followed the Humboldt River. They had cut down the pinion pines, main harvest and principal winter food of the Paiute, and also had killed all the deer and wild game for many miles on both sides of that river. And although the Paiutes had been very cruel to Tewa, she understood that what had been happening to them along the Humboldt River was now happening to all western Indian people.

Seeing the Conestoga wagons again was a painful reminder for Tewa of her earlier journey to Yellowstone with Hawk, Juanita, Inez, and Quinn. Now, Hawk was dead and probably Quinn as well.

"What about the Blackfeet that we killed in the early winter mountains?" she asked Two Bears on one of the last evenings before they entered Yellowstone. "Will their spirits return to their own people, or will they remain where they were separated from their bodies?"

Two Bears was quiet for some time and all the others waited, just as eager as Tewa to hear his opinion on this troubling subject. Finally, Two Bears said, "Their spirits will return to their people and warn them never again to attack the Nez Perce. And their bones will be broken by the wild animals and scattered by the water, the birds, and all things that eat and move."

"But will the Blackfeet find the bones and *know* what happened?"

"They will know," Two Bears predicted. "But the spirits of the dead will tell them not to seek revenge. Do not fear for our people, Hawk Woman. We had great power before and you have given us even more."

Tewa rocked Little Hawk in her arms. "I will always be friend to you and your Nez Perce people. If ever you need my power again, or that of Little Hawk, you need only to call our names on the west wind and we will hear your voice and come."

"This is good to hear."

"It is the truth," Tewa vowed. "And it will never change as long as one of us is alive."

"You will live long and Little Hawk will become great and strong," Two Bears predicted.

Tewa nodded. She was happy, until she thought of Hawk. If only he had died happy. But that had not been meant to be. Hocina was lost, her spirit taken by the enemy. Instead of Hocina, Little Hawk was now all that remained of Hawk. And Tewa would give her life to make sure Little Hawk would become an important leader. Being of two bloods, he would face many difficult decisions, but he would prevail over all his trials.

"These Sheepeater people," Two Bears said. "Tell me about them for I know little."

"They are few in numbers but good in their hearts."

"Do they own fine horses like ours?"

"No," Tewa said, a little ashamed. "In fact, they prefer to eat horses than to ride them."

Two Bears and the other Nez Perce gasped, obviously

appalled. Seeing this, Tewa quickly added, "But that is only because they have no *good* horses."

"There are no *bad* horses," Two Bears said. "Why would they not ride and use them to hunt buffalo?"

"Because . . . because they are walkers. They live in the mountains and prefer to eat mountain sheep and goats."

"They sound like a strange people," Two Bears said, looking around at his friends, who began to nod in agreement.

"They are just . . . just different," Tewa said, unable to explain it any better. "And when you see their sheepskins and feel their softness, you will want them for your own and be willing to trade much for them."

"Sheepskins?"

"Yes," Tewa said. "They are prized by all the Shoshone and the Bannock, too. Soon, they will be prized by the Nez Perce as well."

Two Bears said nothing for a long, long time. But when he did, he made Tewa smile. "We would never trade them horses . . . even our worst . . . to eat. This would be unforgiveable!"

"Then you will return with other trade goods," Tewa promised.

Two Bears said nothing but it was clear that he doubted her words.

Yellowstone! Tewa could not help but feel the excitement building inside when they came to the great lake and looked all around to see the ring of high mountains.

"This is a good land," Two Bears said, clearly impressed as were his companions. "Where are these smoke holes that you speak of?"

"You will see them very soon, my friend," Tewa promised, knowing they would be arriving at the first geyser basin that very day.

And so, late that afternoon when they did come upon the geysers, Tewa had the joy and satisfaction of watching the Nez Perce as they stared in amazement at the steamy basins, the spouting geysers, and the boiling mud pots.

"This is the land of evil spirits!" one of the Nez Perce cried.

"No," Tewa argued, "it is the land of the Sheepeater people. There are evil spirits here only for enemies, like the Blackfeet."

"But maybe the evil spirits think we are Blackfeet!"

Tewa said in her most solemn voice, "To make sure that they know, I will speak to them in prayer. This way, you will always be safe in the Yellowstone country."

And so, as Two Bears and his Nez Perce warriors watched, Tewa dismounted from her horse, took Little Hawk in her arms, and began to chant. She chanted about the sun and the moon. About the trees and the soft summer wind and the beauty of earth and the sweetness of the Yellowstone waters, and again she asked the Great Spirit to always protect Little Hawk and the Nez Perce, who were their friends. These good prayers made Tewa very happy; Little Hawk giggled to show that he was happy, too.

"You will always be welcome and protected in Yellowstone," she told the worried Nez Perce. "For Hawk Woman has spoken to the spirits and they have agreed that this always is to be so."

* * *

Tewa was glad when they finally saw the Sheepeater village. Her arrival, coupled with that of the proud Nez Perce on their beautiful spotted horses, caused quite a commotion.

"It is a very small village," Two Bears said, obviously unimpressed, "and they do not have even one horse!"

"These people are few," Tewa explained, "and I told you they had no horses. They are poor but good and generous and they will treat you as brothers."

"Are there buffalo to hunt in this country?"

"Yes," Tewa said, "and their meat would be much appreciated."

"Then tomorrow we hunt Yellowstone buffalo," Two Bears declared, looking to his companions, who nodded in eager agreement.

"Tewa!" Inez cried, racing ahead to greet her along with the other children. Then, Inez skidded to a halt and her mouth fell open. "You have a baby!"

"Yes," she said, seeing Juanita and Xavier as well as all the villagers coming to greet them. Tewa dismounted with care. "His name is Little Hawk."

The children crowded around Tewa, laughing, giggling and vying for a chance to touch Tewa and her new baby.

When Juanita and the others arrived, Tewa hugged them and showed off her baby, then turned to the waiting Nez Perce, who had not dismounted because to do so without invitation was considered disrespectful.

"This is Chief Two Bears," Tewa announced to all the Sheepeaters, "and his friends, who I bring to you as my friends."

The eldest of the Sheepeaters, Mitosa, was bent and nearly blind but very dignified when he bowed and said,

"Rest yourselves and your horses. We have food for all and welcome you."

Two Bears was pleased by the solemnity and obvious sincerity of the invitation. Soon, everyone was talking and showing off many things. The Nez Perce were proudest of their spotted horses but the Sheepeaters were famous for their beautifully tanned hides, many of which were brought out from the wickiups and displayed.

"This is good," Tewa said, taking Juanita's arm and walking down to the village, knowing how anxious she must be about news of Quinn.

"Where is Quinn? And Hawk?" Juanita asked the moment they were apart from the crowd.

Tewa felt the need for a few moments of distraction so she looked at Xavier. "You have mended well. I would have thought you would walk with a limp, but you do not."

"Your medicine and that of Juanita has done wonders for me," the handsome vaquero said, looking fit as well as pleased. "My legs mended well, but my shoulder is too stiff now to use a reata."

"Let's go into a wickiup," Tewa suggested, still avoiding Juanita's question, "and I will tell you what happened in the Blackfeet country."

"Quinn is dead, isn't he?" Juanita cried, tears filling her eyes.

"I am not sure."

"What do you mean?" Xavier asked.

Tewa sat down on a blanket and opened the front of her buckskin blouse so Little Hawk could nurse. He began to feed greedily, which made her feel better and somehow gave her the courage to explain the difficulty and sadness she had known since leaving this place.

"Hawk is dead," she told them. "Quinn saved my life

at the Blackfeet village by bringing horses so we could escape. The spirits were with us because there was a bad rainstorm which washed out our tracks so the Blackfeet would have difficulty following."

"I'm sorry about Hawk," Juanita said. "Did he get to see his daughter?"

"She is no longer his daughter," Tewa said quietly. "She is Blackfeet now with husband and child."

"What happened after you and Quinn ran away from their village?"

"We were both wounded, he worse than I. I knew that the Blackfeet would not rest until they had picked up our tracks after the storm, then followed and killed us. That is why we separated. I covered the hooves of his horses, although I knew this would not long trick the enemy. Quinn rode south and I tried to draw the Blackfeet to the west."

Tewa closed her eyes and began to rock back and forth, remembering her fear and how she had almost given up . . . would have given up if it had not been for the life of Little Hawk growing inside. "I found the Nez Perce and they set a trap for the Blackfeet and killed them all. Then we traveled to their hunting grounds where I wintered and gave birth."

"But what about Quinn?" Juanita repeated.

"I do not know of his fate."

Xavier expelled a deep breath. "But you said the Blackfeet followed you, not Quinn."

"I believe they would have separated and followed us both."

"Then he's probably dead," Juanita whispered. "If he were alive, he would have come back to Yellowstone."

"Yes, I think this is true."

Juanita reached out and touched Little Hawk's head,

stroking it while the infant fed. "I am glad you still have something of Hawk to love."

Before Tewa could think of a reply, Juanita hurried outside, leaving Xavier behind. "I'd better go see after her," he said, starting to rise.

"It would be better if you left her alone."

"But Señor Wallace might still be alive. A little hope . . ."

"No," Tewa said. "He was badly wounded and the Blackfeet would have caught up with him in a few days, if he had not already fallen from his horse and died."

"Then you shouldn't have left him." Xavier said.

"I did what I did for Little Hawk and also for Quinn. He was hurt too bad to gallop for long."

Xavier sighed deeply. "I'm sorry. Of course you did what was best. I had no right to question your motives. And I'm sorry about Hawk."

"Hawk still lives," Tewa told the handsome young Mexican. "Only now he lives not only in my heart, but in his son."

"But there *is* a chance that Quinn . . ."

"No," Tewa said, interrupting. "Juanita was right. Quinn loved her and would have returned."

"I know and . . . and so do I."

Tewa could see by the sadness in Xavier's face that this was true. Not knowing what to say, she closed her eyes again and gave her son her strength.

Chapter Nineteen

Quinn had a severe case of malaria. He'd contracted it while trying to heal his wounds back in the riverfront dampness of St. Louis. Though ill, he'd managed to reach Independence the following spring with the full intention of hiring on with Zeke to help guide the season's first wagon train west. Zeke had taken one look at the emaciated Quinn and pronounced him far too weak to return westward, but Quinn's insistence had finally won the rough trail boss over and he'd been hired on as a scout.

Some scout.

During the first month on the trail, Quinn had only felt strong enough to shoot a few buffalo and spot a small band of Sioux before they could steal any oxen or horses. After that, his fevers had become so persistent that he'd been forced to spend most of his days flat on his back in a wagon owned by the Reverend Thomas Whitlow, a well-to-do Indiana farmer who'd decided to become a missionary in Oregon. Mr. Whitlow had no sons but he did have a good wife and two beautiful daughters. The oldest of the daughters was Mattie, a happy and energetic brown-eyed girl whose laughter was both loud and contagious. To Quinn's surprise, Mattie had fallen in love with him. During the months of April and May, she was all that had kept him from wasting away with the chills and fever as they'd followed the Platte River across the wide, sweeping Nebraska plains.

"I don't know what we're going to do with you," Zeke said one evening in early June when the wagons were circled just ten miles east of South Pass, the crossing of the great Continental Divide. "I sure can't pay you wages when you're half-delirious most of the time with the ague."

"You don't have to pay me a thing, Zeke. You saved my life once and Mattie seems determined to do it again."

"She's a handsome young woman and you're spending a lot of time alone with her. Must be nice."

"She's easy to be with."

"Yeah, well, I don't like to meddle, but Mrs. Whitlow confided to me that she's worried that Mattie could turn up in a family way."

"What?" Quinn sat up, got dizzy, and lay back down. "Zeke, look at me! I'm not strong enough to do anything, even if I had a mind to, which I do not."

"You could do a lot worse. Thomas Whitlow is also worried about his daughter but he likes you. In fact, he confided to me that you've become like the son he never had."

Quinn flushed with embarrassment. "Mr. Whitlow is one of the finest men I've ever had the pleasure of knowing. He's been more than kind to me through my illness. I couldn't ask for anything more."

"Well, he thinks you'd make a good son-in-law, if you beat the fever."

"There's just one problem."

"What?"

"I told you right from the start that I'm in love with a woman in Yellowstone. And that's why, come hell or high water, I'm leaving this wagon train when we get to Fort Bridger in another week or two."

"Exactly how do you propose to do that?" Zeke asked quietly.

"What do you mean?"

"As far as I know, you're flat busted. I can't pay you any wages because you haven't earned them and even I don't get paid much until we get to Oregon City."

"I don't expect charity."

"Then what are you going to use to outfit yourself for the Yellowstone country?" Zeke asked point-blank. "You've got no money, no horse, no provisions, and your health is poor."

"I'll find a way."

"Like hell you will. Son, with no outfit and in poor health, you wouldn't make it a hundred miles before you came down with the chills and fever again. Then what would happen? You'd be out there alone and you'd die!"

"I can make my own decisions."

"Then use your head and make smart ones that will keep you alive. Give yourself a chance for some happiness. Forget Yellowstone and start thinking about Miss Whitlow. I don't know why she'd want you when there's at least a dozen handsome fellas on this wagon train that would sell their souls to marry that girl. But you're her choice, so if you've got a lick of good sense, marry her!"

Quinn expelled a deep breath. "Zeke, I do owe you plenty but it only goes so far. I'm surprised you'd urge me to marry a girl I *don't* love and forget the one I *do* love."

"What's love?" Zeke said philosophically. "It's as fickle as the prairie wind and usually don't last as long as sweet fruit on the vine. It's hot one day, cold the next. At your age, I loved a different girl every week and at least two on Sundays."

"Zeke, I . . ."

"Hear me out because this is important. Love makes a young man feel full of sap and song one week but he's howlin' like a lonesome coyote and feeling just as ugly the next. Love makes a fella feel like a king even as he sweats like a pig and moans like a constipated cow."

"Oh, for crissakes, Zeke! In the first place, I'm not some lovesick kid anymore. And in the second place, I really do love Juanita. We went through hell together and came to understand each other in ways that most men and women don't."

"I'm gonna puke, if you keep talking. Besides, if Juanita *really* loved you, then why did she let you go off alone and damn near get scalped?"

"Because . . ."

"Ain't no *because*. The Indian woman didn't let Hawk go, did she?"

"That was different! We needed Tewa."

"Well, excuse me, but the first time I saw you all shot up with that swarm of howlin' Blackfeet about to run you down and lift your scalp, well, I thought you needed plenty of help."

"Let's change the subject."

"All right," Zeke said, "but I'll be damned upset if you leave us at Fort Bridger to go off and die on your lonesome. I pegged you as someone who's had a rough time of it the past year or so, but with enough brains and guts to change your misfortunes."

"Thanks for that at least."

Zeke muttered something, then said, "I understand you've been repairing people's furniture when you're up to the effort. Everyone says you've a gift when it comes to working with wood."

Quinn had been carving and sanding a new leg for a broken piano that would bring him ten dollars cash. Now he ran his fingers over the smooth grain and said, "Woodworking gives me something useful to do when I'm feeling puny and it takes my mind off my troubles. I just wish I had better wood than what I've been able to find along the Platte River."

"If you return to Yellowstone, you'd better start making your own coffin because that cold weather will kill you," Zeke groused.

"Drop it, Zeke. Besides, I'm getting stronger."

"If you were going to die you would have by now, but you'll never be up to living in that Yellowstone wilderness. Once you get the ague, it comes and goes."

"I'm tough."

"Yeah, you are," Zeke conceded. "I haven't forgotten how you rode a couple hundred miles with a bullet wound, trying to reach my wagons. You also brought the Blackfeet with you and it cost me some damn good men."

"I've told you I'm sorry."

"I know, and I don't hold you to blame. You were just trying to save your hide. But my point is it would gall me plenty to think that we saved you last fall at the expense of several good men but then I lost you this spring trying to get to a place where you don't belong."

"Zeke, I owe you my life and you're a good friend, but you don't know what you're talking about."

"I've lost others to the fever," Zeke said, the skin tightening around his eyes as he gazed back the long way they'd come from Missouri. "The truth is, I lost my wife and eighteen-year-old son three years ago."

"I'm sorry," Quinn said, noting sudden and intense pain in Zeke's expression.

"Wasn't nobody's fault. Nora and Mike contracted the river fever one spring when the weather turned hot and the mosquitos swarmed. Nora died quick, but not easy. Mike was young and strong and he whipped it for a year and then decided to settle in the Oregon Territory. He was sick and thin but I thought new country might save him and so—against my better judgment—I brought him along."

"But it didn't."

"No," Zeke said, blinking rapidly. "We've already passed where he's buried along the Sweetwater River."

"Why didn't you say something?"

"Nothing much to say, is there? And I didn't mark his grave because Mike said that graves made people sad and things were already tough enough on the Oregon Trail. I respected his wishes."

"Mike sounds like a fine young man."

"Like you, the kid made a lot of mistakes. He fell in and out of love about a hundred times before he was twenty. But like you, he was all right," Zeke said with a quick dip of his quivering chin. "Hell, he was *better'n* all right. Anyway, when you found me this spring in Independence, I saw how sick you were, and worried about getting to Yellowstone. You reminded me of Mike and I got scared. Figured the same might happen and that you'd up and die on the trail, like my son.''

"You said no at first. What changed your mind?''

Zeke looked up, eyes watery. "Your determination. I could see you were going west with or without my wagon train. I knew if you couldn't come along with me, you'd talk your way onto another wagon train.''

"I would have.''

"But you won't survive in the northern wilderness living among poor Indians. And there's something else you had better consider.''

Quinn had a feeling he didn't want to hear what Zeke was going to tell him. "All right,'' he said, "spit it out.''

"Indians get fevers real easy. Whole tribes of 'em have been wiped out for the last hundred years or more. It happened all along the East Coast and it's happening out here in the West.''

"I don't think malaria is . . .''

"Dammit, son, you don't *know* what you really got!'' Zeke argued, passion rising. "It acts like river fever, the ague, or malaria—call it whatever you want—but it could be something entirely different. It could be a pox or even a plague. You don't know. I don't know. Nobody knows.''

"You're damn sure not a doctor!''

"I don't need to be a doctor. I talked to every doctor I could find about my wife and son. After Nora died, I did everything in my power to get out of Missouri but not before I thought I had the ague all figured out. Thought we'd leave it behind just like an enemy or a piece of hard-luck land.''

Zeke's laugh was brittle and bitter. "Every doctor I could find gave me a different story about fevers but none of them really knew anything. The one thing they all agreed on is that fevers and diseases afflict us in strange ways that we probably never will understand.''

"I'm going to live," Quinn said. "I can feel myself getting stronger and stronger and I know a lot of people that have had poxes and fevers that survived."

"Yes," Zeke said, "but none of 'em were Indians."

The remark caught Quinn off guard. "What do you mean?"

"Everyone knows that Indians have no resistance to fevers, poxes, and all sorts of other diseases that white people can sometimes survive. So you had better ask yourself one damn hard question before you leave this wagon train at Fort Bridger."

"And that is?"

"That is—even if I am willing to throw my own life away for the love of a pretty woman, am I also willing to risk the lives of all those Yellowstone Indians?"

"Goddamn you, Zeke, just stop it!"

Zeke turned away to leave. "You can damn me all you want. But even if you did manage to reach the Sheepeaters and then they got your sickness and died, you can bet that *you're* the one that would feel damned. Think about that real careful."

That night Quinn couldn't eat his supper, no matter how hard Mattie pleaded. After she and her family had gone to sleep, Quinn managed to climb out of their wagon and stumble off a little ways to collapse on the grass, then gaze up at the stars. He didn't know exactly why. Maybe, he thought, the glittering stars would offer him some truth or clarity because his fevered mind couldn't.

Quinn struggled to pray for more than an hour, getting weaker and more confused until he finally lapsed into a restless, troubled sleep.

"Quinn!"

He looked up to see Mattie. Behind her, the sky was just beginning to turn salmon. Mattie appeared stricken and distraught. Angry, even. "What are you doing out here cold and all alone! You aren't strong enough to be this foolish!"

She began to cry. Really cry.

Quinn wrapped his arms around Mattie and whispered, "I'm sorry. I . . . I wasn't thinking."

"No, you weren't," Mattie sniffled, hugging him with all her might. "I'm sorry to be angry, but I don't want you to die!"

"Die?"

"Yes, so we can go live together in Oregon."

"Mattie, wait, we . . ."

"Let me finish," she gushed. "You see, I've already talked to my father and everything will be perfect!"

Curious, he said, "You think so?"

"Of course! We'll buy a small house for starters and get you back to good health. After that, my father is going to loan us enough money to start a woodworking business."

Mattie absently sleeved away tears and now she was beaming like this morning's Wyoming sunrise. "And Quinn, I hope you don't object because I know this is unusual, but I'd like . . ."

She was blushing. "Come on," he said, "let's hear the rest of it."

"Well," she told him almost shyly, "I'd like to be your woodworking apprentice."

Despite feeling so bad, Quinn had to laugh. He'd

never heard of a woman woodworking apprentice. But then, he'd never met anyone quite like Mattie Whitlow.

Mattie's words became a torrent. "I could do it! You see, I'm also really good with my hands. I'll be a great helper and we'll work so well together. And ... and when we get older and have lots of grown children and grandchildren, we'll hire every last one of them—if they want—and our family will build fine furniture, boats, wagons, all those things! Whatever is needed in Oregon, we can make together and we'll become ever so happy and prosperous!"

Quinn stared up at Mattie. He gave in to a powerful impulse to stroke her hair, then her cheek and, when he spoke, he was surprised at his own rising excitement. "You really do love me, don't you?"

"Of course! I'm the only one that's really meant for you, not someone living out in the wilderness in an awful little wickiup made of poles, leaves, and branches and ..."

"Wherever did you hear about wickiups?"

"From you, in your sleep. You've talked a lot when you've been fevered. I know all about that and ... and what happened with you before you went to find Hocina and about Hawk and Inez and ..."

"Oh," Quinn said, shaking his head. "I guess I really have spilled my life story."

"It doesn't matter!" She blushed with shyness. "Actually, Quinn, I've had a beau or two myself."

He feigned surprise. "You have?"

"Sure! I even left one behind in Indiana. In fact, I left *two* that wanted to marry me."

"Mattie, please help me to my feet. I'm cold."

Mattie was strong and she easily pulled him up.

"Being newly ordained, my father could marry us today, you know."

"I think that would be . . ."

"Wonderful!" Mattie cried, hugging him so hard that Quinn couldn't breathe. "I'll go get him right now before you change your mind!"

"Mattie, wait!"

"No! I've waited for two months and I've nursed you back to health, almost."

"Please," he begged, grabbing her hand. "Just wait a little longer."

Her smile wilted and her voice cracked with disappointment. "So you can get to Fort Laramie and disappear? Is that it?"

"No," he said. "That's not it at all."

"It's what you plan, isn't it? Isn't it?"

"It's what I *planned*. My plans have changed. Just now, in fact."

Mattie's face became transfixed with joy. "You have? Really?"

"Yes." Quinn buried his face in her sweet-smelling hair. Zeke had been right. And although he loved Juanita, he also loved life and now Mattie was his life. Hell, Oregon was going to be his life. He'd never have been happy in the wilderness. Never.

Quinn breathed in the scent of Mattie's hair and closed his eyes. *Forgive me, Juanita. I don't want to die and I don't want to bring a sickness into Yellowstone, either. So . . . forgive me.*

Fort Bridger was a handsome collection of log houses and buildings on the picturesque Black Fork of the Green River. Their wagon train had been the first to arrive in need of replenishing both livestock and food supplies.

Jim Bridger and his partner, Louis Vasquez, were thriving and very congenial. Like everyone else, Quinn felt in awe of the legendary mountain man. Bridger was a hatchet-faced mountain man of about fifty with a wide grin and barking laugh. Quinn remembered that Hawk had told him the man had been in the Yellowstone country and, with that in mind, he waited until he could get a few minutes alone with the famous trapper and explorer.

"I'd like to have a few words with you, Mr. Bridger."

"Sure," Bridger replied, "Zeke told me about you and Hawk and how you went to live in Yellowstone. I was real sad to hear that Hawk was killed by the Blackfeet, but it didn't surprise me none."

"It didn't?"

"Nope. Damn foolish to try to find Hocina, but I'd have done the same."

"Zeke says I'll die if I return to Yellowstone and I might bring disease and death onto the Sheepeaters."

"That's right, on both counts. I've seen that Whitlow girl and although my eyes aren't what they once were, she's a looker! Zeke says she wants to marry you and her pa has money and ain't against the idea."

"Yes, but . . ."

"Then marry her! We only got one life. Why would you want to throw it away in Yellowstone? You'll also break the Whitlow girl's heart."

"If I don't return to Yellowstone, I'll break Juanita's heart. I'm not worth it, but either way someone gets hurt."

"Don't worry so much, young fella. People your age

always think their hearts will never mend—but they always do. And those that don't mend are weak.''

"There's nothing 'weak' about Juanita.''

"Then she'll be fine.''

"Mr. Bridger?''

"Yeah?''

"You ever see any sign of gold in Yellowstone?''

"Nary a trace. Good fur country. Good timber country, if you could get the stuff outta that big basin. Other than that, it ain't worth much but to feast your eyes upon.''

Quinn would have liked to ask Bridger more questions, but the frontiersman saw a customer enter his general store and hurried off to make some money.

The evening before they were to continue to the Columbia River, which would take them all the way to the mouth of the Willamette River leading into the fertile farmlands of Oregon, Quinn had another important conversation. This one, however, was not one of his choosing.

"I'd like a word with you,'' Whitlow said to him in his usual quiet way.

"Why, of course,'' Quinn answered.

The Reverend Whitlow was of medium height, but strong and fit from many years of successful farming. His face was deeply lined and he had a soft manner of speaking. But when Thomas Whitlow spoke, people listened.

"Alone,'' the reverend added, strolling away from the fort and out across the grassy meadowland with its meandering streams.

Quinn knew that this conversation was going to concern himself and Mattie and he wasn't exactly sure what he was going to say. He was still confused, though he'd decided that he could not afford to return to Yellowstone either for his own sake or that of the Sheepeaters.

Whitlow reached out and took both of Quinn's hands in his own. "Could we pray together before we talk?"

"Sure!"

They prayed. Actually, Quinn's mind was too agitated to pray so he left that to the reverend while he closed his eyes and let his mind run in wild circles.

"Amen."

"Amen, Reverend."

"Son, let's get right to the point because I know we both have business to take care of before leaving tomorrow."

"Yes, sir."

"All I need to know is if you are going to love and honor, according to the word of God and his Holy Bible, my darling Mattie. If you will do that and always forsake all others, then I will marry you myself when we reach Oregon. But, if you still love this other Yellowstone woman, then you must be honest and say so. It will hurt Mattie, but she'll recover."

"I don't yet love Mattie," Quinn said, picking his words very carefully. "And I do still love Juanita."

Whitlow's face fell with disappointment. "I'm sorry but that . . ."

"But, Reverend, I've decided to go on to Oregon, if you'll have me along."

Whitlow's brows knitted together. "Why would you do that?"

"Because I've decided to put Juanita behind me forever." Quinn struggled to clarify his thoughts. "It's hard to explain, but I believe when you finally decide to put a thing into your past, you begin to look at the new things in your future—and to see them much more clearly.''

"And that would be my daughter.''

"Yes.''

"And what about the Lord? I need to know if you are a God-fearing Christian.''

"I was taught that God is love.''

"He is, but much, much more.''

"Yes,'' Quinn agreed. "And I hope, with your patience, help, and understanding, to discover some of that which He is. Will you help me?''

The reverend smiled. "You are a very clever young man. You knew that I couldn't refuse you.''

"Then everything will work out just fine with all of us. But that would be in the Lord's hands, wouldn't it, sir?''

"Yes, it would. But you won't sin against the Lord, will you Quinn?''

"You mean with Mattie?''

"That's right. She loves you very much and so is . . . is vulnerable.''

"No, sir, I won't dishonor Mattie, you, or your God. I give you my word on that.''

"That's all I could ask,'' Whitlow said, clapping him on the back. "Now let's talk about what kind of woodworking shop you will need to prosper in Oregon.''

Quinn blinked, then he began to outline some of the thoughts he'd had since the night Mattie told him of her dreams for their beautiful future together.

Chapter Twenty

"Xavier," Inez said one afternoon shortly after Tewa's return with her baby, "why do you look so unhappy all the time?"

"Ah," the former California vaquero said, forcing a smile, "I am not unhappy. Maybe it is just that you are so very happy that I seem unhappy by comparison."

"Maybe you look sad because Juanita doesn't love you," Inez said.

"It is more than that," Xavier replied, massaging his scarred shoulder, a habit that he had acquired in order to keep it from stiffening up. If he failed to do that every few hours, his arm would become nearly useless until he went through some painful exercises.

"You see, I miss my mother, father, and older sisters who are all happily married. They have children who love their uncle and I am sure that all my family think both Chaco and I are dead."

Inez sat down and studied Xavier intently. "Are you going back to Santa Barbara?"

"I have to," Xavier said without hesitation.

"But what about Señor King? He would want to punish and perhaps even kill you!"

"I do not kill easily," Xavier told her.

"Señor King is a very evil man," Inez said. "I would *never* go back."

"Are you happy here among the Sheepeaters?"

"I am," Inez replied. "I have many friends here."

"But it is a much harder life than in California," Xavier argued. "Have you already forgotten how cold it was last winter?"

"Of course not. But remember how we went to the hot springs every day to get warm?. And how you and Juanita would sit for hours talking beside the steaming pools that made your shoulder feel so good?"

"Yes."

"Xavier, don't leave us. If you go back to California, I would miss you and so would Juanita."

"I think you would," he said, "but I am not so sure about Juanita."

"She would miss you very much!"

"How do you know this?"

"Because, when you do not see her, Juanita watches you."

Xavier wanted to hear more. Much more. "She does?" he asked shamelessly.

"Oh, yes! Juanita is sad about Quinn being killed, but she has become very fond of you."

" 'Fond'," the vaquero spat out the bitter word. "I'm afraid that is not enough."

"I know. You are in love with her and you need her to love you in return."

"Exactly." Xavier shook his head. "How did one so young become so wise?"

"I watch people and learn."

He took a deep breath. "All right, wise one, do you think Juanita will ever forget Quinn and learn to love me?"

"Yes. But first, you have to tell her that Señor King is dead so she doesn't worry about what the priests would say."

"But what if he is not dead?"

Inez shrugged. "Then I think you would have to commit a small sin in order to correct an even bigger one."

"Are you telling me I would have to lie?" Xavier leaned forward, dark eyes intent, because despite the fact that Inez was still a girl, he found himself intensely curious to hear her answer.

"I am saying that Juanita is learning new ways to look at everything, but the Church is still very strong in her heart."

"As it is in mine!"

To demonstrate his great sincerity, Xavier made the sign of the cross. Inez did not look impressed. In fact, she giggled. Offended, Xavier stammered with indignation, "And what is so damn funny?"

"You are," Inez told him. "You would lie to the Pope himself if it would win you Juanita's love."

Protest welled up in Xavier's mind, but he realized that this girl was right. He *would* lie to the Pope, if that was what he had to do to win Juanita.

"Inez," he said, "I am going back to Santa Barbara."

"Quinn went away," she said, "and he never came back."

"He ran into the Blackfeet," Xavier replied. "The

Paiutes are not the Blackfeet. I can outrun them on horseback, or kill them if I must."

"There are the Sierras to cross."

"I am not worried about mountains."

"And then there is Señor King."

"Yes," Xavier said, "he *does* worry me."

Inez frowned. "What will you say to him?"

"I will ask him to introduce me to the bishop in Santa Barbara and seek a marriage annulment."

"He will refuse you."

Xavier nodded. "Probably. But maybe I can talk Señor King into giving the bishop a large gift in exchange for the annulment."

"The bishop would never do such a thing."

Xavier threw his hands up and let them fall in a gesture of complete futility. "Then what else can I do?"

Inez looked him squarely in the eye and said, "Kill Señor King."

Xavier blinked, too surprised to speak.

"Kill him!" Inez repeated, tears welling up in her eyes as she clenched her fists so hard the knuckles turned white. "He is evil!"

"What did he do to you, Little One?" Xavier asked. He reached out to comfort the girl, but she suddenly jumped up and ran away.

Xavier was shaken by the hatred he'd heard in Inez's voice. That such a young girl could hate someone so much told him that she must have been violated in ways that were unspeakable. And with that realization, a cold fury welled up inside him.

If I have to, Xavier thought, *I will kill that monster, because to end the life of such a man would not really be a sin.*

Troubled by Inez's words and reaction, Xavier went

out into the meadow to say goodbye to Lucky. The yearling was getting large but still behaved more like a dog than a wild bear. Lucky nuzzled his arm, indicating that he wished to be scratched behind the ears. Xavier scratched Lucky, explaining why he had decided to go to Santa Barbara and have a showdown with Señor King.

"It is not just Señor King that I must see, but also my family. My mother and father are old. They must grieve very much for myself and for Chaco, thinking us lost. My return, if only for a short while, will bring them the great joy they deserve."

Lucky nudged Xavier hard enough to knock him backward a few steps. "Oh, yes," the Mexican said, "I was so busy talking that I forgot to scratch you some more."

Xavier scratched harder. "I am leaving today. If not, then I might change my mind and nothing would happen for Juanita and me. But first I must ask you not to kill any more of the Sheepeater's dogs. And stay away from their meat, for it makes them very angry and they might have to shoot you. Better that you go away and act like a real bear, huh?"

Lucky made contented little "woofing" sounds. Having said his piece and made up his mind, Xavier went to collect his meager belongings and say goodbye to Juanita before he rode away.

"Xavier!" Juanita called, hurrying to his side. "Why are you going back to Santa Barbara?"

"I must tell my family I am alive. I know they are grieving."

"I think there is more to it than that," she said, looking down at the saddlebags in his fist.

"All right, I also intend to visit Señor King," Xavier admitted, finding it impossible to lie to this woman.

"For what good purpose?"

Xavier shrugged and tried to make his voice sound light. "I want to tell him not to send anyone else after us."

"And, if he refuses?"

"Then we will have a disagreement." Xavier took Juanita into his arms and brazenly kissed her lips, then released her with a smile and the words, "Goodbye, my love."

"This leaving is really about me, isn't it?" Juanita asked.

"About *us,* Señora. But also about my parents. They gave me life and much love. I cannot bear the idea of now giving them sadness."

"Xavier, please don't go away now."

"Shhh," he whispered, gently placing his hand over her lips. "There has been too much said already."

"I don't want you to go!"

"I will be back."

"That's what Quinn said the last time I saw him alive. But now he is dead. I don't want you to die, too!"

"Death has many faces," Xavier said, his eyes bleak, his expression grim. "I promise you I will return, because I am not Quinn and never can be Quinn. Do you understand me?"

When she dipped her chin and scrubbed her eyes dry of tears, Xavier suddenly felt much better—so good that he kissed her once more and then went to saddle his horse.

The desert crossing had been easier than he'd remembered, and the Paiutes more pathetic. He had befriended them and they had given him safe passage.

The Sierras were warm and green, their highest passes clear of snow. The great Central Valley of California was becoming settled; when Xavier crossed the coastal range and inhaled the salty tang of the Pacific Ocean, he cried unashamedly. Santa Barbara was even more beautiful than he had remembered, and when he strode into the humble little abode of his parents and found them napping one cool afternoon, he pulled up a chair and watched them for a blissful hour, happier than he'd been in a long, long while.

"I have come to visit you," Xavier said softly as they awakened and then cried out with joy, "but I cannot stay long."

His parents were so excited that his father lost his breath and began to wheeze and choke. That scared Xavier but the fit soon passed and then they were hugging and kissing him as if he were a girl.

"My son," his mother cried, "we thought you were dead! I have prayed and prayed for you and Chaco."

"Your prayers were answered," he said. "I felt them every day that we have been gone."

"Where is Chaco?" his father asked, looking out through the open doorway. "Is he putting away the horses?"

"No," Xavier said, still not sure how to handle the matter of his brother even though the question had haunted him all the while of his long, difficult journey.

"Then he must be visiting his sisters or perhaps Señor King. He should have come to visit us first," his mother said with unmistakable disapproval. "Oh, I can't tell you how worried we have been for your safety."

"As you can see," Xavier said, forcing a smile, "I am fine."

"You are much too skinny," his mother decided, eyebrows knitted in stern disapproval.

"And what is wrong with your left shoulder?" his father asked, his hand reaching out to explore.

Xavier recoiled. In truth, the scars where Lucky's mother had bitten and clawed him were so ugly that he did not want to upset his parents.

"It is nothing," he told them.

"Then why is that shoulder drooping a little?"

"I . . . I was bitten by a grizzly," Xavier admitted. "But, as you can see, I am well now."

"You never should have gone to such a faraway place. And," his father added, "I will not allow you and Chaco to go back to that place."

Xavier knew he had to be firm. "Chaco is . . . is still in Yellowstone."

"No!" his mother cried, running over to the doorway and looking about in their yard filled with weeds, flowers, and chickens. "Tell me this is not so."

"It is," Xavier told them. "He has decided to stay."

"But . . . but why?" his father wanted to know.

"He has . . . has changed," Xavier stammered. "Chaco has really changed."

"For the good, I hope," said his mother. "I have always worried about Chaco. Never you, but always for Chaco."

"My brother is finally happy. And tell me about things here," Xavier said, wanting to change the subject. "And about my sisters and their children!"

"Everyone is well, thanks be to God," his father said. "Your sister Teresita had another baby."

"Boy or girl?"

"Boy," said his father. "And Donita a girl."

"This is good," Xavier said.

"We will send for everyone today," his mother said, hugging him tightly.

"I will go find them right now," his father added, reaching for his sandals.

"And I will prepare food for you. Xavier, you are much too skinny."

"I have come a long way," he told her as his father hurried away, calling the names of his sisters even before he was out on the street.

"So what happened?" his mother asked.

"It is a long story."

"Then start now."

"I need to eat first," Xavier said.

His mother nodded in agreement. "Yes, before all the rest come and the talking begins. Eat!"

Xavier sat down and was soon enjoying a big plate of corn tortillas which he dipped sometimes in honey, sometimes in a hot mix of beans and peppers.

Soon, his sisters and their families began to arrive and the day passed all too quickly in animated conversations. Xavier was pleased with the way he was able to deflect questions about Chaco so that it seemed his brother was still alive and well in Yellowstone. God forgive him, he even made it sound as if his poor brother had fallen for a Sheepeater woman and gotten married. By midnight, there were still at least two dozen people in the small two-room adobe. Guitars, singing, and dancing followed and the remainder of the night quickly passed.

Just before dawn, everyone went home to sleep for awhile, which was the way of their happy Mexican people. When Xavier's parents fell into exhausted slumber, he went outside and bathed, then changed his clothes and dusted off his boots. In the back yard there was a pole corral where his family kept several fine horses.

Xavier exchanged his weary, footsore animals for a pair of strong and fast buckskins that he had ridden many times and knew well. These were young geldings that would last him many years in Yellowstone, if they were not killed by a grizzly or some other predator.

"We are going far away," he told them, saddling one and putting a braided horsehair lead rope and halter on the other. "Very far away. And I will teach you both to become prized buffalo ponies."

The sun was rising warm and bright over the coastal range when Xavier lashed down his saddlebags. He mounted one of the buckskins and then led the other off down the familiar streets of Santa Barbara until he came to the great hacienda of Señor King.

Tying his horses behind the large, two-storied house, Xavier checked the gun stuffed into his waistband as well as the knife that rested securely just inside his boot top. The hacienda was dark and Xavier knew that there was a fair possibility that Señor King would be away on business. Still, he had to find out, so he entered the back door leading into the huge kitchen where Inez had worked as a cook's helper.

When Lupita saw him, she let out a squeal of delight, then hurried over to throw her arms around Xavier's neck.

"I thought you were dead! We all did. The others came back last year but you and Chaco did not."

"We went on a much longer journey," Xavier said. "Is Señor King at home?"

"Si, but sleeping. He was up very late last night with guests. They drank much wine and he will not awaken at least until noon."

"I need to speak with him now."

"Oh, no!" the cook exclaimed. "Señor King would become very angry."

"Lupita, I have suffered much and will not wait while that man sleeps."

"Then awaken him at your own risk," the cook said, looking anxious.

"How is his health?"

"If you mean from the fight out in the street last year before you left, he recovered."

Xavier took a deep breath. "Lupita," he said, seeing a side of beef hanging from a butcher's hook, "Can you cut off some beef and pack it in something for me?"

"Of course! All that you wish."

"Put it in a big cloth sack," Xavier instructed, "and then go outside and tie it behind my saddle that rests on the buckskin horse."

Lupita was not one to be easily fooled. "Xavier," she said, looking at him with sudden concern, "are you in bad trouble?"

"No."

"But you are leaving again very soon."

"I may have to," Xavier told her. "I don't know yet."

"I wish you would come later when Señor King will be awake and in a better mood."

"I can't.

Before the woman could ask him any more difficult questions, Xavier hurried across her kitchen and down the hallway. He entered the great living room with the big horsehide-covered chairs and sofas and glanced up at the horned heads of dozens of animals mounted on the walls.

Xavier knew where to find Lucius King. The only question was if the man would be sleeping alone, or with one of his servants, some as young and helpless as poor Inez. He hesitated at King's door for only a moment, then plunged inside before he lost his nerve. The room was cloaked in darkness but there were a few cracks of light showing through some heavy velvet curtains. Xavier marched over to them and yanked the curtains open wide to flood the room with brilliant sunlight and reveal King sleeping beside another young Chumash Indian girl.

"Get out," he ordered her in a voice so cold and strained that it seemed foreign.

The Indian girl leaped out of the large four-poster bed, snatched up her cotton dress, and hurried away, bare feet whispering on the polished red tile floors.

King's face was blotched and bloated, his eyes dull and blinking in the sudden burst of morning sunlight. "What the hell is going on?" he roared, shielding his eyes from the glare.

"It is Xavier Diaz," Xavier hissed. "I have come to ask you to speak to Bishop Montez at the church and seek a marriage annulment from Juanita."

The man was still half asleep and very confused. "Huh?"

Xavier felt a mixture of hatred and loathing rise up in his throat. He strode over to the man's bedside table, snatched up a pitcher of water, and hurled it into King's face.

"Wake up, Devil!"

Lucius King spluttered and cursed. He sat up and threw off the covers, then yanked open a drawer and grabbed a waiting six-gun. Too late, Xavier saw the gun and went for his own resting tight in his waistband.

King fired too hastily and that was the only thing that saved Xavier's life. The retort of the gun was close between them but the bullet only grazed Xavier's forearm. Then he was slashing the barrel of his own gun down hard against King's forehead, opening up a deep gash.

"Gawdamn you!" the man howled. "I'll have you quartered for this!"

"Shut up," Xavier ordered, feeling emotions more powerful than any he had felt before. "I want you to write a letter to the bishop now, telling him you sleep with girls and are unfit to be called a Christian or to have a Christian wife."

But King shook his head. "You finally found that slut, didn't you?"

When Xavier couldn't answer because of his over-whelming rage, King shouted, "You found her and fell in love with my *wife*. That's it, isn't it?"

"A letter for the bishop or, as God is my witness, I will kill you right now!"

"No, you won't," King countered, glaring at him with utter contempt. "Chaco would have, but not his weak brother. Where is Chaco?"

"Dead."

"Too bad. He was worth ten of you."

Mocking laughter bubbled out of the man's mouth. "You'd better run for your life, Xavier. But by damned, you won't get far!"

"I think I'll kill you," Xavier said.

"If you pull that trigger, my men will come running and you won't even get outside. I've lived long and well, Xavier, but you are still a very young man."

"The letter!" Xavier dared to look around for writing materials but saw none.

"Put it away and tell me where Juanita and that bitch Inez have gone into hiding. Take me there and I'll pay you well."

"It is too far for you to travel."

"Then I'll just send another man like your brother to bring my wife back home. One that won't get himself killed."

"Why would you do that?"

"Because what is mine once will always be mine unless I sell or give it away. That's how men keep their power. Losing Juanita brought me disgrace. Bringing her and Inez back will change all that."

"What if . . . if I told you she is dead?"

King laughed. "After just asking me to help her get an annulment? You are stupid, Xavier. Very, very stupid."

Xavier saw that this was true. He had been stupid thinking he could reason with this devil.

"Put the gun away."

"No."

"Look, do you want money? Maybe a nice, juicy young girl to sleep with? Or a prize horse from my stables? Or both, eh?"

King shrugged as if none of these things were of any consequence and climbed out of bed. He reached for a silk shirt and used it to wipe the blood that was still streaming down his face. "That's easy. You'll have them if you do as I ask."

"I want Juanita."

"All right, we can share her. Might be fun, even. Share her at the same time in this bed."

Xavier choked with outrage and shoved the gun back into his waistband.

"Oh," King said, misreading his intentions, "so you like that idea, huh?"

In reply, Xavier stooped low, pulled the long dagger from inside his boot top, and slashed the man's throat from ear to ear.

King collapsed on his bed making strangling noises but Xavier didn't stick around to hear them. He was already racing down the dim hallway and through the warm kitchen. From the corner of his eye, he saw Lupita and how her hand flew to her open mouth. He ran to his horses and one of the stable hands gaped at the blood that covered Xavier's shirtfront.

A moment later, he was racing down the streets of Santa Barbara, heading north. Yellowstone was a long, long way but he would get there and stay there with Juanita forever, God willing and forgiving.

Xavier rode into the Sheepeater's camp forty-two days later, thin and weak but resolved in what he'd had to do in order to claim Juanita and love her until the end of his life.

"What happened to you?" she cried, hugging him tightly.

"I have come back to be your husband," he heard himself say.

"But I am married."

"Not anymore."

Juanita looked at him, not understanding. "Is Lucius dead?"

"Yes," Xavier said, handing the reins of his two played-out horses to Inez and her best friend.

"But . . ."

"It was God's will," Xavier said as he took her into his arms. "All is right now, and I have come back as promised."

"Did you . . ."

"Shhh," he whispered, brushing the question from her lips with his own. "It is *our* time to love now."

Juanita studied Xavier's once handsome but now thin and haggard face. "I always thought that you had the kindest and most beautiful eyes. And a warm and loving heart."

"Your heart, Querida."

Juanita laid her head against his chest for a moment . . . listening. *Yes, she thought, his heart is my heart and now my heart is his. And this is the way it was always meant to be.*

"Please come and stay with me," she said, feeling the warm smiles of the Sheepeaters and hearing the giggles of their little children. "For as long as I live, I will take care of you."

Xavier kissed her mouth and the giggles became laughter. He also felt like laughing out loud but said, "When I am strong again, I promise always to take care of you."

They kissed, and then the grinning Sheepeater people parted as Juanita took his hand and led him to her wickiup.

Chapter Twenty-One

My Diary
Summer of 1861

I have only a few pages left in my diary, having recorded something during each of these past thirteen years while living in Yellowstone among the Shoshone Sheepeater People. I am no longer young or attractive because the weather and life here is hard, especially in winter. And yet, I am well contented and happy. Xavier and I were blessed with a daughter and son. Our girl died of the winter cold but our son, Mando, is now twelve, strong of mind and body with an adventurous spirit.

Too adventurous, I fear, to remain always in Yellowstone. Mando and Little Hawk are inseparable but constantly into mischief. To occupy their minds, Xavier has given them his knowledge and love for horses, but this separates them from the other village boys. I cannot say if this is good or bad. I only know that Xavier has remained a vaquero at heart. He still braids reatas and halters and hunts the last buffalo in this country from horseback. Over

*the years, Xavier has raised many fine horses but the Sheepeaters
still have no interest in riding so he sells or trades them to the
Shoshone, the Bannock, Nez Perce, and others. I admit to also
loving horses and we often trade and travel together, sometimes
with Tewa and Little Hawk.*

*Over these last thirteen years, there has been much joy but also
much sadness. Eight summers ago, many of the Bannock people
related to Tewa died of a terrible pox. Because of this, all the
Sheepeaters live in constant fear that death will soon come to them
here in Yellowstone. We are so few that a pox would kill nearly
everyone and then the gentle Sheepeater people would be no more.
Perhaps saddest of all, besides the death of my five-year-old daughter, Hawk, and Quinn, is that Inez fell from a cliff while helping
her husband bring sheep meat down from the highest mountains.
She is buried in a meadow near the big lake and I often visit her
grave. I loved Inez so much and wish she had lived long enough
to have brought a child into this world so that we had something
of her beauty and spirit left to hold.*

*Today, as ever, I trust in God's forgiveness. Abandoning my
Catholic Church, I embrace the gift of being Xavier's wife and a
Sheepeater. I am no longer plagued by either shame or regret. God
will be my judge but He knows that I have loved two very different
men. Quinn was good and brave but Xavier is my life's greatest
joy. Sometimes we talk of California and we have learned from a
few who come into this country looking for their fortunes that
everything there has changed. As Hawk predicted many years ago,
the Americans have defeated the Mexicans and taken California
just as the Mexicans took it from the Spaniards and they took it
from Inez's gentle Chumash.*

*There was also a big gold rush in California and we know
from speaking to visitors that it brought far too many whites from
the East. I pray often that no gold will ever be discovered in
Yellowstone because it is a curse upon Mother Earth just as much
as a pox is upon the Indian people.*

*A few gold hunters sometimes visit Yellowstone and seek that
precious metal. If one should ever find it, I think some of The
People would want to kill that person in order to save Yellowstone
but, God willing, that will never come to pass. There are two
Americans in our village right now, but they act and talk like
fools. Both are from Oregon, the rough sons of farmers. They seem
nice enough but every outsider is dangerous to us because of the
chance that they carry the pox, so The People are afraid. Some
run and hide in the mountains until whites grow weary of gold-
hunting and finally go away.*

*Tomorrow, they will leave, tired and discouraged. Maybe they
will decide that farming in Oregon is not so bad after all.*

"And so, Xavier said, looking across their campfire
at the two exhausted prospectors from Oregon and also
thinking it would be good when they were gone, "you
are going home to the Oregon Territory tomorrow?"

Pete, the taller one with the bobbing Adam's apple,
nodded wearily. "We'd been told there was gold in these
parts. But that didn't prove to be so."

"We lost our stake," Jason added, looking even more
hangdog, "and our horses are plumb played out. You
sure got some fine ones. Don't suppose you'd be willin'
to do a little tradin', would you?"

"No," Xavier said, "your horses are fit only for the
plow. My horses are very different."

"How so?" Jason asked.

"They are very fast," Mando proudly explained. "We
hunt on them, don't we, Little Hawk?"

The taller, more powerful boy nodded quietly.

Pete said, "You folks could sell some of your horses
to the Pony Express for a lot of money."

"What is that?" Xavier asked, suddenly looking interested.

"Well, it's this relay operation that carries the mail all the way from Missouri to California in ten days."

"Señor, that's impossible."

"No, it ain't!" Pete exclaimed.

"Ten days?" Xavier shook his head. "That's unbelievable."

"It's the God's honest truth, Señor Diaz. They've built relay stations every twenty miles or so all across the West. They got the fastest horses money can buy and they hired about a hundred lightweight fellas to be riders, most not much bigger than your son Mando."

"A hundred and twenty-five pounds is what the ad in the paper said," Jason added. "I remember some of our friends wanted to try out but were too heavy. The Pony Express also has special saddles that are real light and have mail pouches that they call *mochilas* that can be switched on the run."

"On the run?" Xavier asked, trying to picture this in his mind.

"Yep, on the run! When they gallop into a relay station, the handler has the next horse all saddled. All the rider has to do is jump off his tired horse and onto its replacement, changing only the *mochila*. They're real quick about it, too!"

Xavier could visualize this exchange of horses and the thundering hoofbeats that would drum across a thousand miles of wilderness. Why, if he were young again and smaller, he would hire on just for the fun and adventure. "What route do they take?"

"They leave St. Joe, Missouri, and follow the old Oregon Trail along the Platte River all the way to South Pass and on to Fort Bridger here in the Wyoming Territory," Jason told them. "After that, they go to Salt Lake and then straight across Nevada. They run through Carson

City and over the Sierras and on down to Sacramento, California.''

"They don't follow the Humboldt River?'' Xavier asked, wondering how they could go any other route and have enough water to cross the blistering Nevada desert.

"Nope,'' Pete said.

"What about Indian attacks?'' Little Hawk asked. "Do the Paiutes allow this to happen?''

"The Pony has had some trouble with 'em,'' Jason admitted, looking uneasy. "But they have orders never to stop and fight but always to run. You see, they *grain-feed* those racing Pony Express horses—grass-fed Indian ponies are no match for 'em.''

"My father's ponies could catch them,'' Little Hawk declared, feeling insulted. "Catch and pass them with ease.''

"Oh, no,'' Pete vowed, shaking his shaggy head, "and I mean no offense 'cause you've fine horses here, but they sure ain't equal to them that the express riders use. We saw The Pony come racin' through the army post at Fort Bridger. You can't hardly believe how fast they move and how quick they change mounts.''

"I would *really* like to see that,'' Xavier announced.

"I'd like to race and beat 'em,'' Little Hawk added, dark eyes shining with anticipation.

"Me, too!'' Mando grinned. "I'll bet all three of us could give 'em a run for their money!''

"Again, no offense intended, but they'd leave you chokin' in their dust,'' Pete said confidently. "A lot of people have tried to outrun The Pony but they all get beat. If not in the first mile, then in the second or third because the Pony Express mounts have too much stamina. They're conditioned to run hard for ten or fifteen tough miles. That's why they pay two hundred dollars each for their relay horses."

"Two hundred dollars," Xavier whispered in amazement. "I sell *my* fine horses for only fifty."

"I expect that you do," Pete said, "and we'd be lucky to get thirty dollars for our plugs but The Pony is payin' that much and sometimes more. They advertise for fast horses that can run long distances."

"My horses can run for twenty miles," Xavier proudly declared. "These boys and I do it often when we travel."

The two Americans exchanged skeptical glances, then got up, excusing themselves for the night. "We're headin' out early. Could use some smoked meat. Can't pay you anything but we'd be willing to trade."

Xavier wondered if these two tattered farm boys had anything of value. "Trade for what?"

"How about a couple of good knives?" Jason asked as he and Pete reached into their pockets.

Xavier inspected the knives and agreed to the trade in exchange for twenty pounds of smoked elk meat.

"Where are you going first when you leave?" he asked the two discouraged prospectors.

"To Fort Bridger, where we hope to earn enough money to buy fresh horses and enough food to cross the desert and go home," Jason said. "Right now, marchin' behind a mule from sunup until sundown doesn't seem as bad as it did last year."

"Amen," Pete said vigorously. "Pa told me to come back to our farm when I got sense. I don't know about the sense but I sure am lookin' forward to some regular meals."

Xavier turned to the boys. "Maybe we should round up some horses to sell and follow them down to Fort Bridger."

"We don't need their money," Little Hawk answered. "But I'd like to race and beat a Pony Express rider."

"So would I," Mando agreed. "Father, could we do that?"

"Sure we can," Xavier replied, deciding that would be a great test for his horse-breeding skills, practiced over many years in this harsh country.

"You're welcome to tag along," Jason told them. "But I wouldn't place any bets on outrunnin' The Pony or you'll lose your shirt *and* your horses."

"He's right," Pete agreed, his Adam's apple bobbing like a cork. "As good as your horses are, you might even beat them for a mile or two but you'd never go the distance to the next relay station."

"We'll see about that," Xavier said, winking at the boys. "We'll just see."

When Little Hawk told his mother about their plans to go to Fort Bridger, Tewa said, "I will come along with you and trade skins."

"But . . ."

"Don't argue with me," Tewa told him. "I have need of trading post things."

"I will come along as well to trade," Juanita said when she heard of the plan.

"It will be a long trip," Xavier said.

"Not so long," Juanita replied, "and you can use some help with our horses. Besides, Tewa will never allow her only son to go with you unless she comes, too."

"She should have remarried after Hawk was killed."

"Why?" Juanita asked. "Tewa is revered by these people and is a skilled hunter herself. Besides, some people give away their hearts only once."

"I am such a person!" Xavier was hurt and insulted.

"My dear husband," Juanita said, only half teasing, "you have a good and generous heart that is full of love, but I think you often gave it to the Santa Barbara señoritas many years ago."

"Not true, Querida!"

"Xavier, let us not talk of such things because they are the past and no longer of any importance. Now, I must prepare for this trip. How many days' travel is it to Fort Bridger?"

"I don't know."

"Then go ask the Americans."

Xavier nodded dutifully and found them asleep. He awakened Pete and learned that the trip would take about five days, maybe six because of the poor condition of the Oregon plow horses.

Xavier returned to his wickiup. "Juanita, besides the horses we ride, I will take five to sell to the Pony Express."

"How much money would that be?" Mando asked.

Xavier thought about it for a few moments but was too excited to calculate the amount in his head. "At two hundred dollars each, a lot of money."

"A thousand dollars," Juanita said, kissing him good night. "Such money has never been seen by our Sheepeater people. We would not know what to do with so much money."

"I could think of something," Xavier assured her.

"It is too much money for us ever to spend, my husband. But if you have five good horses to spare, then bring them and we will see."

"We will race the Pony Express and beat them," Mando exclaimed. "We will show them what *real* mountain-bred horses can do when they run hard!"

"The hour is late, the journey long," Juanita told them, "So go to sleep, both of you."

They left soon after sunrise, with the entire village up and wishing them well. The story of the Pony Express had been told by Little Hawk to his friend, Running Elk, who told it to Barks-in-the-Wind, who told it to others so that the legend of the Pony Express grew very large through the night and was discussed in every wickiup.

After only a few hours of travel, Xavier, Mando, and Little Hawk quickly grew impatient with the slowness of the Oregon plow horses but they said nothing because Tewa and Juanita were in no hurry. In fact, they often stopped to collect medicinal herbs which they placed in their buckskin medicine bags. Or they found nuts and other things to eat because Tewa knew everything good that was wild.

So it took them a full seven days to reach Fort Bridger. When they arrived, they learned that the Pony Express was due to arrive the very next afternoon.

"They want to race the Pony Express," Pete told Captain Fairchild, the commanding officer of the army post. Fairchild was a tall, spare man in his mid-fifties with wavy gray hair and ice-blue eyes. "All five of them?"

"No," Xavier said, after introducing himself and the other Sheepeaters, "just me and these two boys."

Fairfield shrugged and flicked off a little lint from his handsome officer's uniform with his fingernail. "I have no objections, as long as you don't interfere with the job they are doing. How far will you race?"

"To the next station."

"That's about fifteen miles over some real rough

country," Fairchild said, looking skeptical. "Even our cavalry horses can't run for more than five miles at a stretch and they're not nearly as fast as those owned by the Pony Express."

Xavier measured the readiness of his son and Little Hawk, who were standing beside their best horses. Then he turned back to the captain. "We will make it a good race, Captain. But now, I seek the honor of finally meeting the great explorer, Jim Bridger, who was also a friend of Hawk."

"I'm afraid that will be impossible,"

"Why?"

"Because Mr. Bridger sold out to his partner, Luis Vasquez, who then sold this property to the Mormons. The army bought it from their church three years ago and we've been trying to fix it up ever since. Lot of work to be done here yet but it's a good duty station, except in the winter. What kind of Indians are you?"

"Sheepeaters," Xavier said, squaring his shoulders.

"Then where did you get such fine-looking horses?"

Xavier sensed the sudden challenge and glanced at Juanita for help, then back to the captain. "It's a very long story."

"I've never met a Sheepeater Indian before," Fairchild said, frowning. "But I was told that they didn't own horses. You didn't *steal* those fine animals, did you?"

"No, sir!" Xavier said, becoming very nervous.

Juanita had kept quiet but now she could tell things were in danger of turning bad. Stepping forward, she smiled, bowed slightly, and said, "Captain Fairchild, permit me to introduce myself. I am Señora Juanita Diaz, wife of this fine gentleman. Many years ago, we brought good Spanish horses from Santa Barbara, California. My husband has been raising them in Yellowstone ever since, among our adopted people."

Fairchild nodded, but did not appear convinced. "What about them two?" he asked, pointing to Tewa and Little Hawk.

"They are also Sheepeaters, although the boy's father was a white man."

"He don't look all Indian. In fact, *none* of you do."

"Tewa is Shoshone and Bannock," Juanita explained. "I am Mexican and American. I will swear to you on the Holy Bible that these horses belong to my family. Captain, if you will find a Bible . . ."

"Well, that's not going to be necessary," Fairchild quickly decided. "You people sure don't look like horse thieves. I'll take your word on ownership. But it would be better if you had a Bill of Sale."

"What is that?" Mando blurted.

"It just says you have legal ownership of your horses," the captain replied.

"But what would such a thing say?" Little Hawk had to ask.

"Never mind," Tewa said, nodding deferentially to the army officer. "It is about things that we cannot understand."

Captain Fairchild glanced around to make sure that none of his men were close enough to hear his next suggestion. Lowering his voice, he said, "For a dollar each, I'd be willing to write up Bills of Sale for all of your fine Yellowstone mounts."

"No," Juanita said, "that will not be necessary."

But Xavier disagreed. "If we beat the Pony Express horses, I would like to sell our faster ones. Would they need this . . ."

"Bills of Sale," Fairchild repeated. "And yes, they definitely would. Do you have any cash money?"

"Not yet," Xavier admitted.

"Tell you what," Fairchild said, grinning. "I'll give you ... thirty dollars ... minus the dollar a horse I mentioned, for that sorrel you rode in on. That way, you'd have ten Bills of Sale and twenty dollars cash in your pocket and that's a lot of wampum for beads, firewater, or whatever you want to buy!"

"You are indeed generous," Xavier said tightly, for he felt very insulted. "but my wife and Tewa have skins to sell ... or trade, and that is how we will pay you the ten dollars for writing Bills of Sale."

"Okay," Fairchild said, not even attempting to hide his disappointment. "Take your goods over to our commissary and show them to Corporal Williams. He'll probably find you enough takers to pay for the Bills of Sale. When you got the cash, come on back and I'll write them up in my office and then everything will be legal and proper as far as ownership."

"Thank you," Juanita said as they left.

Their tanned skins were of such high quality that Tewa and Juanita had no trouble selling them and making far more money than was needed to pay Captain Fairchild as well as to buy many fine things in the commissary.

"I think these Bills of Sale are worthless," Juanita complained after reading them over one by one.

"It is better to be safe," Xavier told her. "If we can sell five horses for a thousand dollars ..."

"That is crazy talk."

"Maybe not," Xavier replied, "especially if we win the race."

"Are you sure that will happen?"

"No," Xavier admitted.

"I am," Mando blurted.

"You and the boys be careful," Juanita warned. "And we would expect you back by tomorrow night."

"With ease," Xavier told her, figuring they could race the fifteen miles and return by late afternoon.

That night, Little Hawk and Mando hardly slept because of the growing excitement at Fort Bridger. As in their own village, news of the race had created quite a stir. Fort Bridger was not a large garrison, but there were at least fifty soldiers and almost every one of them had inspected the Sheepeaters' remarkable horses. None seriously believed that the Yellowstone Indians had a real chance of keeping up with tomorrow's Pony Express rider, but they were cavalrymen who recognized and appreciated the quality of Xavier's horses. Horses whose Spanish blood he had mixed with the finest of the Nez Perce spotted horses as well as an occasional and especially fine animal he had traded among Chief Washakie's Wind River Shoshone.

Daybreak brought reveille and a thrill to Mando and Little Hawk, who had never before heard a bugle or seen men rushing about and then lining up in perfect columns for roll call. It all seemed quite silly to the two Sheepeater boys; they had to cover their mouths in order not to start giggling.

Breakfast was followed by hasty preparations for the arrival of the Pony Express. Pete and Jason had assumed the roles of Indian ambassadors. And then, right at the promised time, they saw the Pony Express rider topping a ridge about a half mile to the east.

"Get ready!" a sergeant bellowed a warning. A fine black horse with a gleaming coat and four white stockings was escorted out of a barn wearing a saddle especially made for the Pony Express mounts. "Everyone stand back and stay out of the way!"

"Christ almighty!" a corporal missing his front teeth whistled. "When that Pony rider sees these Indians stampedin' out of here on his tail feathers, he's goin' to circle back around yellin' at us to shoot 'em!"

Everyone except Sheepeaters thought that was very funny and howled with laughter.

"You've got to let him leave ahead of you," the sergeant shouted, hurrying over to Xavier. "Understand?"

"Yes," Xavier coolly replied, checking his cinch and then glancing at Mando and Little Hawk, who were already mounted but having serious problems with their horses because of all the commotion.

"Relax," Xavier instructed, his voice loud over the throng. "Find peace inside."

"Yes," Tewa agreed, struggling to hold onto the reins of her son's prancing and rearing mount.

"Here he comes!"

Little Hawk, like Mando, had decided to ride bareback but now he was regretting that decision because of all the noise and excitement. It was all that he could do to hang onto his gelding. He noted that Mando was having even greater problems and that Juanita was hanging onto the bit, but being jerked around like a child's play doll.

"Here he is! Stand back!"

Little Hawk twisted around to see that the Pony Express rider was very young and slender. Like himself, the youth wore buckskins but also a wide-brimmed hat pulled low over his eyes with a leather thong tight under his chin to keep it from blowing away. There was no time to notice anything else as the rider shot through the stockade gates and dragged his lathered horse into a dusty, sliding stop.

The Pony Express rider didn't waste an instant despite all the confusion. He probably didn't even see Little Hawk, Mando, and Xavier struggling to control their terrified mounts. Instead, he leapt off his exhausted horse with the *mochila* in his fist and then jumped onto the waiting mount with all the grace and agility of a mountain lion moving swiftly from rock to rock.

"Ya!" he shouted, almost before his feet were buried in his stirrups and his horse was digging hard for the stockade gates, ears flat, eyes on fire.

Little Hawk looked to Xavier for the signal to go, but suddenly someone tossed a string of burning and smoking sticks under Mando's horse. The sticks exploded like pistol shots. Mando's horse reared, its front hooves striking Juanita in the face and knocking her over backward before it fell down, kicking and squealing. Little Hawk saw blood on her face and then saw Xavier leaping off his mount to run to Juanita and drag her and their son to safety. Mando appeared lifeless; his crazed horse jumped up, then shot out of the fort and raced after the vanishing Pony Express rider.

"I'm okay!" Mando shouted, trying to stand as he gestured wildly toward the open gate. "Catch them, Little Hawk!"

"Yes," Tewa cried, releasing his horse and slapping it on the rump. "Catch them!"

Little Hawk leaned forward over his mount's withers and kicked it hard in the ribs with the heels of his moccasins. His tall chestnut responded by lunging forward and almost trampling a soldier. With the roar of the wind and the soldier's frenzied cries in his ears, Little Hawk shot through the gates, seeing the Pony

Express rider already a half mile ahead with Mando's horse following right along behind.

"Run!" Little Hawk shouted in his mount's ear as he clung to the animal like a badger on a bear. "Run!"

They flew across the open meadowland, leaping gentle streams and, in less than a mile, Little Hawk passed Mando's riderless horse. However, the animal joined the chase, moving up to run neck and neck beside Little Hawk, probably because it and his horse were brothers born with a love of running.

"Yiiii!" Little Hawk screeched when he realized he was actually narrowing the distance between himself and the rider up ahead. "Yiii-yip-yiiii!"

He overtook The Pony two miles later. When the rider glanced sideways and saw him and Mando's riderless horse, he shouted something and quirted his mount, forcing it to run even faster.

Little Hawk and Mando's horses stayed even, mile after mile. It was so much fun that he could not help but laugh and let out frequent yips and screeches of joy. If it had not been for the worry about Juanita and Mando, Little Hawk would have been completely, deliriously happy.

Time passed swiftly against the rolling thunder of racing hearts and hoofbeats. The Pony Express rider finally gave up trying to leave the Sheepeater behind and he also began to grin. At the completion of ten miles, they were *both* laughing and they didn't stop until the very last mile into the relay station when they each called upon the final reserves of their horses and tried to win the race. Little Hawk and Mando's horses pulled ahead and left The Pony in their dust.

* * *

"Little Hawk," the weary Pony Express rider said later as they sat at the relay station's crude dining table before a plate of food while his replacement raced westward with the mail, "I never saw the likes of you and those Yellowstone horses!"

Little Hawk toyed with his food, then got up. "I have to hurry back to Fort Laramie to find out about the trouble."

"Yeah," the young Pony Express rider said, looking angry but greedily mopping up his plate of thin gravy and hard biscuits, "I heard the firecrackers go off as I left Fort Bridger. Damn fool thing someone done to you people!"

"Yes," Little Hawk agreed.

"But listen, I'll write a note to Captain Fairchild telling him that you and your ponies really won the race."

"I can read," Little Hawk said, glad he had suffered all those long, tedious hours as Juanita had schooled him and Mando so they would be important if the whites ever came to Yellowstone in force to make big trouble.

"Okay, then," the Pony Express rider said, writing the notes in a large, flourishing hand and then handing them to Little Hawk. "Just deliver these to the captain."

"Why two?"

"The second one is for our official Pony Express horse buyer. His name is Clyde Eakins—he passes along the whole route every three or four months looking for replacement horses."

"Are they really worth two hundred dollars?"

"At least! And don't take a red cent less!"

Little Hawk thanked the rider, took the notes, and

trotted his horses all the way back to Fort Laramie. He arrived long before sundown and was saddened to learn that Juanita's nose was broken but glad to hear that Mando had only suffered chest bruises. When he told everyone about winning the race and showed them the letters he'd brought, they were very happy. Especially Xavier, who acted as if he had just fathered another son.

Mando grimaced. "I only wish we were old enough to become Pony Express riders on our own horses."

"No," Little Hawk told him. "The food they have to eat is very bad. Even Lucky would have turned up his nose at it before he went wild and ran away. It was all I could do to choke a little of it down in politeness."

"Oh."

"And there is something else," Little Hawk said, his expression troubled.

Xavier and the mothers leaned forward with concern. "What is that?" the former vaquero asked.

"The Pony rider told me something very strange was happening."

They waited. Finally, Mando lost patience. "What?"

"There is an evil coming across this land from where the sun rises to where it sets."

"What kind of evil?" Xavier asked.

"It will sound crazy if I tell you what I was told by the rider."

"Tell us anyway," Tewa demanded.

Little Hawk stammered and toed the dirt for a few seconds in embarrassment. Then he whispered, "Talking wires on tall sticks."

Chapter Twenty-Two

Ten years later

A cold, icy wind was blowing and the last stubborn leaves on the aspen trees were spinning against a pewter-gray sky. Fresh snow blanketed the snowcapped mountains ringing the Yellowstone basin. Xavier knew it was going to be an early winter and the Sheepeater people would run short of winter meat. The buffalo were all gone now, the last shot out by white hunters several years earlier.

"Mando, you and Little Hawk must take those four mares to Chief Washakie," Xavier said, riding across a frosty meadow and studying his band of more than thirty horses. "They are some of our best and you'll get enough smoked meat to carry us through the winter. Too bad the Pony Express went out of business."

Long gone were the days when they had been paid two hundred dollars each for their superior horses by

The Pony. Thanks to the Iron Horse and the telegraph lines, even the stagecoach companies were now going out of business.

From astride their mounts, the two young men exchanged glances. Mando said, "But Father, those are your favorite mares."

"I know, but Chief Washakie is a very good judge of horses. I would not insult him with less than my finest. And besides, the weather is better down south where Chief Washakie and his people winter. These mares are all between the ages of eight and ten years old and have suffered more than their share of deep mountain snows."

Xavier looked up toward the towering mountains with a troubled expression. "I wonder what happened when Mr. Moran and Mr. Jackson presented their paintings and photographs before the United States Congress this fall."

Every summer for the last few years, Mando and Little Hawk had been helping and guiding American scientific expeditions which arrived in Yellowstone to collect and record detailed botanical and geographical information. Thomas Moran and William Jackson had been here this past summer and the Hayden expedition had spent several enjoyable weeks camped beside the Grand Canyon of the Yellowstone. The previous winter had been one of exceptional heavy snowfall—both the Upper and Lower Falls had been thunderous. Afterward, they had traveled down to Yellowstone Lake, where Jackson and Moran continued to create vivid images of the basin's natural wonders.

Neither Mando nor Little Hawk had ever seen such paintings and drawings as Moran created effortlessly with pen and ink or a palette splashed with brilliantly colored oils. They had also been amazed to see a camera and the images it created at the hands of the great American photographer.

"We're going to take our art back to the United States Congress in Washington D.C.", Jackson had declared, "and show them the most magnificent country ever created on this or any other continent by God."

"That's right," Moran had agreed, "and we'll see if we can get it protected for your Sheepeater people and all future generations of Americans so it will never be mined, logged, fenced, or otherwise defiled."

"Thank you," Mando had told the two great artists. "Our people have always lived here and would not be happy in any other place."

"Of course you wouldn't!" Moran had exclaimed. "And who could expect you ever to leave this paradise on earth?"

Moran had even presented Mando and Little Hawk with handsome pen-and-ink sketches of the waterfalls. But the Hayden Expedition, like the others before, had departed with the first frost of autumn; life in Yellowstone had returned to the familiar ways and the struggle to meet the demands of another long, cold winter.

"I hope nothing will come of their plan with the United States Congress," Little Hawk announced.

"Why?" Mando asked. "They want to make our home a protected place. This is good, for we have both seen how the Americans have ruined good land with fences and cattle."

"What I think Little Hawk means," Xavier injected, "is that a national park or preserve might bring problems that we can't even anticipate."

Mando could not imagine such problems but he respected his father's and Little Hawk's concerns.

"After trading with Chief Washakie," Xavier said, changing the subject, "stop at nearby Fort Brown to buy ammunition, flour, salt, butcher knives, and whatever else your mother tells you the women need before next spring. But do not remain there any longer than is required. And do not let the soldiers know I have given you dollars until after they have been spent on supplies."

Mando felt a bit offended because he was a man and would soon take a wife and become a father, like Little Hawk. But he said, "We will be careful."

Little Hawk placed his hand on the stock of a repeating rifle that Xavier had purchased with money earned from the sale of horses to the Pony Express. His mountain man father's ancient trade rifles, blunderbusses, outdated pepperboxes, and other weapons once expected to defeat the mighty Blackfeet had long ago rusted into scrap. "Now we are well armed."

"And well mounted," Xavier reminded Tewa's spirited son. "So use horses—not weapons—to put trouble behind. The Shoshone meat you bring back is important. More important than matters of honor."

Xavier turned to Mando. "Do I also have your word on this?"

"Yes."

"Good," Xavier told them. "Little Hawk, your wife and mother are not happy about your leaving but I would not trust my horses to any others and . . . I have no choice but to remain here."

Mando knew that his father wanted very much to journey with them to visit the great Shoshone chief and then to dicker over his mares. Afterward, he would enjoy a short stay at the newly created but unimpressive Fort Brown to talk of worldly matters with the soldiers and their officers. But Juanita had been feeling unwell, so Xavier would remain by her side while Tewa made strong medicine.

The four mares were caught and put on lead ropes and then, after many farewells, Mando and Little Hawk set out to trade with the Wind River Shoshone. Although the weather was cold and threatening, they were well dressed, mounted, and armed.

For three days, they followed the eastern slope of the Continental Divide on down to the Wind River. It grew warm again and the high mountain spruce, aspen, lodgepole, and other tall pines gave way to the scrubby pinion and juniper. After a gentle rain, the high desert air sweetened with the scent of wet sage.

"I like this country," Mando said, turning his face to the bright sun and closing his eyes to bask in the unaccustomed warmth.

"It is ugly," Little Hawk said with contempt.

"No, it is good, especially in the winter." Mando opened his eyes and looked around as if to confirm his conviction. "And sometimes I think I would like to go out and join the white man's world. I have yet to see the Iron Horse."

"It is evil!"

"No," Mando argued, "it is just a thing made by man like a gun or a rifle. It has no life or spirit."

"The Iron Horse brings too many whites. We have heard from others of The People that it has brought the hunters that killed all the buffalo for their hides. That is evil. Evil bringing evil where before there was only good and harmony."

"Maybe all good," Mando said, "but never in com-

plete harmony. Remember how our fathers died long
ago at the hand of the Blackfeet enemies? How Shoshone always fought Arapaho and Crow?"

Little Hawk remembered but wasn't willing to con-
cede the point. "The whites are like so many swarms
of stinging insects."

Mando gave him a sharp, questioning look. "I
thought you liked those who hired us to be their summer
expedition guides."

"I did," Little Hawk reluctantly admitted, "but they
are not the ones I fear."

"Who, then?" Mando asked, deciding that Little
Hawk was being too critical. "The soldiers? They have
always been good to us and our people."

"Have you forgotten the one that threw the barking
sticks under your horse at Fort Bridger?"

Mando shrugged. "That was long ago and the act of
only one soldier—who was tied to a whipping post and
punished by Captain Fairchild. I still remember the
blood on his back . . . and his screams."

"Yes," Little Hawk admitted, "but the captains who
came afterward were never as honorable."

Mando was disappointed that Little Hawk was so dis-
trustful and suspicious. "If Moran and Jackson are successful in Washington, perhaps we will never have to
worry."

"Perhaps," Little Hawk agreed, though he did not
sound convinced.

The large Wind River Shoshone village was easy to
spot from a distance because these people lived in tepees
rather than wickiups. Mando and Little Hawk were
greeted enthusiastically by many dogs and children and
then escorted to Chief Washakie, who sat before his
own tepee attended to by his wives, children, and even

his grandchildren. Washakie was far past his prime, but still a tall, imposing figure. He had a prominent scar on his left cheek, inflicted during his youth by a Blackfoot arrow, and very broad shoulders. In respect to his guests, Washakie wore an eagle feather headdress, brightly beaded moccasins, fringed buckskin leggings, and his favorite red plaid shirt. His hair was silver, thick, and shoulder-length. A blue scarf was tied around his neck, the ends passed through holes pierced in a seashell. He sat cross-legged on a checkered mackinaw blanket, smoking a corncob pipe.

"How is your mother?" he asked Little Hawk, for the legendary Blackfoot-killer, Tewa, was considered a great woman among all the Shoshone and Bannock.

"She is well and sends her greetings," Little Hawk replied, proud to be the son of one so famous.

"And yours?" the chief asked Mando.

"Very well, as is my father," Mando answered, knowing that this chief considered Xavier a good friend as well as a superior judge and breeder of horses.

Washakie returned his attention to Little Hawk. "I understand you have brought me horses to trade."

"Yes. Four of Xavier's best mares. They will bring added speed and strength to your fine band."

"I am getting too old to mount my horses but not yet my wives," the famous chief said, grinning mischievously.

Mando felt his cheeks warm, although he should have expected such a remark because it was typical of Washakie. For a while, they talked of many things. Washakie was upset because the United States Army was forcing him onto a reservation, but at least it was nearby and a favorite place of his own choosing.

"They also wish to put our enemies, the Arapaho,

among us but I do not want this to happen. The Arapaho are 'dog eaters' and cannot be trusted. The whites promised me money and a house of my own if I will let the dog eaters stay on our reservation until they have one of their own.''

"The Arapaho are as bad as Blackfeet," Little Hawk said. "You are right to refuse them. And what would you do with a house when you have a fine tepee?"

"This is true!" Washakie agreed. "Last summer they built this house of wood near the hot springs where I soak my aching bones. They wanted to show me that a house was good. The Agency people said that if I lived in a family house, it would set a very good example."

"And you did this?" Little Hawk asked with surprise.

"The Indian Agent brought many people to celebrate the first day I was to live in the wooden house. Finally, they all went away with smiles. I spent two days in that house but I could never sleep! When the wind blew, the wood protested until I thought it would fall down. So I went back to the tepee and slept two nights and one whole day because I was so tired!"

"What happened to the house?"

Washakie shrugged and puffed on his pipe. "It is still standing. So that the Agency people would not become angry, I put some of my oldest ponies inside ... but they don't like it much either."

Mando and Little Hawk dared not grin. "So you are going to take your people to live on a reservation?"

"Of *my* choosing," Washakie said with pride. "And what else can I do?"

"Some would fight," Little Hawk dared to suggest.

"Then they would die," Washakie said, his eyes narrowing with remembered pain. "That is no good. I have watched the Iron Horse. There is nothing we can do to stop it. My powerful enemies, the Sioux, tried to stop it but were defeated as were their brothers, the Cheyenne.''

He let his words sink in and then made a violent slashing motion. "All defeated! I want my people to live. To do this, they must be in peace with the white man because he is here to stay. Our children must go to his schools and we must learn to plant, to move water in ditches, and to raise crops and cattle as well as fast horses.''

"That is it then," Little Hawk said, looking disappointed.

"Yes," Washakie said with sadness. "The Great Spirit gave The People this earth but not the wisdom to defeat the white man. The white man brought better weapons than bows and arrows and so our fathers died. We, their sons, are being forced to live on little spots of this earth surrounded by soldiers who want to kill us all so they can go away and forget about The People. We are cornered on these reservations, fed bad Agency beef and expected to say thank you as if we were prisoners.''

"I would rather die free," Little Hawk said, his voice tight with emotion.

"You are a man," Washaki said, "and I heard you took a wife and have fathered a boy child. So who will feed your woman and son when you are killed for honor? Mando?''

Washakie caught Mando admiring his prettiest granddaughter, Tularia, and he smiled. "I think maybe your friend wants his own wife and child.''

Washakie emptied the ashes from his corncob pipe and slowly refilled it with strong black tobacco. After it was lighted, he said, "Today, I smoke the white man's tobacco and this ugly pipe. But it is not so bad and my grandchildren will live to grow old, like me.''

Mando looked at Washakie's grandchildren and then at Little Hawk, whose lips were pressed tightly together so that angry words would not defile this great war chief turned peacemaker.

"We need meat," Mando said, "for our people."

"We have only bad Agency beef to trade," Washakie said. "Our women have smoked and added things so that it can be swallowed."

"Then that will have to do," Mando replied, trying to hide his disappointment that they would not be getting good buffalo meat.

"Is there a white man's sickness among the Sheepeaters yet?" the chief of the Shoshone asked.

"No."

"There are many Indian peoples who are no more because of the white man's sicknesses."

"I know that," Mando said, "and I hope our people never die of those sicknesses. Also, I am glad you were given the land of your choice."

"But why did you choose land that is *not* mountain and forest?" Little Hawk asked.

Mando quickly stepped in front of his best friend. "Chief Washakie, we are grateful for your generous ways and for the meat."

"As I am grateful to have your father's best old mares." Washakie came to his feet and then, without further conversation, he went into his tepee.

"You are hungry," Tularia said, looking only at Mando. "Come with me and you will be well fed."

The girl was maybe sixteen, tall like her grandfather and possessing exceptional beauty. Mando started to follow her like a dutiful puppy but Little Hawk grabbed his arm. "This talk of whites robbed me of my hunger. I will get the Agency beef packed. You eat, then we go to the fort and move on before darkness."

"All right," Mando said, not wanting to show disagreement in front of this girl and but also not liking being given orders. "I will be done soon."

"Do not waste time," Little Hawk replied, still angered by the conversation with Washakie.

Mando was fed buffalo meat instead of the Agency beef being loaded on pack mules and travois to be pulled by their two horses. Tularia was very attentive. "Your friend has poor manners," she said.

"He is angry about reservations," Mando told her. "And he does not like this country as well as Yellowstone."

"It is beautiful there?"

"Very," Mando told her. "The trees are almost as tall as the mountains and there is much game and boiling waters to keep us warm in the wintertime."

"If there is so much game, why do you want our old beef?"

"In the winter," Mando confessed, "the snow can be very deep and the game difficult to find. The cold must be fought with heavy robes and much food."

"I see." Tularia was silent for a few moments, then asked, "I have seen the boiling waters, too. There are many that way."

She pointed to the northeast and added, "The whites call that place Thermopolis and say there are no larger boiling waters to be found."

"The whites are wrong again," Mando said. "Our boiling waters are bigger and hotter. And there are tall water shoots that go way up into the sky. Does this place you speak of have such things?"

"No," Tularia admitted.

Mando was pleased to hear this and went on to tell the girl about all the mountains, the waterfalls and canyons. And about the boiling mud pots as well.

"Your Yellowstone sounds very beautiful."

"Yes," Mando told her. "As you are beautiful."

The Shoshone girl blushed and then refilled his bowl of buffalo meat. "You should stay a few days and rest with us."

"I would like to do that," Mando said, "but it is not possible. The snows could come any time now and that would make it very difficult to get the Agency beef back to my people."

"Maybe next spring you will come back," she said shyly. "I would wait to see you then."

Mando forgot all about the food. He even forgot his manners and reached out to touch her hands. "Yes," he said, "I will come back next spring."

"Good," Tularia replied, unable to hide her joy. "Then I will see you then!"

She rushed away, leaving him flustered and feeling a little dazed with surprise and happiness. It was in his mind to go find and touch her hands again but then Little Hawk was calling his name and it was time to leave for nearby Fort Brown.

But, Mando vowed, when the snow first melted and the passes were clear, he would return to see this girl and then he would stay for a while and learn more about the beautiful Tularia.

Fort Brown was treeless and primitive. It consisted of a rectangle of blockhouses, corrals, barracks, mess hall, and storage without benefit or protection of the usual

impressive log stockade. It possessed none of the picturesque charm of Fort Bridger and its soldiers were mostly
misfits who resented being sent to such a bleak outpost.

Mando and Little Hawk knew nothing of these men
when they arrived with Agency beef packed on two
mules and a pair of travois borrowed from Washakie's
generous people.

"Who the hell are you?" a young lieutenant breathing
an unmistakable whiff of whiskey demanded as they
drew up before the quartermaster's building.

"I am Mando and this is my friend, Little Hawk. We
come to buy salt, flour, and ammunition."

"Ammunition?" The lieutenant sneered. "Who do
you think you are to ask for Army ammunition!"

"I have dollars," Mando said in a lowered voice so
all would not hear.

"Yeah, I'll bet! Do you boys belong to Washakie's
crowd of beggars?"

Little Hawk's voice sounded strange when he hissed,
"We are Sheepeaters."

"Never heard of 'em. But an Injun is an Injun and
by damn if we'll sell you any firewater, guns, or bullets.
I lost three men a month ago out on patrol. You Sheepeaters know anything about that? Maybe you're Arapaho
. . . or Crow or even the gawdamn Sioux!"

"Sheepeaters," Mando snapped, feeling the hair on
his neck begin to rise as the lieutenant marched around
them and their horses before demanding, "What are
you packing?"

"Beef."

"Beef, huh?" The officer drew a knife from his pocket
and cut away the leather bindings, then pulled back the
skins to stare at the poor-quality meat.

He rocked backward on his heels and swore, "Pee-yewww! Where'd you get this?"

Mando hesitated but knew he'd be caught in a lie if he did not tell the truth. "From Chief Washakie."

"Well, sonofabitch! We give them buggers so much good beef and they let it spoil and then sell it off to any rabble that has a dollar or two."

"Lieutenant?"

They all looked over to see a sergeant, the only soldier among them with polished boots and a clean uniform.

"What?" the officer demanded.

"If these boys have money, maybe we ought to sell 'em a few supplies, but no ammunition." The sergeant looked at Mando. "Are you sure you can pay in cash?"

Mando reached into his pocket and dragged out a wad of money. He was so upset that all he could do was nod.

"Then, Lieutenant, I reckon we could sell them a few things and . . . well, who knows, maybe even make a little profit for the Army." He winked. "What do you think?"

The officer hadn't been thinking but now he finally saw the sergeant's line of reasoning. "Uh, sure! Take 'em over to the commissary and bring their money to my office when you're finished."

"Yes, sir."

Mando was not sure if either man could be trusted, but he suddenly felt a huge relief because it was obvious that the lieutenant was drunk and mean-spirited.

For two hundred dollars of Xavier's money, they got fifty pounds of flour and sugar, a hundred pounds of salt, a box of knives, four good axes for wood-cutting, and a half dozen heavy metal buckets that would have all sorts of good uses in Yellowstone.

"This is all?" Little Hawk shouted in anger after realizing they were being shamefully swindled.

"That's right," the sergeant told him. "And you'd better be glad I stepped in when I did or by now you'd either be dead or whipped down to a nubbin. Or maybe you didn't notice that the lieutenant has a pretty big hate going for all Indians right now."

"Come on," Mando said, trying to drag his furious friend outside. "We promised Xavier we would leave without trouble."

"But this is wrong!"

"Life ain't fair, Injun," the sergeant said with a loose grin and a shrug of his heavy shoulders. "And, if you don't take heed of your friend's good advice, it's about to suddenly get a lot *more* unfair."

But Little Hawk had passed beyond the limit of reason. Mando saw his friend's fists clench at his sides and realized that Little Hawk was about to attack the big sergeant. Without fully realizing his intent, Mando swung one of the heavy buckets and smashed Little Hawk behind the head, knocking him to his knees.

When Little Hawk cursed, shook his head, and reached for his knife, Mando hit him again, this time knocking him out cold.

The sergeant's fists were knotted but now he relaxed. "If I tell the lieutenant that your friend was planning to put a knife in my belly, he'll be hanged before our regular commanding officer, Major Talbot, returns from Fort Steele."

Mando could feel icy sweat beading across his body. "Sergeant, after I hit Little Hawk, he did not know what he was about to do."

"Oh, yes, he did. But I guess he probably learned an important lesson. Drag him outside and pitch him and these supplies on one of your travois. Then bust out of this fort as if your ass was a'fire."

"Yes, sir!"

"I ain't no 'sir'," the sergeant growled, stuffing half of the money in his polished boot tops. "I'm just a poor, misfortunate Irishman trying to make a nice profit."

Mando got Little Hawk and their army supplies lashed down on the travois in a hurry and mounted his horse.

"Sergeant O'Leary, what happened to that Injun?" the lieutenant shouted as he stumbled outside, gaping at the unconscious Little Hawk.

The sergeant took a deep breath, smiling to show a lot of fine white teeth. "He was so happy about the deal we made him I guess he just fainted outta pure joy, Lieutenant!"

All of the onlooking soldiers guffawed ... until O'Leary shot them a murderous glance and whispered to Mando, "Now git!"

Mando didn't need any urging. Taking up a long lead line, he departed Fort Brown, vowing never to return or to trust the white man again.

Chapter Twenty-Three

My Diary
Early Summer of 1872

There is great excitement among our people and I can hardly contain my joy. We have just learned that the United States of America Congress and President have made Yellowstone its first National Park. This is wonderful news as it means our home will never be cross-fenced, logged, mined, or farmed. The land is to be set aside forever for The People and all people. No longer will we live in fear of the whites finding gold and coming in droves as they did to California and other places at the news of a mining strike.

Xavier and I have tried to explain to The People how this will be a blessing for all of us but they don't seem to care very much. Perhaps that is to be expected because they do not read or write, or have any idea of the white man's world. When I think of how fortunate they are not to have to suffer the same fate as so many Indian peoples I praise the Lord for His goodness and mercy.

Word has reached us that a delegation from Washington will arrive to commemorate this historic event. The Sheepeaters have been asked to attend. There will be much food, dancing, and celebrating although The People are not sure how they should act among such important officials. I wish I owned a proper dress and that Xavier and Mando had suits and shoes to wear for our distinguished guests. However, I am sure it will not matter and everyone will have a wonderful time.

I will write again when I return from this celebration.

My Diary
Late Summer of 1872

I have been unable to write, or think, or even feel since learning from the Army and the Washington officials that all the Sheepeaters will have to leave Yellowstone National Park . . . forever. The new Park Superintendent believes our presence will scare off or insult white tourists. Xavier and I have spoken to this man with all the passion that is in our hearts, begging him not to make us leave our beloved Yellowstone, but his ears are deaf and his heart is stone.

No date has been set for our removal. We are so few that some of The People are determined to remain and hide in the mountains. But we have already been warned that if any Sheepeaters do this, the soldiers would hunt us down and put all of us on a bad reservation. There is great sadness among our people and great fear. I am asked a hundred times each day what will become of the Sheepeater people. How will we survive? Will they send us to the terrible desert or put us among our enemies like the Arapaho among Chief Washakie's Wind River Shoshone?

Mando and Little Hawk have vowed never to leave but Mando has fallen in love with Chief Washakie's beautiful daughter, Tularia. Little Hawk has two more children and his wife is afraid to hide in the mountaintops.

Xavier is not too sad. He loves his horses almost as much as he loves me and believe they will do even better where the winters are not so hard. I do not know what to think anymore. Sometimes I feel as if this is all my fault, a punishment from God for my many mortal sins. But then, I walk into the mountains and look at the sky and all the beauty and think that a God who could create so much beauty could never be spiteful, only loving and forgiving.

I am confused. All of us are confused. We do not know what will become of us anymore or what to do when the soldiers come to round us up like cattle and drive us away.

Tewa went to Xavier to borrow a horse and saddle, saying, "I must go away."

"Where?" Xavier asked.

"I have need to go to another place."

Xavier frowned. Tewa's medicine had saved his life after the mauling he'd taken many years ago from Lucky's mother. And Xavier knew that the Shoshone woman was very special. Also, it was not uncommon for Tewa to go away for a month or two at a time in the summer, sometimes to visit the Nez Perce or Bannock in Idaho. But always before, Tewa had gone in the spring, never late in the fall when she might be trapped by an early winter storm.

"I will give you a horse and saddle and anything else you need," Xavier told her. "Are you going to see your Nez Perce?"

"No."

"Ah, then the Bannock?"

Instead of answering, Tewa said, "Which horse?"

Xavier was caught off guard by the unexpected question. "I . . . well, which one would you like?"

"The bay mare with the blaze face."

"An excellent choice! She is older but a very good mountain horse."

"I will leave tomorrow," Tewa said before she turned and went back to make her preparations.

Xavier returned to his wickiup, which was finer than any of the others because he had added a large extra room and even a small porch. He said to Juanita, "Tewa is going away but will not tell me where."

"Then she must have a good reason. Did she ask for a horse?"

"Yes. She chose the bay mare with the blaze on her face and the two white front stockings. It is surprising that she would know that this mare is one of my own personal favorites. I remember the time I was riding this mare in the mountains and . . ."

"When is she leaving?" Juanita asked, not interested in hearing the oft-repeated story.

"Tomorrow." Xavier shook his head. "It is getting close to the first snowfall. I think Tewa is making a big mistake. Something could happen to her out there alone. But I remember I was riding this same mare once when it began to snow very hard! Well, the first thing I knew, the mare was . . ."

"I think I will go and talk to her now," Juanita declared.

"Yes," Xavier said, losing track of his story. "That would be a good idea."

Juanita found Tewa busy with preparations. They had been good friends for so long she could tell that Tewa was up to something important. So important that she did not want to speak of it yet.

"I think I know where you are going," Juanita said to her old friend.

"Away. That is all. Just away."

"Have you told Little Hawk about this?"

"No. Little Hawk is off with a hunting party."

"Mando or Xavier could go with you," Juanita offered, then softly added, "Mando wishes very much to see Tularia."

Tewa had been packing something into a leather pouch but now she paused and smiled. "You are a wise woman, Juanita. If Mando wants to come with me to the Wind River Reservation, this he may do. But I want no one else to know where I am going."

"Why?"

"I have my reasons."

"I think I know your reasons," Juanita replied. "But it will not be easy to hide such a secret. Everyone will talk."

"That is why I am first riding north," Tewa confided.

"I will tell Mando to pretend to go hunting, then meet you in the forest up beyond the big geysers."

And that was where Mando met the legendary Shoshone woman who had once been a Paiute slave, the wife of Hawk, then the slayer of Blackfeet enemies.

"Little Hawk will follow when he returns from hunting and finds us away," Mando said.

"If he chooses."

Tewa said no more as they followed the Yellowstone River south toward the Wind River country.

Mando was curious about Tewa's secrecy but also happy, for he had been thinking only of Tularia. In fact, he had decided to ask for her hand in marriage. But then had come the shocking news that all the Sheepeaters were to be removed from Yellowstone and

Mando's whole world had turned upside down. Like Little Hawk, his emotions had swung back and forth from great sadness to rage. They had agreed to remain isolated from all whites but to resist any attempts at removal. But now, he might again meet soldiers and this caused him worry.

A cold wind drove them onto the Wind River Reservation, where autumn leaves from the many cottonwood trees swirled along the cold river. Tewa went to see Chief Washakie and spoke from her heart. "Great Chief," she began, "you must know that the Sheepeater people are few but good friends. Like yourselves, we have always lived in peace and harmony with the white man and all the Shoshone."

"Yes," Washakie said, smoking his corncob pipe. "This I know to be true. We are brothers and sisters. And you, especially, are great in the eyes of my people."

"As you are," Tewa said, feeling her spirits lift. "And that is why I ask for your permission to bring the Sheepeater people to live on this reservation."

"There are enemies here," Washakie said after a long while. "And I listened to your son, Little Hawk. He does not like this valley land."

"It is true that my son loves the mountains and the streams. Maybe he will choose to live on the Fort Hall reservation or stay in the mountains of Yellowstone and hide with his family. I do not know. That is up to Little Hawk. I ask now for myself and many other Sheepeaters to live on your Wind River Reservation."

"Will Xavier bring all of his fine Spanish-blooded horses?"

"Yes, all of them."

Washakie could not hide his pleasure. "And what about Mando?"

"He is going to ask Broken Bow for permission to marry Tularia."

"That will cost him many good horses. How many Sheepeaters will come to live at Wind River?"

Tewa had anticipated this question. "No more than two hundred. More women and children than hunters."

"They will be welcome," Washakie decided. "But maybe one day I will ask them to help me drive away the 'dog eating' Arapaho."

"Those who come would never refuse you," Tewa promised.

"Then it is done," Washakie pronounced. "I will give you good land, enough to farm."

"Sheepeaters cannot farm."

"They must," Washakie told her with gentleness. "They must farm and send their children to the Agency schools and learn to raise cattle and grow potatoes."

When Tewa paled, Washakie reached out and touched her on the arm. "But in fall before the deep snows, we will sneak away and go hunting in your Yellowstone country. Maybe kill some mountain sheep and goats, elk, deer, and the great moose."

"The whites would allow this?"

Washakie grinned and pointed the stem of his pipe at her for emphasis. "No longer do we tell the whites everything. And *that* is also something that the Indian people must learn!"

For the first time in a long time, Tewa was unable to keep from smiling because she, too, had also learned that hard lesson.

Epilogue

My Diary
Spring of 1878

The Sheepeater people are no more. Some like my son, Mando, are counted among the Wild River Shoshone. Others, like Little Hawk, live among Bannock and a few among the Lemhi in Idaho Territory. All scattered. All gone from Yellowstone except when they sneak into the mountains and hunt mountain sheep and goats.

I am not sad. When I was young, I believed nothing was more beautiful than Santa Barbara. Then later, I fell in love with Yellowstone and thought it the most beautiful place on God's earth. In Wind River, I appreciate the beauty of a different country where the winters are mild and the air sweet, warm, and pure. I have learned that happiness is in the heart and you can take it with you everywhere. Xavier's health remains strong and he has become close to Chief Washakie, who shares his love of horses. Mando has two daughters and expects soon to have a son.

Little Hawk alone runs free now and he was with Chief Joseph this summer, helping the Nez Perce try to escape the army of Colonel Miles. Most were caught before they could reach Canada. Many were shot or died of starvation in the snow. None will ever forget Chief Joseph's sad surrender words told to me by Little Hawk:

"I am tired of fighting. Our chiefs are killed . . . the old men are all dead . . . it is cold and we have no blankets. The little children are freezing to death. My people, some of them, have run away to the hills and have no blankets, no food; no one knows where they are—perhaps freezing to death. I want to have time to look for my children and see how many I can find. Maybe I shall find them among the dead. Hear me, my chiefs. I am tired; my heart is sick and sad. From where the sun now stands, I will fight no more forever."

Only the great Chief Washakie was right to make a lasting peace with the white man. So while Xavier breeds horses and Mando raises strong children, I will just plant potatoes and grow old in peace.

WINGMAN
BY MACK MALONEY

THE SEVENTH CARRIER SERIES
BY PETER ALBANO

THE SEVENTH CARRIER   (0-8217-3612-4, $4.50)

The original novel of this exciting, best-selling series. Imprisoned in a cave of ice since 1941, the great carrier *Yonaga* finally breaks free in 1983, her maddened crew of samurai determined to carry out their orders to destroy Pearl Harbor.

RETURN OF THE SEVENTH CARRIER

(0-8217-2093-7, $3.95)

With the war technology of the former superpowers still crippled by Red China's orbital defense system, a terrorist beast runs rampant across the planet. Outarmed and outnumbered, the target of crack saboteurs and fanatical assassins, only the *Yonaga* and its brave samurai crew stand between a Libyan madman and his fiendish goal of global domination.

ASSAULT OF THE SUPER CARRIER

(0-8217-5314-2, $4.99)

A Libyan madman, the world's single most dangerous and fanatical despot, controls the fate of the free world. The brave samurai crew of the *Yonaga* are ready for the ultimate kamikaze mission.

Available wherever paperbacks are sold, or order direct from the Publisher. Send cover price plus 50¢ per copy for mailing and handling to Kensington Publishing Corp., Consumer Orders, or call (toll free) 888-345-BOOK, to place your order using Mastercard or Visa. Residents of New York and Tennessee must include sales tax. DO NOT SEND CASH.

HORROR FROM HAUTALA

SHADES OF NIGHT   (0-8217-5097-6, $4.99)
Stalked by a madman, Lara DeSalvo is unaware that she is
most in danger in the one place she thinks she is safe—
home.

TWILIGHT TIME   (0-8217-4713-4, $4.99)
Jeff Wagner comes home for his sister's funeral and uncov-
ers long-buried memories of childhood sexual abuse and
murder.

DARK SILENCE   (0-8217-3923-9, $5.99)
Dianne Fraser fights for her family—and her sanity—
against the evil forces that haunt an abandoned mill.

COLD WHISPER   (0-8217-3464-4, $5.95)
Tully can make Sarah's wishes come true, but Sarah lives
in terror because Tully doesn't understand that some wishes
aren't meant to come true.

LITTLE BROTHERS   (0-8217-4020-2, $4.50)
Kip saw the "little brothers" kill his mother five years ago.
Now they have returned, and this time there will be no es-
cape.

MOONBOG   (0-8217-3356-7, $4.95)
Someone—or some*thing*—is killing the children in the little
town of Holland, Maine.